The Parting

BEVERLY LEWIS

The Parting

BETHANYHOUSE
MINNEAPOLIS, MINNESOTA

BY BEVERLY LEWIS

ABRAM'S DAUGHTERS
The Covenant • *The Betrayal*
The Sacrifice • *The Prodigal*
The Revelation

※

THE HERITAGE OF LANCASTER COUNTY
The Shunning • *The Confession* • *The Reckoning*

※

ANNIE'S PEOPLE
The Preacher's Daughter
The Englisher • *The Brethren*

※

THE COURTSHIP OF NELLIE FISHER
The Parting

※

The Postcard • *The Crossroad*

※

The Redemption of Sarah Cain
October Song • *Sanctuary** • *The Sunroom*

※

The Beverly Lewis Amish Heritage Cookbook

www.beverlylewis.com

*with David Lewis

BEVERLY LEWIS, born in the heart of Pennsylvania Dutch country, fondly recalls her growing-up years. A keen interest in her mother's Plain family heritage has inspired Beverly to set many of her popular stories in Amish country, beginning with her inaugural novel, the *Shunning*.

A former schoolteacher and accomplished pianist, Beverly has written over eighty books for adults and children. Five of her blockbuster novels have received the Gold Book Award for sales over 500,000 copies, and *The Brethren* won a 2007 Christy Award.

Beverly and her husband, David, make their home in Colorado, where they enjoy hiking, biking, reading, writing, making music, and spending time with their three grandchildren.

PROLOGUE

——

Autumn 1966

For as long as I can remember, I've eagerly awaited the harvest. Oh, the tantalizing scents wafting from *Mamma*'s kitchen, come autumn. But it's not my mother's baking as much as it is my own that fills the house with mouth-watering aromas. Each year I entertain myself, seeing how many ways I can use pumpkin in an array of baked goodies. Naturally there are pumpkin pies and pumpkin breads. But I also delight in making pumpkin cookies with walnut pieces and brown sugar sprinkled atop. And there is spicy pumpkin custard, too, and gooey pumpkin cinnamon rolls—sticky buns, of course—cinnamon pumpkin muffins, and the most popular item of all: pumpkin cheesecake.

As I wait for pies to bubble and cookies to turn golden brown in the old cast-iron oven in Mamma's kitchen, I thrill to the world beyond our tall windows, watching for the first hint of shimmering reds on the sugar maples along the west side of our lane. I catch sight, too, of the glistening stream as it runs under Beaver Dam Road and across our wide meadow. It's here, near Honeybrook, northeast of White Horse and smack-dab in the Garden Spot of the World, where I live with *Dat* and Mamma and my two older sisters, Rhoda and Nan.

But garden spot that this may be, this year I am not able to use our own pumpkins for baking, nor am I as aware of the usually melodious brook, or the growing excitement of the fun to come—youth frolics and hayrides. All the pairing up beneath the harvest moon.

Sadly our own harvest has already occurred—stunted stalks of sweet corn, acres and acres of it all around us, cut early. Dat said the fact it never got taller than knee-high was an omen of bad things to come. *"Time will tell, as in all things,"* he declared. And time did tell.

Accepting our loss, we salvaged what was left of the life-less stalks, using them for fodder. Even so, some are still standing brown in the field. Rows of short scattered stumps, a cruel reminder of what might have been.

Though I'm only seventeen, I've already made some obser-vations about the passing of years. Some are marked by loss more than others. As for this season, never before have we lost so many of the People to jumping the fence to greener pastures—our own cousin Jonathan and his family among them. But losing a crop, or some of our own to the world, pales in comparison to the greatest loss of all.

I still remember clearly that early June Saturday. The day had begun with anticipation, as all market days do. Grief was the furthest thing from my mind the morning Caleb Yoder smiled at me for the first time ever. I was minding my own business, selling my baked goods to eager customers, when I had a tingling awareness of someone nearby watching me.

I looked up . . . and there he was. I felt a rush of energy, as if something inside me was saying: *Is he the one?*

Caleb's admiring gaze lingered after his handsome smile, and by afternoon, my next oldest sister, nineteen-year-old Nan, was telling me something Caleb's own sister Rebekah had whispered to her—that Rebekah wished Caleb might court me. Such a wonderful-good thing to hear!

Now, if I hadn't secretly liked him for several years, the smile and the whisper would have meant little and the day would have been like any other. Instead, it was the collision of the best and worst days of my life.

My sister Suzy died that evening. Younger than me by just eleven months, she drowned before she had a chance to be baptized and join church—a giant strike against our souls. Mamma and I were alone in the bakery shop when the policeman came with the wretched news, and I could not stop shaking long into the night.

Nearly a hundred days have come and gone, and at times it seems Suzy's untimely death has started a whole chain of unusual events. I'm aware of a hole in my middle, like someone reached in and pulled a big part of me out. This, mixed with a measure of anger. Surely the Lord God and heavenly Father could have done something to protect her, to keep her from dying. Yet I must learn to accept this terrible thing that has come across my path. It is our way. At all costs, we must trust in divine sovereignty, even when, secretly, doing so is just plain hard.

Am I alone in this?

My sister was daring, truth be told. Mamma sometimes said such characteristics in a pretty girl were a recipe for danger, and trouble certainly seemed to follow Suzy during her last months. Losing her was bad enough, but my own guilt tears me apart, too. I've heard tell of survivor's guilt—when you feel responsible because someone you loved has died, and you've survived. But that isn't my guilt. No, mine is ever so much worse.

Most times I'm able to push it deep down, where I can scarcely feel it, but every so often the blame rises unexpectedly. If not for me, Suzy would be alive. *Jah*, I know her death wasn't my fault, but if I'd stopped her from going with her friends that day—and I would've done so if I'd known she'd a mind to take dangerous risks—I could have saved her. I can only hope someday I'll be able to forget all of that. Forgetting Suzy will be impossible.

As for dear Mamma, it seems she can't think on much else. All of us miss Suzy's presence dreadfully—her constant whistling on washday, as well as her cheerful, even mischievous smile while weeding the vegetable garden. Like she knew something we didn't.

I daresay it is Rhoda and Nan . . . and myself—all of a sudden the youngest—who must help carry poor Mamma through this sorrowful time. Nearly all her energy still seems spent on Suzy. I see her pining in the set of her jaw, the way she shies away from social gatherings, longing for the comfort of silence . . . for her cherished aloneness. No doubt she yearns to talk to Suzy again, to cup her freckled face in both her hands and hold her near.

Sometimes I want to hug Mamma and whisper, "I'm so sorry. Please forgive me." But she wouldn't understand, and my words wouldn't change anything.

Truth is, Suzy's gone. The ground holds her body now. The ground holds her diary, as well. I broke my promise to burn it if anything ever happened to her, the kind of talk between sisters who never think they'll have to honor their frivolously spoken vow. Instead, I walked to the wooded area behind the paddock and buried it deep in the ground, as good as destroyed. Better that we remember the Suzy we all knew as sweet, innocent, laughing—the truest friend—and not who she became.

While Mamma grieves in her own way, Dat scarcely talks of Suzy. He acts almost as if nothing's changed, as if he isn't affected by her death. Yet I can't bring myself to believe he is cold toward the loss of his youngest daughter. Surely he is merely sad and simply unable to express his grief openly as his womenfolk do. I see flickers of pain and worry around his dark brown eyes. Jah, at the heart of him, he must suffer the searing, constant ache the rest of us feel when we whisper amongst ourselves of lovable Suzy and the mystery surrounding her life . . . and death. Daily, we struggle to face the future without her.

There's but a single bright spot on my horizon: Caleb Yoder. Now, I must admit to having spent time at Singings and youth frolics with plenty of fellas, but none who holds a candle to Caleb as I imagine him. Though the days continue to pass, I'm still holding out hope that he might yet invite me to go riding after a Sunday night Singing or other gathering. Such a fine driving horse he has, too. He might chuckle if he knew I thought such things!

I may be just fuzzy brained enough to think my affection for him is enough to keep me going when I feel this sad. Maybe Caleb has figured things out for himself about Suzy's final weeks and her death—who knows what he's heard, what with the rumor mill hard at work. Could be that's why he hasn't asked me to ride with him sooner, unless he is seeing someone else. If he is, I can hardly blame him.

Even so, I hold my breath, reminding myself that he might be honoring my time of grieving, a noble thing if true. Then again, maybe I'm mistaken that he ever noticed me at all, and I'm simply engaging in wishful thinking born of a wounded heart. Either way, I realize how important it is to yearn for the best, as Mamma used to say . . . before she lost her Suzy.

To my thinking, Caleb *is* the best. He is admirable and good from the inside out. I only hope he might choose to smile at me again, for hope is all I have.

"Therefore we do not lose heart. . . . We fix our eyes not on what is seen, but on what is unseen. For what is seen is temporary, but what is unseen is eternal."

—2 CORINTHIANS 4:16, 18 NIV

CHAPTER 1

She sometimes wondered what her life might have been like had she been given only one first name. Instead, she had two—Nellie, after her great-grandmother on her father's side, and Mae, for Mamma's youngest sister.

Despite the near-fancy ring to them, Mamma had often said the names were a good fit, and what with the special attention Nellie Mae gave to creating her pies, cakes, and other pastries, she guessed her mother was right.

But I'm not fancy, not one bit! She hurried across the drive toward the bakery shop set back behind the house, where Dat had made an area for parking both automobiles and horses and buggies. Nellie Mae glanced at the hand-painted sign atop the bakery shop and smiled.

Nellie's Simple Sweets.

The cozy place was considered hers because of her near-constant baking as a girl. By the time she could roll out pie dough or see to it that a two-layer cake did not fall, she was baking more than her family could possibly consume. It was Dat who had suggested building a small shop right on the premises to offer Nellie's delectable treats to the rest of Honeybrook. Of course, it never hurt to bring in some

17

extra cash, which the shop certainly did, thanks to word of mouth from Nellie's many satisfied customers.

This nippy September morning, Nellie Mae raised the green shades on each window and quickly turned the sign on the door to Open. In less than five minutes, the regulars started to arrive, all *Englischers,* two by car, and the other on foot. The brass bell on the door jingled merrily as they each entered, all smiles.

"*Willkumm,*" Nellie greeted first Mrs. Hensley, a woman with a distinct southern accent; then Miss Bachman, who was known for her peanut butter cravings; and Rhoda's employer, Mrs. Kraybill, two of her children in tow.

Not wanting to appear overly eager, Nellie Mae stood primly behind the counter while the ladies perused the display case. Mrs. Hensley scrutinized the array of baked goods, a canary yellow dress resembling a sack beneath her sweater. Rhoda had spoken of such tent dresses, as they were called by the English, and Nellie was polite not to stare at what surely was the brightest dress she'd ever seen. With her swept-over bangs and pouffy hair, Mrs. Hensley couldn't have looked more like an Englischer.

Mrs. Kraybill blinked her pretty eyes over her rimless glasses and asked, "Would you mind if I purchased all four dozen of the pumpkin cookies?"

"Why no, not at all," Nellie was quick to say.

Mrs. Hensley pointed to the cinnamon-raisin cake front and center on the counter, tapping her manicured fingernails on the glass. It was nearly all Nellie could do to keep from leaning forward and telling her how wonderful-*gut* the cake tasted.

"How do you bake all this yourself?" Mrs. Hensley asked, her fingernails still resting on the glass. "It's perfectly lovely."

"Melts in your mouth, too," added Miss Bachman, eyeing the peanut butter fudge on the left. "How you manage to bake everything without so much as a recipe amazes me, Miss Nellie Mae. You're a walking cookbook!" Glancing at Mrs. Hensley, she smiled. "If you want the recipe, just ask. Nellie's as generous with her know-how as she is with the sugar on her cookies."

Nellie Mae blushed. She had always had a good memory. When it came to listing off ingredients and correct measurements, she could do so in her sleep.

Rooting in her purse, Mrs. Hensley pulled out her wallet and a small tablet. "Would you mind terribly, dear? I'd love to try my hand at that cake." Her eyes pleaded for the recipe.

Quickly Nellie rattled off the ingredients and the measurements, feeling somewhat self-conscious, even though she didn't mind one iota sharing such things with her regular customers.

If only Caleb Yoder would stop by sometime, she thought before catching herself. It was wrong to boast, and she would surely be doing so by showing off her baking ability for the sake of male admiration. Still, Nellie could hope.

She turned her attention to making correct change. When she'd finished with Mrs. Hensley's purchases, she assisted the other two women, who, much to Nellie Mae's delight, were now fussing over who would have the fudge.

———

Nellie Mae sat fidgeting in her elder brother Ephram's carriage early Thursday morning, thankful Mamma had sent Nan to oversee the bakery shop so she could make this visit. She adjusted her black outer bonnet while Ephram sat silently on the right-hand side of the carriage, his eyes focused on the road as they drove toward his house.

Snug under her heavy woolen lap robe, she tucked her hands into the gray muff and shivered, wishing it were summer again. She daydreamed of lying in a green meadow, the delicious scent of wildflowers perfuming the air.

Will Caleb ask me home from Singing by next summer, at least?

So much time had passed already. Regardless, she was tired of going with boys she didn't much care for, even though she had been guilty of stringing two young men along. While she'd enjoyed their company, most of the boys she'd gone with were ho-hum; none of them made her heart sing the way Caleb had the day he'd smiled at her. As with every boy around here, all had plans to farm. That was right fine with Nellie Mae. She wasn't hoping for someone who would do things differently. All she wanted was someone who had opinions of his own, and was not only appealing but who was smitten with her, as well.

Is that too much to ask?

Lots of girls married simply to get hitched, and she had no interest in that. She would not marry if it meant settling for someone to cook and clean for and having a whole string of babies. She wanted what Mamma had with Dat—a steady fire between them. Even after all these years, she could see it when her parents looked at each other from across a room.

Willing herself to relax, she sensed the buggy was warmer today than yesterday, when she'd gone with her mother to the general store in Honeybrook after closing her shop for the day. She always felt more secure when either her father or one of her five older brothers drove the team. Of course their driving was not nearly as much fun as the wild buggy driving the fellows she'd dated liked to do. No doubt such recklessness was partly to blame for several fatal accidents involving buggies and cars in recent years, not all on the more congested main roads. Surely it was good that today her elder brother—responsible husband and father of four, with another on the way—steadily held the reins, just as he did for his family.

Who will hold the reins of my life?

She shifted her feet, conscious of the tremor of the wheels on the road through the high-topped black shoes her mother had insisted she wear. *"Too late in the season for bare feet,"* Mamma had said before sending her off. *"Tell your sister-in-law hullo for me, won't ya?"*

Nellie sighed, watching the trees as the horse and buggy carried her along. She dreaded the coming winter with its lash of ice and wind. She wriggled her toes in the confining shoes, longing for the freedom of bare feet.

Farmers up and down the long road—Amish and English alike—were busy baling hay . . . what little there was, due to the regional drought. Farther up the road, the neighbors' apple orchard came into view. Immediately she wondered if the orchard had been affected, too. Would there be enough fruit for cider-making frolics and apple butter, come late fall? The apple harvest always meant a large gathering of young people—perhaps Caleb would be among them. A work frolic was one of the ways the young people mingled during the daytime, but it was under the covering of night that courting took place.

She tried to shut out the surroundings and let her mind wander, imagining what it would be like to encounter Caleb at such a lively get-together. She found herself lost in the reverie, wishing something might come of it. Hoping, too, he might not be as curious about Suzy's death as certain others seemed to be.

Her brother spoke just then, startling her. "You're awful quiet, Nellie Mae."

Ephram did not gawk at her the way he sometimes did when they traveled to and from his house. Though the visits were rather infrequent, he had been kind enough to offer to bring her back with him this morning, sparing her the two-mile walk to visit her sister-in-law Maryann. If time permitted, Nellie wanted to see her best friend, Rosanna King, too.

Her brother's blond hair stuck out beneath his black felt hat. The straw hats of summer had recently disappeared on the menfolk, something that nearly always caught Nellie Mae by surprise every autumn.

"You're brooding," he said.

"Maybe so." Absently she rubbed her forehead, wondering if her frowning into the morning light had given her away.

"Aw, Nellie, what's troubling you?"

But she couldn't say, though she hadn't been brooding; she was simply pondering things.

She glimpsed at him, averting her eyes before daring to ask, "Did ya hear anything 'bout that meeting Dat went to two weeks ago?"

Ephram turned right quick to look at her.

She smiled. "Seems you *did* hear, then."

His rounded jaw fell and he turned his attention back to the road. Even though she rarely interacted with him, Nellie could see right through this brother. His dairy cattle and growing family kept him plenty well occupied these days, but Ephram had always worn his feelings on his plump face. "What're you talkin' about?" he asked.

"I heard there was a gathering. All hushed up, too."

He shook his head. Whether it was in disgust or out of reserve, she didn't know. Fact was, she wanted to know, but she wouldn't press him further. Not fitting for a woman, Mamma would say—though Nellie didn't always embrace everything Mamma thought or suggested. Even so, today there was no sense dredging up the tittle-tattle she'd heard at the bakery shop about the menfolk and their secret meeting. Likely they'd meant it to remain just that.

Nellie wondered if this summer's stunted crops hadn't caused some of the recent turmoil. She'd heard there were some who were convinced the failed crops were a dreadful prophecy to the area of Honeybrook. Limited as the problem was to their area, it was as if God had issued them a warning.

She recalled the upheaval the phenomenon had caused. As farmers, their very livelihood depended upon the success of their crops. Feed for livestock and chickens had been trucked in. And the bakery shop felt the pinch, as well, from the need to purchase ingredients, tapping into the family's profits.

Shifting her weight a bit, she stared out the other window. The heavy dew looked much like frost, with the biting cold to go with it; the harsh air must have sneaked up on them and fallen into the hollow while they slept last night. Summer's end though it was, it felt like the middle of winter. And even though that meant ice and snow and wind and cold, Nellie Mae longed for this year to be over and a brand spanking new one to begin.

Looking at her brother now, she wished he would say what he surely knew about the meeting in the bishop's barn.

What's the big secret?

Ephram was turning in where the tree-lined lane led to his house. Right away Nellie spied Maryann standing in the door, clearly in the family way as she waved a hankie-welcome.

"Now, don't be fillin' *her* head with your s'posings and all," Ephram warned, stepping down to tie the horse to the hitching post.

Nellie wondered why he hardly ever referred to his wife by her name. So many of their men referred to their wives as "she" or "her," instead of by their lovely names.

I sure wouldn't want to marry a man like that.

Nellie Mae thought again of Caleb, wondering what he would say to all the gossip. Should he ever be available to talk to, would she dare ask? Or would he treat her the same distant way Ephram seemingly treated Maryann?

CHAPTER 2

⸻

"Oh, Nellie Mae, ever so nice to see ya. Do come in." A glowing Maryann kissed her cheek as she came through the door.

Nellie gave her tall sister-in-law a quick hug. "Hullo, Maryann. Nice seein' you, too." She shed her shawl in the welcoming warmth of the house.

"You should come more often. Before you know it, we'll have another little one in our midst." Maryann's hand briefly went to her middle.

"Jah, and I'm looking forward to meeting him or her." Nellie sighed. "*Ach,* but it seems so hard to get away these days." With Mamma grieving hard and tongues still wagging about Suzy, Dat had made it clear to Nellie that she and she alone was in charge of handling the bakery's customers—at least for now.

"How is your dear mamma?"

"Well, she struggles." *We all do.*

Maryann reached for her hand, her hazel eyes serious. "'Tis not surprising. Tell her I asked 'bout her, will ya?"

Nellie nodded.

"It's good of you to visit." Maryann ushered her to the kitchen, where some sassafras tea was brewing and a plateful of warm oatmeal and raisin cookies graced the long table. "Care for a treat?"

Nellie sat down, glad to be inside after the chilly buggy ride. Maryann was known to bake new cookies well before the former batch was eaten. "Don't mind if I do." Nellie reached for two.

Maryann eyed her. "Oh, take more than that. You can stand a few more pounds, jah?"

Nellie was content with what she had, as well as the cup of tea sweetened with a few drops of honey. The pair talked of all the canning Maryann had already accomplished, and the recent sewing she was doing for the children, especially for the two older ones enjoying school this fall. As they sipped tea, Maryann periodically added more honey to hers, her fondness for sweets evidently heightened by her pregnancy.

Mindful of Ephram's earlier warning, Nellie shied away from discussing any hearsay. Even so, she was on pins and needles trying to comply with her older brother's wishes, all the while anxious to discover what Maryann might know.

The house seemed too quiet, although she was sure Ephram had camped out in the front room—doing what, she didn't know. Aside from that, the house was a large and comfortable place with a small *Dawdi Haus* built on one side for Maryann's grandparents, ready for whenever they might need to live closer.

Nellie made small talk. "Katie and Becky must be napping?"

"Jah, tired little girlies they are. Katie's tryin' to catch herself a cold, seems."

"Sure would like to see them before I leave."

"I wouldn't expect them to sleep too much longer," Maryann said with a smile. "By the way, your friend across the road would be happy for a visit, if you have the time," she added, as if she were aware of Nellie's intentions. "Rosanna said as much this morning . . . almost like she guessed you were comin'." Maryann chuckled. "The two of you have always known each other so well."

Nellie nodded at that. Though never as close to her as Suzy, Rosanna was as dear as a flesh-and-blood sister. The only girl in a family with a whole line of boys, Rosanna had frequently sought out Nellie's company over the years.

"Rosanna works hard makin' all those quilts," Maryann said.

"Jah, close to fifty a year."

Nellie had sometimes assisted Rosanna and two of her sisters-in-law to get a quilt in the frame and done up right quick for customers. But since Suzy's death, Nellie had been too busy with her own work to help out or visit. Now that she was here in Maryann's kitchen, she realized how much she'd missed both women, especially Rosanna.

Nellie finished drinking her tea silently as Maryann began talking of upcoming work frolics and the November wedding season, an obvious twinkle in her eye.

Of course, it was best for Nellie to follow tradition and keep her interest in Caleb to herself, especially with Iva Beiler and Susannah Lapp fondly glancing his way at the last few Sunday Singings. Caleb was mighty good-looking; no one would argue that. And while he wasn't one to flirt like some fellows, he certainly had an engaging way. No question that the deacon's pushy daughter was set on capturing his attentions. Nellie would never admit to disliking Susannah, but watching the way she batted her eyes at Caleb made Nellie's fingers tingle to wipe that syrupy smile from her pretty face.

For all Nellie knew, Susannah had already laid her trap and caught Caleb. Maybe that's why Nellie hadn't heard from him—he'd been stolen out from under her nose while she was mourning Suzy . . . before she'd even had a fair chance.

She accepted a second cup of tea and glanced out the window, captivated by the first hints of fall color. "Seems autumn has snuck up on us, ain't so?" Nellie said wistfully.

The splendor of the season seemed less important to Maryann. "Have you heard any of the latest church rumors?" she asked in a sudden whisper.

"Some."

"There's dissension." Maryann was solemn, leaning as close as her growing stomach allowed. "Some of the brethren don't see eye to eye on the *Ordnung*."

Nellie moved nearer, pleased Maryann had offered this without any prompting.

"Trouble's brewing, Nellie Mae. For nearly a month now."

While Nellie was sure such trouble did not concern her and her family, she tensed up at this admission from Maryann. She chided herself. *'Tis a sin to worry.*

Afraid Ephram might overhear them, Nellie purposely stared down at the green-checked tablecloth. "Best not be sayin' more . . ."

Maryann slowly rose to pour more tea for herself. Then, sitting again, she glanced at Nellie and tilted her head nervously toward the doorway between the kitchen and the large front room. Likely Ephram was but a few yards away.

Nellie changed the subject. "When do ya think you'll be goin' to another quilting?" She hoped to finish their gossiping elsewhere, far from her brother's listening ears.

At that Maryann held her sides, seemingly bursting with repressed mirth. "Aren't you a good one, Nellie Mae."

Nellie smiled and gave an anxious little chuckle. She lifted her teacup to her lips, hoping her eyes might relay what was on her mind. There was precious little freedom to visit in *this* house.

For that reason, she could hardly wait to bid Maryann farewell. In a few minutes she would hurry across the road and look in on dear Rosanna, who would give most anything to be expecting her *first* baby, let alone the fifth, as was Maryann.

Reuben Fisher wouldn't have thought of telling a soul, but he found himself grinding his teeth whenever one of his daughters got to talking about missing Suzy. Heavyhearted as he felt, especially when Betsy wept in his arms for their youngest, he could not bring himself to speak of Suzy. Not to anyone.

He had heard the whisperings of the grapevine—Suzy had died because of her contrariness . . . her sightings with worldly boys, her growing secrets. It was becoming all too common for young people in *Rumschpringe*, the running-around years, to sow wild oats; their Suzy's mistake was dying in that carefree state. For that and for missing out on baptism into the church, she was damned for eternity.

He was a father in need of solace, with no one to turn to. No one who might offer understanding for the increasing fear that filled him. No one who might give him hope. No, all he was offered was the standard answer: "This is our belief . . . and 'tis the sovereign will of God."

Everything within Reuben cried out against the image of his youngest burning in fire and brimstone. She was young, for pity's sake—just sixteen . . . not quite ready for weighty matters such as joining church. Betwixt and between.

He considered his cousin Jonathan and what he might have to say on this matter. Recently Jonathan had embraced beliefs foreign to the church's guidelines for living—their Ordnung—and was therefore deemed dangerous. What a man chose to think about such things independent of the membership was not trustworthy at all.

Jonathan's wife and grown children had followed in his beliefs, standing with him in his choice of an "alien gospel," as the bishop had declared whatever nonsense Jonathan now embraced. In fact, Jonathan's offspring had so united with him, the People had voted to excommunicate the whole bunch.

At least his kin sympathize, thought Reuben sadly, wishing there was some way around the shunning practices that meant ostracizing long-standing church members, treating church brothers—in this case Reuben's own relatives—nearly as outcasts. The longer Jonathan refused to renounce his new belief and repent of it, the harder life would become. The purpose of the *Bann* was to bring wayward ones back to the church, where they were expected to obey the Ordnung, never to turn away again.

Yet as dire as Jonathan's present circumstances looked to be, Reuben could not ignore the fact his cousin fairly reeked with joy, even after suffering the shock of excommunication at the vote of the brethren and the membership. Reuben often wondered exactly what had gripped his cousin so thoroughly that he had found strength to walk away from all he knew and loved.

Could it help me cope with Suzy's death? His grief intertwined with an intense curiosity, driving him now to visit his errant cousin. Such fellowship was still allowed by the bishop, for the time being, provided there was no exchange of money or eating at the same table. Eventually, Jonathan would be cut off.

Jonathan and his wife, Linda, greeted Reuben warmly, and after making small talk about the weather and whatnot, Reuben had nearly forgotten the bishop's prohibition—that is, until Jonathan began reading Scripture.

Despite Reuben's protestations, Jonathan insisted on holding up the Bible and reading portions of it Reuben had never heard. As was their way, the ministerial brethren preached from the same biblical texts each time they gathered. Even Reuben's own father and grandfather had kept to those limited passages during nightly Scripture reading when Reuben was growing up. Only certain chapters were sanctioned by the bishop.

Jonathan continued to read from Galatians, chapter one. " ' . . . the gospel which was preached of me is not after man. For I neither received it of man, neither was I taught it, but by the revelation of Jesus Christ.' " He raised his eyes toward Reuben. "See? It's right there." Jonathan sighed, tears welling up. "The Lord's in those words. He's revealing himself directly to us."

"You're sure it says that?" Reuben leaned over to have a look-see. He peered at verses eleven and twelve, muttering as he read them aloud. Jonathan was not pulling his leg about what the Scriptures said, but Reuben felt his mind resist. This was *not* the teaching imparted to him in his youth.

Jonathan gripped his arm. "You should look at the third chapter of John, too. It could be the difference 'tween—"

"What?" Reuben shot back, suddenly alarmed. He'd never before witnessed such intensity in his cousin's eyes.

Jonathan released his hold and ran his hand through his dark beard. "Just read it, cousin."

Reuben was torn. Here he was talking with a blemished man, one who was no doubt trying to recruit him to the wrong side of the fence. It was a line Reuben wasn't willing to cross.

"You goin' to please the Lord God or the brethren?" asked Jonathan.

"Ain't that simple."

"Well, 'tis so . . . the way I see it." Jonathan held his old Bible out to him. "Everything we need to know is here, Reuben—*all* we need for life and godliness. I beg of you, read it. For the sake of your children and grandchildren. So they don't end up . . . like Suzy."

Reuben trembled. "What's that?"

"I'm sorry, cousin. I never should've—"

Reuben felt his ire surge within him. "Getting myself shunned won't bring my daughter back," he interrupted, putting on his hat. "Sorry to take up your time, Jonathan."

He bade his cousin a terse farewell, hurrying to the horse and buggy.

Out on the road, he seethed, needing the space of miles between Jonathan's house and Bishop Joseph's to quiet his thoughts. He'd brought along his eldest brother's shovel to return and was mighty glad he had. Time to put some distance between himself and his shunned cousin.

A group of steers were on the move near the side of the road to the south. He noticed several cattle bunched together, vying for clumps of green sage. The yearlings stayed close to their mothers, some of them bawling as they went.

It was hard to take his eyes off the cows and their calves. His sons raised large herds of cattle, though he had always preferred horses. He observed the cattle crossing the stream, as if following him, some eyeing his horse while others paid no mind.

At the next junction, Reuben spotted a row of bedraggled late roses, the last blossoms of summer hanging on. The bishop's place came into view, and he looked forward to exchanging a few kind words with his eldest brother before heading on home to Betsy and his work.

But as he tied up the horse and headed to the bishop's barn, he happened upon another spur-of-the-moment meeting—the second such debate over the Ordnung in two weeks.

Several men were talking about tractors, and others were raising their voices in favor of electricity and cars, too. "We don't just want 'em, we need 'em!" huffed one man.

Reuben's own first cousin, Preacher Manny—short for Emmanuel—shook his head in response. "We can't be unified for the upcoming communion if yous don't stop and listen to yourselves. It's impossible to make any headway with the order of things . . . not with such discord."

Ephram's neighbor, Abraham Zook, seemed bent on change, his eyes squeezing nearly shut as he spoke. "I call for an altering of the Ordnung come next month, before communion service and foot washin'."

The bishop next district over and his two preachers—all from Chester County—raised their voices in accord with Preacher Manny against what looked to be a growing faction of discontented farmers.

But Abraham ignored them. "It's high time we get some help. That freak summer drought nearly did some of us in."

"That's God's business," said Preacher Manny.

"Well, I say the Good Lord gave us brains and we oughta use 'em." Abraham turned toward his three sons, who muttered their agreement. One of them egged him on by cuffing him lightly on the back. "We could use the tractor power. Now more than ever."

When will it end? Reuben wondered, slowly stepping back to remove himself from the ruckus. Struggling from dawn till dusk was the expected way of the People—the way things had always been done.

Then Old Joe Glick and four of his brothers, along with a handful of their fired-up cousins, started defending the Ordnung. One of the younger men pointed his finger, and several more near Reuben mimicked the gesture, their eyes intent on Abraham and his sons. For sure and for certain, this meeting was even more heated than the last one, where many of these same men had gathered to voice frustration.

Placing his hat on his head, Reuben turned to go. But right then his brother spoke up from behind him. "'Tis time all of us head on home. We've got plenty-a work to be done, seems to me," the bishop said.

Abraham frowned. "Jah, we've plenty-a work, Bishop . . . and tractors would ease the burden. We're losin' ground in more ways than one."

"Such things are of the devil, the way I see it." The bishop caught Reuben's eye as he faced Abraham and the others. "'Tis best to do what you know you're s'posed to, following what we all know is right and good. And, Abe—and those of you of like mind—you best be watchin' your rebellious spirit."

Abraham looked down at the floor, working his foot on something Reuben couldn't see.

Their sixty-year-old bishop shook his head. "I must say, there's far more to this than meets the eye. And it can't be solved in these dog-and-cat fights."

Reuben was moved to speak at last. "Why not call the membership together? We'll put this thing to rest."

Both the bishop's and Preacher Manny's expression changed mighty fast. "Reuben, you have no idea what you're talkin' 'bout," said his brother.

The preachers from Chester County nodded, seemingly in agreement.

Then Bishop Joseph spoke again. "The die is cast . . . no turnin' back to voting and such. Here lately, if it's not one thing, it's another: men wanting tractors . . . others wanting to do away with shunning practices." He folded his arms over his stocky chest. "Seems we need more than just another gathering."

"Jah, but 'tis best to keep the women out of this for the time bein'," Preacher Manny said, eyeing Reuben.

"Well, our wives ain't deaf, nor are they dumb." Reuben stepped forward. "They surely know something's a-brewin'." He was tired of all this talking in circles; time to draw a line in the dirt. He was *for* the Ordnung as it stood, so why was Manny singling him out, anyway?

Manny's eyes shot daggers. "Best be keepin' your thoughts to yourself, cousin."

Ach, I'm with ya, Preacher, don't misunderstand, Reuben wanted to say.

Well, he was with Manny on *most* aspects of the Ordnung. He thought again of Suzy, departed before she could take the kneeling vow. It was impossible to erase from his mind the painful knowledge that baptism into the church was essential for any hope of heaven.

To think that some folk, in other churches, were allowed to say they belonged to the Lord—*saved,* as it were—and could rejoice in that assurance. His cousin Jonathan believed exactly that. Oh, to know where you were going when you died!

Poor, dear Suzy . . .

Reuben had a gnawing emptiness in his very soul, a festering grief he refused to express. Following the Old Ways had not fulfilled his spiritual longing, and his discussion this morning with Cousin Jonathan hadn't made things any better.

CHAPTER 3

Betsy Fisher, mother of nine, thought of herself as a percep-
tive soul, though she would never boast of it. Reuben had
surprised her once by saying she had an uncanny way of
deciphering the things folk said, could cut right through to
the truth.

Fact was, she sometimes felt most everything right and
good had ceased when her youngest daughter drowned.
She assumed this was how other mothers felt when their
children's lives were cut short . . . taken away too soon from
those who loved them.

Sighing, Betsy gazed out the kitchen window at the clear
sky, as blue as a piece of fine pottery she'd seen over at a shop
north of Strasburg not so long ago. The color had stood out
because it was so unlike the blue of the fabric sanctioned by
the brethren. Not the royal blue of their cape dresses, but
the soft yet distinct blue of a robin's egg.

She found herself glad for the lack of rain this day—the
weather made traveling pleasant, and Ephram had already
come to drop off some preserves from Maryann, offering to
take Nellie Mae over to see her when he was headed home
again. It was awful nice how that worked out, seeing as how
Nellie scarcely got a chance to visit with Maryann.

Betsy realized anew that she disliked having Nellie Mae farther away than the bakery shop. Since Suzy's death, Nellie was the daughter who had watched over her most closely, as if more aware of the depth of her mother's loss. When Nellie left a room, she took something along with her. *Something I sorely need,* Betsy thought.

There had been times lately when she felt sure Nellie Mae was stronger than she herself, even as a grown woman. Betsy had known it in her bones from her daughter's earliest days just how confident Nellie was—at least since Nellie's first determined baby steps at only nine-and-a-half months. It was no surprise that such a determined child had grown into the kind of young woman capable of running a shop almost single-handedly. Few girls could handle such responsibility, let alone thrive under its weight.

Jah, Nellie's a strong one. Ever so steady on her feet . . . and otherwise, thought Betsy. *Till recently.*

She wiped her hands on her long black apron and hurried down the center hall of the farmhouse, heading for the back door. She had been awake since before sunup, glad for the few tender moments of Reuben's usual morning natter and nuzzling before he arose for a long day of work.

Sighing once more as she opened the door, Betsy breathed deeply of the crisp air. Just yesterday she'd noticed moths had clustered in the dark trees like tiny umbrellas, foretelling the cold snap. She looked out over their vast spread of land, a gem of a place nestled in a green hollow—"away from it all," as Reuben liked to say. His grandfather had bestowed this land upon them when they'd decided to up and marry nearly the second they'd started courting. Their youth had stunned the bishop, but he was happy enough when the babies started coming a full year later.

Betsy smiled. *Such a long time ago, but, oh, the good days of hard work and raising youngsters.* The familiar lump in her throat threatened to return, but she willed herself not to cry. *One step at a time,* someone had told her. You didn't get over the loss of a child in a mere three months. It could take years and even longer.

Whatever might come, Betsy must not let this crush her heart as she'd seen happen to others. Grief-ridden mothers, some who'd lost little ones at the hands of Englischers who drove recklessly around the buggies, speeding up on purpose, or so it seemed.

Does this pain the Lord God, too?

She was squinting hard, knowing she ought not to give place to anger. Even so-called accidents were the will of the Sovereign One, Jehovah God, whose ways were lofty—higher than her own. Trials made one stronger, didn't they?

The Good Book itself spoke of such profound sadness— weeping only lasting so long, then joy coming in the morning. Even for her, the time for the singing of the birds and spring would come eventually, if the Lord God saw fit to turn her sorrow into gladness. When dear Reuben read Scriptures like these, she often felt comforted, and she took refuge in the fact.

Betsy whispered to the air, "Are there others who fret like me?" She expected there were, even though they, too, had been taught to adhere to the Ordnung; many of its rules had been handed down for generations. They embraced whatever life brought, knowing that in God's providence, it was meant to be.

Forcing her mind on to the task now at hand, Betsy headed toward the chicken house. The old frame structure had recently been made sturdier by her husband's frugal ingenuity. She recalled her days as a young bride, gladdened by

Reuben's natural skill in breeding and raising horses. He had gotten his start by purchasing half a dozen lame racing horses at local stockyard auctions, mostly Morgan trotters, taking care to flawlessly mend their injuries. Over time those horses and their offspring became some of the best for harness use, thanks to Reuben's gentle, yet persistent nature and knack for training colts. His reputation was such now that Amish farmers from all around the area turned to him whenever they required a reliable horse. Truly, Betsy knew she'd married a good man; one with a good heart, too.

She caught herself in a rare smile and stopped to glance across the yard at the bakery shop, all freshly painted and done up. *Wonder how Nan's faring today.* Most days, she'd much rather help Nellie Mae's customers than tend to the chickens. Who wouldn't? Nice warm, cheery room. Friendly faces, pleasant chatter . . . a bit of gossip. She felt too alone here lately, but all of that was another thing yet. 'Twas Reuben's say-so where she spent her days for now.

She made her way across the yard, still wet in patches from the heavy dew. She remembered sitting there on the lawn with five-year-old Emma, her son James's daughter. How she'd enjoyed eating strawberries from Kauffman's Fruit Farm in the shade of their old maple.

Was it just this past June—before Suzy died?

A sudden longing sprang up for the youngster who looked ever so much like Suzy, but who possessed more sense of right and wrong, hopefully. She wished Emma would slow down some and not grow up so quicklike. The times she crawled onto her *Mammi's* lap were already becoming scarce. *Thinks she's too big for that now,* Betsy supposed.

What was it about summertime? Children and weeds.

Sighing loudly, she pushed open the door to the chicken house. The hens flapped and cackled greedily. "*Kumm* get it." She reached for the sack of feed, knowing right then why she cared not one bit for this job. She'd only begun doing Suzy's chore the day after she'd drowned, reluctant to let anyone else take it on.

Several times since, she'd considered stepping aside. "Think like Nellie Mae . . . be strong," Betsy urged herself. Still, it was all she could do to complete the chore and get herself back into the house to sit awhile. If only her now-youngest might somehow sense how much she was needed at home.

Rosanna King's blue eyes shone brightly with tears, and her blond hair was pulled back tightly in a large bun beneath her white head covering—her prayer *Kapp*. The expression on her face made it clear to Nellie her friend's tears were joyful ones. "Oh, Nellie Mae, you'll never guess what I have to tell ya. You just never will."

"Well, what on earth?"

"Nearly too good to be true, it is." Rosanna reached for Nellie's hand. "Ach . . . but my cousin Kate has offered Elias and me a most remarkable gift."

The first thing that came to mind was Kate Beiler's antique hope chest, which was a lovely sight to see. Handcrafted from the finest wood, it was perhaps the prettiest piece of furniture Nellie had ever seen. Was Kate going to part with it?

"Kate's in the family way—due near Christmas."

She's had many-a baby, thought Nellie, not quite sure what Rosanna meant to say.

"Kate wants to give the baby to *me* . . . to Elias and me."

Witnessing the joy-light in Rosanna's eyes, Nellie Mae's heart leaped. "What unbelievable news, Rosie!" She had heard of an Amish mother in another state offering to give an infant to relatives, but learning her barren friend was to receive such a gift was another thing altogether.

"Ain't it, though? And to think the Good Lord told my cousins to do this—well, put it in their hearts, I s'pose I should say."

"Jah, 'cause God scarcely ever talks to folk, ya know," Nellie said.

"Well, in this case . . . He surely must have."

"I'm ever so happy for you," Nellie said, smiling at this woman who was as dear to her as the day. Though Rosanna was but twenty-one, she knew too well the sorrow of losing her babies to miscarriage. This last time, the presiding doctor had declared she would probably never carry a baby to term. The shock of the news had been terrible for both Rosanna and her young husband, and Nellie wondered if Rosanna had confided the doctor's startling conclusion to Kate just as she had to Nellie.

Suddenly she felt nervous as worrisome thoughts flitted through her head. What if something happened and Kate couldn't . . . or didn't follow through with her offer? But Nellie held her peace, not wanting to bring a sad thought to her friend, who had yearned for a little one with no success.

"Please sit, Nellie Mae. Have some hot cocoa with me. Time to rejoice." Rosanna didn't wait for her to agree. She scurried over to the stove and set a kettle on the fire. "'Tis such a gift, ain't? There's no other way to look at it."

"I should say so." Yet Nellie could not understand how Rosanna's cousin and her husband could give away their own precious baby—their flesh and blood. She'd seen the adorable wee ones Kate had birthed over the years, six youngsters in all.

How can Kate relinquish her baby? Won't she pine for this child all the days of her life?

Despite her questions, Nellie's spirits had risen at Rosanna's news. She couldn't help but think, and hope, that just maybe Kate's promise of a baby—a Christmas babe—might somehow dispel some of the ridiculous church tittle-tattle. *If a baby can do such a thing.*

CHAPTER 4

—

Betsy rolled out the dough for her chicken and dumplings dinner, glad Nellie Mae was back from her visit over at Ephram's. She had tried her best to chat with Nellie upon her return, but her daughter had seemed distracted. She wondered if Nellie Mae had taken the opportunity to open up to Maryann and share her secret. Close as she had been to Suzy, surely Nellie knew more about Suzy's death than she was telling.

Sighing, Betsy expertly shaped each dough ball, washing her hands at the sink when she was through. How convenient it was to no longer have to carry well water indoors from the pump.

Reuben's doing . . .

Thinking of her husband's insistence on bringing water into the house two months back, she hoped Reuben would not fall prey to the urging of his farmer friends and relatives' current progressive talk. Yet her husband had voiced nary an interest in modern farm equipment over the years, despite their living alongside English neighbors who owned such things. Of course, as a newly married couple, she and Reuben had sometimes talked privately of the hard reality of doing things the Old Way, which kept them working long hours, day in and day out. Truth was, Betsy did sometimes envy the Englischers, who could plow, plant, and cultivate their fields in record time.

With time left to rest of an evening . . .

Momentarily she wondered what that must be like, but immediately she rejected the thought, just as Reuben certainly would. It was not the path they had chosen.

She wrapped her arms around her middle, making her way across the backyard to the paved path that led from the dirt road in front of the house all the way back to Nellie's cozy and quaint bakery. The shop's sign perched above the solid structure, beckoning passersby to drop in. Like the rest of the building, it had been built by her husband and their eldest sons—twins Thomas and Jeremiah—both as strapping as they were dependable.

She smiled thinking of her double blessing, still recalling all the fun—and the seemingly endless work—she'd experienced as a new mother of only eighteen. How thankful she'd been even then for a husband who'd added to her joy with his thoughtful ways. Truly she had cared for handsome Reuben Fisher right from the start of their courting days.

Betsy suspected her daughter Nan was equally ripe for a similarly intense romance, although she had no indication from studying Nan's blue eyes, a striking contrast to her rich brunette hair. Nan was as guarded about whom she liked and disliked as any of Betsy's girls, just as a discreet Amish girl ought to be. No, this daughter was not about to give away any secrets with the stoic look on her face.

But now, there was definitely something going on with Nellie Mae. You couldn't miss the blush on her cheeks. She had always enjoyed playing baseball or volleyball with the boys in the church . . . even climbing trees at times, too, which had never set well with Reuben. He wanted his daughters to be young ladies—none of this tomboy business. God made boys to be tough and hardworking, and girls . . . well, they were supposed to be soft and sweet and mighty submissive.

Of course problems arose when there was a lip and an attitude, like Nellie Mae had at times, especially here lately. Thankfully it wasn't as obvious when Reuben was present. Betsy wished Nellie to be compliant and pleasant, but Suzy's death must have triggered something in her. Betsy had discovered the same angry struggle within herself. "Does the Lord God see the darkness within me?" she muttered, looking at the way the light from the sun cast parallel lines on the lawn.

Suddenly she noticed a black automobile with a white top slow down and stop in front of the house. A tall man got out and stood near the mailbox, as if checking for the address. He eyed the signpost poked deep into the ground—Nellie's Simple Sweets—the only advertising needed on the road, as word of mouth was the best source of customers.

Another Englischer, she thought, glad for the additional business. The Good Lord knew they needed to sell all their baked goods each and every day—this fall especially.

This worldly man did not look like one of Nellie's regulars, however. He had a purpose in his stride, and a stiff brown hat on his head. Even the long tan overcoat that looked like it had leaped off the pages of a Sears, Roebuck, and Co. catalogue spoke of business.

"Hello, there, ma'am." He stopped to tip his fine hat. "I'm looking for Reuben Fisher." His eyes were black coals in a too-pale face.

"Who do you say is lookin' for him?" she spouted before she could stop herself.

"Why, that would be me—Mr. Snavely, ma'am." He quickly extended his hand.

"My husband's runnin' errands, but he'll be back after a bit." She wanted in the worst way to ask what this fancy man wanted with Reuben, all dressed as he was in creased black trousers and a worldly sports jacket beneath his open top coat. Even his long plaid tie was looped just so.

"Would you mind giving this to him?" Mr. Snavely handed her a small white card with the silhouette of a small tractor up in the corner. "I've been in the neighborhood. This tells how to reach me."

She glanced at the telephone number, wishing to set him straight: They did not believe in using the devil's tools for either business or pleasure, no matter the convenience they provided. Besides, the bishop would put the nix on such goings-on in a big hurry.

He continued to stand there, looking her over curiously. Surely it was her Plain attire that he found interesting, being a modern fellow and all. Some Englischers weren't accustomed to the sight of Amish folk. "Thank you, uh, Mrs. Fisher?"

"Jah, that's right." She wasn't about to volunteer her first name, although she herself seldom went by her given name of Elizabeth. Better she encourage this unwanted visitor to be on his way.

When Nellie spotted the Englischer shortly after she'd returned home from Rosanna's, she ought not to have been surprised. After all, it wasn't the first time a stranger had rolled to a stop in front of their roadside sign. All the same, she did wonder why he remained out in the yard talking with Mamma, of all things.

"What the world?" Nellie went to the shop window, glad for the short lull, and watched the man lean forward while talking with her mother, apparently handing her something. Was he someone her father knew?

The moment the man hurried back to his shiny car and took off down the road, Nellie ran straight to the house.

Mamma was shaking her head, fanning her pink face with a hankie. "We've got ourselves a tractor salesman in the neighborhood."

"He wants us to buy *what*?" Nellie asked, shocked that an Englischer like that would feel comfortable going door to door.

Evidently the discord among them had already reached the ears of outsiders. Nellie should have seen this coming. Yet she dared not say she'd hinted at such things with Maryann over tea earlier.

Mamma rose. "Well, we Fishers will be havin' none of this nonsense." She opened the cupboard beneath the sink and dropped the business card into the rubbish. "You're not to breathe a word of this, ya hear? Not even to your Dat. No need for him to know a Mr. Snavely even exists."

Nellie Mae had never seen her mother's eyes so dark. The pupils were nearly black—odd, since Mamma's eyes were normally ever so blue. "Next thing People will be wantin' electric and cars and who knows what. It's the evil one at work among us, I say." She reached for the hem of her apron and began again to fan her face.

"Mamma, you're workin' yourself up." Nellie pulled out her father's chair at the head of the table, helping her into it. "Just sit now."

"You've got a mouth on ya, child."

Nellie Mae huffed. "Try and be still, that's all I'm askin'. You know Dat's not interested in such things."

Her mother kept fussing. "Promise you won't speak of this to anyone. We don't need any more worries."

"Oh, Mamma—"

"Right now, promise me!"

Nellie was silent. Then slowly, she shook her head.

Mamma glowered. "Nellie Mae?"

She gritted her teeth at her mother's resolve.

"Give me your word, daughter."

Nellie had stonewalled long enough. "There—you have it." Abruptly she hurried out the door.

Frustrated by her mother's seemingly irrational concern, she noticed a huge flock of red-winged blackbirds appearing out of the dense grass to the east of the house. Like a small black cloud at first, the flock took shape and flew low to the ground across the expanse of pastureland and meadow before flying up, up to the tallest tree. First one bird, then another plunged in and out of sight, settling into the branches of the mighty oak tree.

Suzy had always been so fond of birds, fascinated by their migration each year, their patterns of life.

If only she were still alive . . .

What would her sister have thought of the tractor talk between their mamma and Mr. Snavely? Life had become complicated indeed since Suzy's death.

———

Nellie cleared the table after supper, glad she'd taken time for a walk to calm herself down after her tiff with Mamma. Glad, too, she'd gone back inside after a while to apologize.

Presently Nan was busy heating some water while Rhoda began sweeping. As she carried dishes to the sink, Nellie observed the contrast in her sisters' hair color—Nan's such a rich brown and Rhoda's a buttery blond. Like Nellie, Nan could eat anything and remain as skinny as a stick, a trait the pleasingly plump Rhoda did not share. Yet despite their physical differences, her two older sisters could not have been closer.

The way Suzy and I used to be . . .

"Mamma's talkin' of having Emma come over for the whole day tomorrow," Nan said suddenly.

"I'm not surprised," said Rhoda, reaching under her Kapp to poke her chubby finger at her blond hair bun.

"Mamma can't seem to get enough of *that* one," Nellie Mae agreed.

"Well, one good look says why." Rhoda had a knowing smile. "She's a little Suzy."

"Just so you know, Emma will have to sleep with *you*, Nellie," Nan said, handing her a dish towel. "Will you dry tonight?"

"Why, sure." Nellie meant she'd dry the dishes, but she didn't mean the wiggle worm could share her bed. "Emma's all over the place when she sleeps."

"Well, why do ya think I suggested you?" To this Nan added a giggle.

"We could put her in James's old bedroom," suggested Rhoda, who stooped down to brush crumbs into the dustpan. "How's that?"

"If she doesn't mind sleepin' in a haunted room," Nan said over her slender shoulder.

"Ain't haunted," Rhoda insisted, pushing up her glasses and heading right to Nan at the sink. "Why do you make up such things?"

Nan grinned. "Ach, I say it is."

"Well, *why*?" Nellie asked, bewildered at the turn in their conversation. She'd never heard Nan talk so.

Nan looked at them both, eyes serious. "Guess you didn't know it, but Suzy went in there sometimes. Quite a lot, really."

"Whatever for?" asked Nellie Mae.

"Maybe to hide the . . . um, smell." Nan held up two fingers to her lips and took an imaginary puff.

Nellie felt her neck burn. "You don't know any such thing."

"Ach, are ya sure?" Rhoda piped up.

Nan shrugged. "I wouldn't be surprised."

Nellie was stunned. "I never saw Suzy smoke."

"Then why did she change clothes in there so often?" Nan smirked.

"You know this for certain?" Nellie asked.

"Jah, I saw her." Nan rolled her eyes, as if to say, *you think I'm fibbing.*

To Nellie the whole conversation seemed irreverent. They had no right to speak of their dead sister this way. Nellie wasn't surprised at Nan's seemingly jealous streak, though.

Nan had always been envious of Suzy's popularity, especially in school in years past. Not to mention the way Dat and Mamma had always held Suzy up as a standard of innocence, much to Nan's consternation—at least until Suzy's last half year.

Still, would she make this up about Suzy?

The teakettle began to shrill. Grimacing, Nan scurried to the stove and carried the kettle to the sink. She poured the boiling water into the cold and added the dish soap, swishing it around to make plenty of suds. As she did, Nan leaned over to whisper in Rhoda's ear, but not so softly that Nellie couldn't hear.

"I daresay Suzy was ready to jump straight to the world," she whispered, "just weeks before she drowned."

Rhoda's hand shot up and clapped over her mouth. "You don't mean it!"

Nan nodded, a glint of sadness in her eye. "Seems so."

Before Nellie could object to the foolish speculation and attempt to scold Nan for such disrespect, Mamma came into the kitchen, hushing them all up.

But for the rest of the evening and long into the night, Nellie thought of Nan's startling words. In some ways, she was glad Suzy's secrets were buried with her—whatever they might have been. She trembled a bit. No, she didn't really mean that. She would give most anything to have Suzy back, laughing and enjoying life, sharing her infectious joy. Nellie Mae would even put up with her apparent fondness for fancy English friends, if only Suzy were alive.

Chapter 5

The first thing Nellie Mae did Friday morning was bake more chocolate chip cookies than usual. Recently they were flying off the shelves, and she wondered why. Were fancy mothers too busy to bake once school started? *Seems they'd have more time, rather than less,* she thought.

Later in the bakery, she set about arranging the day's offerings and considered the number of pies and such she could make through the autumn months if she only had more pumpkins. Perhaps Dat or one of her brothers might pick up some more at market over the weekend.

Hearing footsteps, she looked up and saw a young man wearing a black work coat and black felt hat walking toward the bakery shop. He leaned into the breeze in such a way that she couldn't make out his face.

When he came in the door and raised his head, she was stunned to recognize Caleb Yoder, hazel eyes smiling.

What on earth? She thought her heart might stop beating.

"Hullo, Nellie Mae." He removed his hat.

"Hullo."

He fumbled for something in his pocket, and she assumed he was fishing for his wallet.

"I baked lots of cookies today," she said quickly, wondering what he might like.

He fixed his gaze on her. "Frankly, I'm not here for the goodies." Despite his words, he glanced longingly at the pies. "I stopped by on my way to do an errand for *Daed*." He handed her a piece of paper folded several times. "I want to give this to you personally." His smile spread clear across his handsome face now.

"*Denki*," she said. The note felt warm in her hand, and she wished he might stay.

But Caleb glanced nervously at the door. Was he worried he might encounter other customers?

"Well, I'd better be on my way." His eyes lingered on hers for a moment. "I'll be seein' ya, Nellie Mae." With that he left.

She moved immediately to the window and watched him fairly march all the way down the drive and out to the main road, where she assumed he'd left his horse and buggy.

Jittery with excitement, Nellie Mae returned to her post behind the counter, the folded paper with her name scrawled on the top still in hand.

I was absolutely right last June. He did smile at me!

Trembling, she opened the note and began to read.

Dear Nellie Mae,

Will you go riding with me after the next Singing? If so, please meet me alongside Cambridge Road afterward, about a mile southeast of the barn. There's a sheltered area among some trees and shrubs that will keep you out of the wind.

Sincerely,
Caleb Yoder

He was asking her in a note? This was rather unusual. Even so it was quite sweet, and Nellie felt ever so happy.

"Ach, this is unbelievable!"

She imagined how blushing pink her face must be, and just now there were customers coming up the drive, having missed Caleb by a mere minute.

She tucked the note into her pocket, her heart singing as she went about helping her customers that morning. *He does like me . . . he does!*

"A true miracle," she decided of the invitation. Up until now Caleb had kept his distance, attending the same Sunday Singings but always talking to others. She would have given up all hope if it hadn't been for that single June smile.

And now this note . . . after three months of waiting, it certainly seemed as if he'd finally decided to act. Yet could she allow herself to fully hope? Caleb had caught the eye of nearly every girl in the district, after all.

But I'm the one he asked!

To think he'd stopped by personally to invite her to ride with him after the next Saturday night Singing—one week from tomorrow!

When a break from customers presented itself, she wondered if she dared run to collect her writing paper from the house. But no, Nellie Mae didn't need to drop everything to give Caleb her reply. *He can wait for the Monday mail,* she decided.

———

After Mamma's noontime dinner of creamed dried beef and pan-fried potatoes, Nellie Mae was glad for some time to write her response to Caleb. Here, in the quiet bakery shop, it was private—although with its being the start of the weekend, there was no guarantee things would remain so.

She wrote the date on her lined stationery ever so neatly. How she wished for something prettier, but this paper would have to do. There was no extra money, hers or otherwise, for frivolous things like fine writing paper.

Not like Deacon Lapp's daughter surely has. Truth was, Susannah Lapp's father was earning himself a bank full of money raising tobacco, even in a dry year. Others in the community grew the crop, as well, including Caleb's father and all of her own married brothers. It was the cash crop of choice and had been around Lancaster County for longer than Sam Hippey's ring bologna.

Nellie Mae was glad her father had never grown the smelly crop, for she disliked the suffocating scent of tobacco hanging to dry in the shed. She would never understand why on earth her brother Ephram had decided to take up the pipe when their own father had shunned the habit.

Nan startled her but good, rushing in the shop door. "Do ya need any help?"

"All's quiet for now."

Nan's gaze fell to her paper and poised pen. "Takin' inventory?"

"Not today."

"Writing a circle letter, maybe?"

Nellie held her breath. Since Nan had been the one to bring in the mail today, she surely knew there hadn't been a single newsy letter from their cousins. Nan was pushing.

"What, then?" Nan asked, eyes probing.

"Just a little note is all."

Nan nodded. "Ach, if you'd rather be alone, just say so."

Nellie wondered if she'd seen Caleb come and go, but she wouldn't fret over that. Even if Nan had spotted him, she couldn't know his reason for stopping by. Still, she was relieved when her sister left nearly as quickly as she'd arrived.

Only then did Nellie resume her writing.

Dear Caleb,
  I would be happy to go riding with you next Saturday.
I'll meet you where you said to after Singing and wait
there in the thicket along the roadside.
             Sincerely,
             Nellie Mae Fisher

Perusing Caleb's note to her once more, she was thankful Nan hadn't returned, although she could always use help if business picked up. Typically it did this time of day as English folk stopped by on their way home from school or work.

She folded both notes and slipped them into her dress pocket. There would be plenty of time for addressing an envelope later in her solitary bedroom. She'd always thought Suzy's and her room was large enough for only one person, whereas Rhoda and Nan shared a bigger room. Sometimes she could hear them whispering and giggling into the night.

An uncontrollable shiver caught her off guard as reality sank in: Caleb had finally asked her out. Even as wonderful-good as that was, the feeling was tinged with the ever-present underlying sorrow; in happier days she might have shared her news with Suzy.

She missed sharing a room with her younger sister, something they'd done since their earliest days. The many nights they'd talked quietly late into the wee hours seemed precious to her now. At times she felt as if Suzy might simply come walking through the bedroom door. Today surely she would take one look at Nellie and say, "Ach, you look ever so cheerful—who's the lucky fella?"

Suzy had seemed quite eager to become a wife and a mother, to make a home for her family just as all Amish-women did . . . just as Nellie herself would someday. Truth be told, until lately, Nellie had been rather contented living in her father's house. A comfortable family abode—large enough to bed down the whole family, including the married brothers and their wives and children. Now that there were only three young women left, the place seemed rather empty.

Sometimes while Nellie Mae baked in the early-morning hours, she considered the house and the comfort in its walls to be a safeguard of sorts. She had always loved their home. *A home with character,* Rosanna had said of it years before, after spending more than a week when her parents visited friends in Sugarcreek, Ohio. She and Rosanna had been exceptionally close even then, sharing not only a love of baking, but of quilting. Yet it was not merely the connection to domestic things that tied them together in close fellowship; they simply liked being together. With Suzy gone, Nellie longed for time with Rosanna all the more.

She rose and circled the display counter. Everything had changed, and nearly in the blink of an eye. Their loss of Suzy was enormous.

Perhaps it's missing her so that makes me less content, she thought, knowing she longed for more. But not for material goods. Rather, she yearned for things out of her grasp. Sometimes she went walking deep in the grazing grass or out on the narrow road, heading as far to the east as she could before coming to the busy intersection, then turning again toward home. At times she even caught herself muttering aloud, as if perhaps, in some peculiar way, she was expressing her thoughts to Jehovah God.

She did not quite know what to do about her ongoing yearnings. Often as a girl she had dreamed of the hereafter, wondering what it must be like in God's heaven . . . if the Lord God would see fit to say to her, "Well done, faithful servant," on the Judgment Day. To think Suzy must surely know the answers to these hardest questions of all.

———————

With the shop closed for the day, Nellie made her way to her bedroom, aware of the coolness seeping in through the walls of Dat's big house. The second room down from her parents', hers was a cozy place with plenty of space for a loveseat in one corner, for whenever she might entertain a beau, as was their particular courting tradition, come engagement. Might Caleb ever be of a mind to visit her secretly? But she was getting way ahead of herself, she knew.

Already she was in over her head with hope. Who knew, once they spent time together, if she'd even like him? Or if he'd like her?

Standing now at the dresser she and Suzy had long shared, Nellie Mae put Caleb's and her notes safely inside. He had gone out of his way to hand her the invitation. *It could be the beginning of something special,* she thought. *Or will I be just another step in his path to finding a wife?*

She lifted the pretty blue plate that graced the dresser. Between the size of a saucer and a salad plate, it had been a gift from eight-year-old Suzy for Nellie's ninth birthday. Suzy had spotted the sweet little thing at an antique shop, and Mamma had purchased it. Over the years, Suzy had used it to leave notes for Nellie, and vice versa. Sometimes a joke or a funny saying . . . something for cheering up or saying merely "good-bye, till later." Even as a youngster, Suzy had always been thinking of ways to express her love for Nellie and others.

Nellie traced the plate's floral border before returning it to the dresser, wishing now she'd saved the last few notes Suzy had ever written.

Always wishing . . . wishing following the death of a beloved one, her good friend Rosanna said. Rosanna, too, had regrets, never having gotten over her own mother's tragic death so many years before . . . nor the deaths of her unborn babies.

Nellie picked up the hand mirror. Her eyes looked tired and her hair was a little *schtrubbich,* so she smoothed it some on either side of the middle part.

Her sadness often came in waves. Just when she thought she'd healed a bit, she would begin to miss Suzy all over again. Setting the mirror down, she opened the small box-like compartment on the right side of the dresser. There she found the strings from one of Suzy's white Kapps . . . the last one she'd worn, on the day of her drowning.

Nellie trembled, knowing she had done a wrongful deed in snipping the ties from the sacred covering.

Mamma might not forgive me, she thought. *Yet my deed is nothing compared to the full truth of Suzy's final months, whatever that may be.*

Standing there, she recalled the night of Suzy's viewing here in the house. Mamma and Mamma's sisters had taken great care to bathe Suzy's body. They'd curtained the kitchen off, locked all the doors, and laid Suzy out in the pine box after lovingly clothing her in her best blue Sunday dress and long white apron. Poor Rhoda and Nan could hardly bear to be present and left together after a time to go upstairs. Nellie had suffered through it alone, scarcely knowing how to compose herself.

Not long after, a stream of visitors began coming and going, some staying longer than others. All through the evening this went on, some folk partaking of the great spread of food the women had brought in. Others took nothing more than black coffee before sitting by the open casket, heads bowed. A few of the younger relatives wept softly.

Nellie had kept to herself, wanting to be near her departed sister yet unable to grieve openly. The news of Suzy's death was still terribly fresh—a death she wholly believed might have been avoided.

Long after midnight, when she saw a momentary opportunity—the room's being suddenly empty of people after Mamma stepped away to the outhouse—Nellie crept to her sister's casket. Aware of her own breathing, she felt compelled to place her hand on Suzy's thin wrist, now so cold and lifeless.

Is it really her?

For a moment Nellie was frightened by the lack of vitality, recalling how she and Suzy had reached for each other's warm hands while sharing their bed upstairs. Nellie groaned, her deep sadness enfolding her as she stood, bowed and frozen, so terribly close to her dead sister.

The darling of the family . . .

Nellie refused to cry. She must hurry, for Mamma would not be gone much longer.

Swiftly she pulled the small half page out of her pocket. There was no need to reread the words she had penned earlier, words that had emblazoned themselves onto her heart.

> *Dear Suzy,*
>   *I wish I could've told you this while you were still alive. I'm sorry we argued the morning before you drowned. I was harsh with you, and I wish I could ask for your forgiveness. I miss you, dearest sister.*
>   *With all my love,*
>   *Nellie Mae*

She shook, tears falling fast. Then, hesitating at first, she managed to reach under Suzy to raise her slightly, just enough to slide the folded note beneath her.

With a sorrowful sigh, Nellie stepped back. Suzy's body lay resting on the heartfelt apology, things she'd longed to say since hearing the devastating news. Little good they did her sister now, but perhaps almighty God would see the words she'd written and take them into account. No matter, Nellie had done what she'd set out to do, her heart and head all tangled up with grief and regret.

She moved nearer again, peering down at Suzy's face, so close. "Oh, Suzy . . . why'd you go with them? Why?"

Overwhelmed with both guilt and love, she leaned down and kissed Suzy's cheek. It felt as smooth and hard as the lovely painted faces of English dolls she'd seen and touched at Watt and Shand's department store in downtown Lancaster. She and Suzy had gone with some Mennonite neighbors, but only that once. Nellie remembered observing the many modern teenagers on the sidewalk—boys with hair cut nearly like her own brothers, and girls with free-flowing waist-length hair wearing long, gathered skirts—as though they were trying to be Plain somehow. She'd never told Mamma about their outing, not even to this day.

With a faltering breath, Nellie ceased her reverie and lifted the white ties of Suzy's head covering from the small wooden cubicle. She slipped them into her empty pocket—the same spot where she'd kept Caleb's wonderful note.

She sighed. *When, oh when, will my joy over Caleb overshadow my sadness for Suzy?*

CHAPTER 6

———

Talkative little Emma *did* come to visit that evening, just as Mamma had wished. As Nan had guessed, it was Nellie who was asked to keep the inquisitive child, and she bedded her niece down early in an attempt to get her settled in.

True to form, Emma had more questions than Nellie had answers. "Where's Aunt Suzy right now?" she asked, lying in bed on the side where Suzy had always slept. "When's she comin' back home?"

Nellie was shocked that her brother James and his wife, Martha, had not explained to their young daughter the finality of Suzy's passing. Or had Emma's young mind simply failed to understand?

Emma began to whimper. "Suzy didn't take her doll with her."

Nellie looked around the room, unsure what Emma could mean.

Still sniffling, Emma rubbed her eyes. "She left her little doll behind. She'll come back for it, jah?"

"Aw, dearie." Nellie leaned forward, kissing her niece's soft forehead.

"*Aendi* Suzy made it last summer . . . during Preachin' "
came the explanation. "She made a dolly in a cradle with
her white hankie."

Nellie lifted Emma into her arms. "Of course she did."
Betsy knew exactly what Suzy had done to entertain Emma
during the long, hot Sunday mornings. All the teenage girls
and young mothers knew that useful trick.

"I kept the dolly in her cradle, Aunt Nellie Mae." Emma
leaned back on the pillow.

"Did you bring it with you?"

Emma shook her head, her blue eyes blinking sleepily.
"She's in my room at home. I'll show you next time you
visit, all right?"

"Why, sure." She felt as tuckered out as Emma seemed,
her energy for the day spent.

"I named her Elizabeth."

Nellie smiled. "Didja know that's Mammi Betsy's name,
too?"

"Jah. Mamma told me." Emma closed her eyes. "It's a
right perty one." She opened her eyes again. "But I still want
Aunt Suzy to come home."

Nellie considered the rote prayers she recited in her mind
each night while lying in bed—prayers she'd learned as a
child younger even than Emma.

Now I lay me down to sleep . . .

She wondered if Emma was saying them now, too. Or
had she succumbed too soon to sleep?

*O Lord God and heavenly Father, is my little sister truly
in heaven? Or that other place . . . ?*

———

Betsy was glad for the help she was getting with breakfast
preparations this morning. Rhoda hummed softly, gingerly

tapping the eggs on the frying pan to break them open while Nellie stirred the pancake batter as the griddle heated up. Betsy found it amusing and baffling that a girl who loved to bake sweets was so thin. She supposed it was because Nellie worked so awful hard.

Reuben liked his eggs fried over-easy, with plenty of pancakes on the side. So did Emma, a chip off the older block. She was balanced on her Dawdi's knee, her hands folded expectantly on the table. James was due to come for Emma sometime midmorning, and Betsy hated to think they must say good-bye very soon.

"How many pancakes can you eat?" Reuben asked Emma.

She spun around in his arms. "Ach, you know, Dawdi!" A chorus of giggles spilled out.

He played along, frowning a bit. "Well, now, let's see, was that six or seven?"

Emma grinned and jumped off his lap, going over to watch the pancakes rise on the big griddle, stepping back when Nellie cautioned her.

Betsy moved about the table, pouring freshly squeezed orange juice into each glass. Truly, she couldn't keep her eyes off James's next oldest, such a delight she was. Much blonder than even their Suzy, Emma had oodles of freckles, with one almost exactly where one of Suzy's had been—just left of the tip of her petite nose.

Emma came running. "I wanna wash the dishes, all right, Mammi?"

"You'll have to ask Aunt Rhoda and Auntie Nan. Aunt Nellie will be out at the shop."

As usual, Betsy had heard Nellie Mae rise in the wee hours before dawn, quietly pulling out the many pans in preparation for baking her cookies, pies, and other goodies. Every day she performed the same ritual, except for the Lord's Day. This day, Nellie had baked an abundance of bread, too. How she managed with only a minimum of help from her sisters was anyone's guess.

Rhoda had been employed for quite some time now by the Kraybills, their English neighbors down the road. Other young women in their church district had started doing much the same, with Bishop Joseph's grudging permission. Even Reuben had stated his opinion against Rhoda's arrangement, but by the time he'd known about it, Rhoda had already been working there for several weeks. Truth was, as an unbaptized young adult, Rhoda was to some extent at liberty to do as she pleased.

As for Nan, until recently she had helped Nellie fairly regularly at the bakery shop, although reluctantly. These days she more often cooked and cleaned alongside Betsy in the house, stepping with ease into Suzy's shoes.

"Can I help Aunt Nellie, then, after I wash the dishes?" Emma's question broke into Betsy's thoughts.

Reuben smiled broadly at the wee girl's persistence. "You're a busy bee today, ain't so?"

"Only today?" Nellie Mae commented from across the room. "You should try sleepin' with her." Suddenly she seemed sheepish, like she ought not to have hinted at her sleepless night with Emma within earshot. But the truth of the matter was Emma didn't seem to pay her any mind.

Emma leaped off Betsy's lap and headed over to Reuben again. *Such a busy girl is right,* thought Betsy, getting some paper napkins for Emma to put around the table. "Here, girlie . . . help your ol' Mammi out."

Emma stood and took the napkins, turning her face up to look right at her. "Aw, you ain't so old, Mammi. You're just awful sad."

The innocent words unlocked something inside, and lest she weep in front of them, Betsy inched toward the doorway and stepped into the sitting area. Behind her, she heard her husband call to Emma. Going to the window, she stood there almost out of habit, as she could scarcely see for the tears.

———

Rosanna set to work after the noon meal crocheting a baby blanket with pale yellows, greens, and blues. *Just right for either a boy or a girl,* she thought, although she hoped for a son for her husband, Elias. A firstborn ought to be a boy. Besides, if they were to have only one child, then a son would be ever so nice.

She pressed her hand to her heart. Ever since Cousin Kate's visit and the splendid news, Rosanna had been unable to sleep because of happiness. To think dear Kate would offer up her very own! And now beloved Nellie Mae knew the joyous news, as well.

'Tis God's doing, Kate had told her several times that day she'd come so unexpectedly, her face shining. The day had been one of surprises, to be sure, beginning with Elias's bringing in a whole bushel basket of oversized cucumbers and butternut squash. Rosanna had already set about to making pickles—both sweet and dill—when Cousin Kate had shown up, astonishing her with her words.

"I want to give you a baby, Rosanna," Kate had said. "Seein' you struggle so . . . losin' several wee ones to miscarriage, just nearly broke my heart." Kate had gone on to say she and John had talked it over. "Right away John was in agreement. Something that rarely ever happens, to be sure!"

Sighing now with all the love she already possessed for Kate's little one, Rosanna took pleasure in the feel of the yarn—the softest she could find at the yard goods store. The beauty of it, the way the pastel colors blended so prettily, made her hope this blanket might be as lovely as some she'd seen at Maryann's. Nellie's sister-in-law seemed to have a knack for making baby blankets.

Just as she seems to have wee ones nearly at will.

Rosanna brushed away the thought; she didn't see how she could be any happier if she were expecting her own child.

"Ach, if Nellie Mae wasn't awful surprised," she murmured as her crochet hook made the yarn loops. She let out a gleeful laugh as she recalled Nellie's brown eyes growing wide at the news. Nellie knew well of her pain . . . the heartache of waiting and hoping, month after endless month, for a babe that never lived to see his mother's face. Truly, Nellie was like a sister to her. She remembered the many long-ago times she'd stayed with Nellie and her family; and the same for her friend, spending time at Rosanna's father's house with Rosanna and her brothers. Though life was keeping them farther apart nowadays, their dear friendship had remained strong. For this reason, Rosanna had wanted Nellie to be the first after Elias to know.

As she began the next row on the baby blanket, Rosanna wondered how her friend was really faring here lately. She felt a tremor of sadness at the thought of her own losses, particularly her mother—much too young to die.

And Suzy Fisher dead now, too . . .

Nellie's sister's drowning still caused Rosanna distress from time to time, and she rose and walked into the kitchen. She set her crocheting down on the table and went to stir the beef stew simmering for dinner. How Suzy's death had come about was not at all clear to her. The Fisher family had said only that she had gone boating with some friends and an accident had occurred, although Nellie had shared a bit more privately with Rosanna. More than was necessary to be told around, she had added.

So an Englischer had been Suzy's downfall—her boyfriend, no less. Rosanna leaned over the pot of stew to taste it, adding more seasoning. What would possess a girl to go that route when there were so many nice Amish boys?

For certain, Nellie Mae knew more than she was saying, and it wasn't Rosanna's place to pry. To Nellie's credit, it took some amount of restraint to be tight-lipped—especially when Nellie had always said she felt "ever so comfortable" with Rosanna. From their first encounter as young girls till now, the two had shared openly.

Yet Rosanna had noticed that despite Nellie's sorrow, she looked almost radiant at times. Was Nellie sweet on someone? And if so, why hadn't she confided it as she always had before with every boy Nellie'd liked even a smidgen? There was an air of mystery around Nellie lately, which wasn't like her. If there was a young man, Nellie Mae had evidently decided to keep this one a secret.

Lovingly now, Rosanna touched the unfinished blanket that would warm her baby this winter. Unexpected tears sprang to her eyes. She thought of the last infant she'd seen, at Preaching service last week, and the way the baby had snuggled so blissfully in her mother's arms. She could only imagine what it might feel like to hold the wee one who was to be her own.

"Will it be a son for Elias? Or a daughter for me?" she said softly, bringing the beginnings of the crocheted blanket to her cheek and holding it there.

———

They'd all had their Saturday night baths, thanks to Dat, who'd built on a small washroom at the east side of the

kitchen two months ago. Nellie was most grateful for a bath-
tub with running water where she could enjoy the privacy
of bathing in a locked room. And she secretly liked having
the medicine chest with its small mirror affixed to the wall.
Having such luxuries certainly spoiled one.

Nellie and Mamma were sitting on Nellie's bed after Bible
reading and silent prayers, their long hair still quite damp.
"'Tis best not to yearn for what used to be," Mamma said.
"Even though I'd like to turn back the clock somehow."

"I think we all would, ain't so?"

Mamma nodded sadly. "Every day." She paused and her
face flushed as if she was eager to say something private.

"Aw, Mamma." Nellie touched her mother's hand.

Her mother sniffled. "I dream of Suzy so often."

Nellie rose and picked up her brush from the dresser,
feeling a twinge of regret. *Why don't I dream of Suzy?*

Oh, how she'd longed to. The fact that she hadn't—or
couldn't—troubled her greatly. Did this happen to others
who grieved? Was it because she kept pushing the guilt
away? Was she pushing away the memories, too?

Her mother reached for the brush. "Here . . . sit awhile.
I'll help you get your tangles out." She stood and began to
brush through Nellie's long hair.

Nellie sighed, enjoying Mamma's gentle brushing. She
dared not tell a soul, but she had begun to forget what her
sister looked like. Try as she might, Suzy's features were
beginning to fade, and Nellie felt panicky at the thought.
For the first time, she yearned for one of those fancy photo-
graphs. Yet even without it, how could she forget her own
sister's face? So many things didn't make sense . . . starting
with the stunted sweet corn . . . and now all the talk amongst
the People.

Was this a sign of things to come?

CHAPTER 7

Preaching service seemed longer than usual. Nellie and her family were cooped up in the deacon's stuffy house, instead of gathering for the Sunday meeting in the barn, where the breezes could blow through the wide doors. The weather having begun to turn, it made better sense to meet inside today.

From where she sat, Nellie Mae could see the back of Caleb's head. Susannah Lapp and her mother and three younger sisters all sat primly in a row, off to one side. Normally Nellie wouldn't have paid any mind to the other young woman's whereabouts, but Susannah kept glancing at Caleb.

Wouldn't she be surprised that Caleb likes me? Nellie thought, feeling more smug than she probably ought to on the Lord's Day.

Forcing herself to listen carefully, she wished she could understand the Scripture reading. Both sermons, the shorter first one and the much longer second, were always given in High German, which only the older people like her Dawdi Fisher understood. Her father had also picked it up from hearing it again and again over the years. Nellie, though, would have much preferred Preaching to be in Pennsylvania

Dutch, with occasional English mixed in, the way the People communicated at home and at work.

Because the sermons were not comprehensible, one of the only clues Nellie had as to the subject matter was the preacher's facial expression—at this minute Preacher Lapp, Susannah's uncle, wore a scowl. Susannah's family was certainly well represented among the church brethren, with both a preacher and a deacon in this generation. Of course, that had everything to do with the drawing of lots, the practice through which the Lord God divinely ordained their ministers.

What else will God choose? She hoped Caleb wasn't of the elect, at least not for Susannah's future husband. She wondered again why Caleb had written to her instead of Susannah. Every fellow surely knew Susannah was the prettiest girl in the district.

Nellie pushed the gnawing thoughts away. Slowly she began to relax, the monotone of the preacher's voice fading more and more, until . . .

Nellie's head bobbed, but a hard poke to her arm from Rhoda jolted her. Hoping not to draw attention to herself, she sat up straighter and inhaled deeply, then held her breath, doing what she could to try to stay awake from now till the end of the three-hour service. Why was it so hard?

On the other side of her, Nan seemed to be choking down a chuckle; either that or she was struggling not to cough. No, Nellie was pretty sure Nan had seen her doze off during the unending sermon—just like their mamma, who was nodding off herself. That at least made Nellie feel some better, though she was thankful to be well out of Caleb's view this Preaching service.

During cleanup following the common meal, when the women and some of the older teen girls were putting the kitchen back in order and the men were folding up the tables, Nellie came across two men talking heatedly on the back porch.

Not wanting to eavesdrop, she walked past them with the bag of rubbish she was carrying to the trash receptacle behind the barn, but the angry words followed her across the stillness of the barnyard. For the most part, the People were still gathered in the house.

"Listen here, I've got fifteen children, and four of my sons are out seein' English girls," one of the men said. "Can't get my boys much interested in farmin'—the minute they turn sixteen, seems they're out getting themselves an automobile . . . and, well, who wants to join church after that?"

"'Tis a bigger problem ev'ry year," said the other, an old-timer. He took a puff on his pipe and blew out the smoke before going on. "You just ain't hard enough on your young'uns."

"You've forgotten what it's like," retorted the first man. "All this talk of cars and electric and telephones round here don't help much, neither."

Nellie nearly stopped walking, so badly she wanted to hear the rest of their pointed discussion, but she didn't pause until she'd reached her destination. If men right here in their midst were demanding such things—and she had every reason to suspect they were, despite Ephram's tight-lipped refusal to comment—then surely the bishop would set them all straight. And anyway, why wouldn't a son want to farm with his father? She didn't understand and was quite sure Caleb would never do otherwise as the youngest son in the family. In the Old Order community, the youngest typically inherited the farm.

She thought of Caleb receiving the nearly one hundred acres his father and grandfather had farmed—property that went clear back to his great-grandfather Yoder. Was Caleb itching to claim the land of his ancestors?

Surely he is, she thought. *Just like any son who finds himself on the eve of his father's impending retirement.*

But before Caleb could take on the family farm, he must find himself a bride.

Caleb knew he would remember weeks, maybe months from now, exactly how Nellie Mae Fisher looked as she came walking across the yard toward Deacon Lapp's house. Her face was rosy, like she'd gotten a mite too close to an old cookstove, and a stray slip of hair on her neck made her appear younger than her seventeen years.

Nellie had not been a girl who stuck out in a crowd, at least not until this past summer. As if blossoming overnight, she was suddenly altogether feminine and pretty in a way he couldn't describe. She possessed something more than the curvaceous beauty of some of the girls he'd dated and quickly tired of. The sparkle to her eyes and mystery in her smile made him wonder why he hadn't noticed her before.

He'd gone out to get some fresh air, secretly hoping to encounter Nellie. Instead, he happened upon two men locked in debate. Thankfully the pair were moving now from the interior of the back porch to outside, near the well pump, as their arguing rose to a higher pitch. Unexpectedly three more men marched up, joining the first two as one raised his fist in the air.

"No tellin' where all this will lead." One man's words floated to the sky.

Caleb wanted to spare Nellie the commotion, but she was making a beeline straight for the house. She would have to enter the back doorway and head through the porch to return to the kitchen.

He called to her. "Nellie Mae!"

When her big eyes caught his gaze, her engaging smile spread clear across her face. "Hullo, Caleb," she said right out, not like some girls who seemed nearly afraid of their voices. Of course, he'd expected such composure in a girl capable of running a bakery shop. Surely he could also expect to hear back from her soon regarding his written invitation.

His heart beat more quickly at the thought that, for the first time in more than a year of asking girls to go riding after Singings and such, he couldn't be sure what the answer would be.

"You mind walkin' round the house with me, right quick?" He steered her away from the growing cluster of men.

"Why, sure." She smiled at his request and turned, not waiting for him to smile back. "Did you hear what they were talking 'bout?" she asked.

"Some, jah."

"Well, I didn't like it, not one bit. Did you?" She was straight to the point and it pleased him.

He stopped then, where the Dawdi Haus jutted out from the main house, hiding them well enough. He was glad when she did the same, her eyes squarely on his as she awaited his answer. "There are men who are lookin' for loopholes in the Ordnung," he told her. "Some are willin' to walk away from the beliefs of our forefathers . . . what they laid down as the right way to live and work."

A way of life paid for with the blood of our martyrs . . .

He wouldn't go on; he would spare her too much of his opinion now, alone as they momentarily were in broad daylight.

"Well, I'm altogether sure of one thing," she replied.

"What's that, Nellie Mae?"

"My father will have nothin' of that sort of talk." She did not blink and her pretty, heart-shaped face was mighty sober. "Will yours?"

He grinned at her refreshing frankness. Here was a girl who spoke her mind, not caring to wait first to determine *his* opinion.

"We Yoders are Old Order through and through," he stated.

She nodded and there was a hint of a smile. "Wonderful-good."

They stood there looking at each other. *Has a girl ever intrigued me so?* he wondered.

When Nellie spoke again, he was suddenly aware of her lilac fragrance. "It was nice of you to drop by, Caleb, with your note."

He waited for her response, but she gave no hint of her reply. She merely smiled, turned, and walked away. He watched her head toward the front of the deacon's house, to the seldom-used formal entrance.

That's all?

Never before had a girl treated him so casually—not rudely, but keeping him at an almost measured distance.

When Caleb had waited enough time to prevent people from suspecting he and Nellie Mae had been together, he looped back through the yard and onto the porch, aware only of his great curiosity about Nellie.

Nellie feared her face might be suspiciously rosy as she walked nonchalantly into the house by way of the front door. She retraced her steps in her mind, wondering how she had bumped into Caleb. Was he already outside when she had headed through the porch and down the steps? For the life of her, she could not recall having seen him out there. Had it been an accident, or had he intentionally sought her out? She blushed once more at the thought.

Warning herself to keep her emotions in check, Nellie looked for Nan and Rhoda and found them in the kitchen, still helping Susanna's mother and others redd up.

To think I almost didn't offer to take out the trash today, she thought with a suppressed laugh.

CHAPTER 8

The dawning of Monday's washday was peaceful with Mamma and Rhoda already busying themselves with the laundry. Nellie slipped seven loaves into the belly of the woodstove, wondering why Nan remained in bed at this hour. While her sister slept, Nellie had put her morning to good use making eight pies and ten dozen cookies, mostly chocolate chip.

For a moment, Nellie thought she felt the rumble of a distant train. Pausing from her work, she realized the rumble was instead the sound of the wringer washing machine in the cold cellar below where she stood. If she had a few minutes today sometime during the usual afternoon lull at the bakery shop, she might ask Mamma to tend the store a short time—not breathing a word to Dat, of course. She needed to slip away for some quietude out in the meadow, near the sugar maples, hoping for a glimpse of a deer, rarer these days than she remembered. No doubt the drought had affected them, too.

Strange how wild things and humans can live side by side and yet keep such a distance. She contemplated the mystery of that, and as was often the case lately, her mind made the leap to her deceased sister, fond as she had been of God's creation. *Why hadn't Suzy drawn a line . . . kept herself set apart from the modern world as she'd been taught?*

Nellie shook off the thought. Right or wrong, Suzy had always insisted her friends were wonderful-gut people.

There are good people right here, sister . . . in the hollow.

Nellie shrugged away her opinion and went to check on the cooling cookies. If they were ready to put into her large wicker carrier, she could begin her several trips up the lane to the shop, where she would arrange the day's baked goods and hang the Open sign.

"Another day, another dollar," she muttered, using an expression her father sometimes said in jest. There was more than a grain of truth to the saying.

When she arrived at her shop with the first basket of cookies, someone was already standing outside, waiting for her to open. The woman turned at her arrival—it was Uncle Joseph's wife, Aunt Anna. Uncle Bishop, as she and her sisters sometimes referred to the man of God, certainly loved his sweets.

Anna had come on foot across the cornfield that lay between the families' homes. "Hullo, Nellie Mae," she said right quick. "I saw the light on in your kitchen and decided to pick up some pastries for our trip."

"Oh?" This was the first Nellie had heard they were traveling.

"Joseph says 'tis past due for us to get away for a vacation," Anna explained. "So this afternoon, we're boarding a bus to Iowa . . . Kalona, where I have kinfolk."

"Plain?"

"For the most part."

"Well, come on in." Nellie didn't need to bother with a key, as she never locked the shop; neither did her parents lock the house. She opened the door wide for Anna, who looked awfully glum for someone about to embark on a trip. "I've got plenty of cookies—all nice and warm, too. The pies and such are comin' if you'd care to wait."

Anna shook her head. "Your uncle will be mighty happy with cookies." Anna slowly selected several different kinds—oatmeal raisin, pumpkin, and the bishop's all-time favorite, chocolate chip—almost as if the effort of choosing was too much this morning. Clearly her mind was on other things.

"There'll be no charge," Nellie said when she had carefully wrapped up Anna's requests.

"Aw, Nellie Mae, are ya sure?"

She nodded. "Yous have a wonderful-gut time out where you're goin'."

Anna brightened momentarily. "Denki, we will."

"How long will you be?" Nellie thought to ask.

"'Tis up to the bishop." *And to the Lord God,* Nellie thought she heard Anna murmur with a slight frown on her face.

She watched the gray-haired woman pull her black woolen shawl close around her before heading out the door. Anna made her way toward the desolate cornfield, carefully picking her way among the remaining hard stumps as she moved across the field toward home.

Nellie wondered if Dat knew his elder brother was leaving town for a while. *Why now, for goodness' sake?*

———

When Nellie's Simple Sweets was officially open for the day, Rhoda came to help with customers until she had to leave for her housekeeping job. Nellie was grateful for the assistance, though she wished for some privacy when her friend Rosanna stopped in.

"You're spoilin' us but good, Nellie Mae," Rosanna said after selecting two pies. "These look just delicious."

Nellie slipped away from the counter, delighted to see her again so soon after visiting just last week. "You getting . . . uh, things ready?" she asked, not wanting to say more with Rhoda nearby.

Rosanna nodded. "Oh, goodness, I certainly am. Made an afghan—finished it off early this morning." She whispered, "But I don't have a pattern for baby booties."

"Ah," Nellie said, her voice low. "Walk across the road and see Maryann 'bout that. She'd be glad to help."

"You think so?"

"Well, Maryann's thoughtful that way. And with so many young ones, she prob'ly does have a knitting pattern. No doubt she's making a pair or two herself."

Rosanna touched her arm. "How's your mamma been?"

"Good days and bad."

"'Tis to be expected. Losin' a child is the hardest loss of all." Rosanna smiled weakly. "Word has it . . . well, some of her best friends seem to think she's in need of some peace and quiet."

"Jah, 'spect so." Nellie frowned, glancing out the window. "Aren't we all?"

Rosanna leaned on the display case. "Ach, are you all right, Nellie Mae?"

She didn't want to gossip, but she figured Rosanna had no idea of the bishop's plan to travel to Iowa. "Oh, I'm doin' fine, jah."

"Well, you don't look it, if I may be so bold."

Nellie brushed off her apron and eyed her friend. "What's a-matter with me?"

Rosanna came around behind the counter to her. "Didn't mean any harm. You just don't seem yourself."

"Well, *who,* then?"

To this, they both chuckled. And because she was not about to share any news that might upset either Rosanna or Rhoda, who was surely listening in even though she feigned busyness at the far end of the counter, Nellie kept to herself what she knew of Uncle Bishop and her aunt's trip.

Switching the subject, she asked, "Who else knows?"

"Only Elias and our parents. That's all for now." Rosanna nodded her head toward Rhoda. "So if you don't mind . . ."

"That's fine," Nellie agreed, waving good-bye to Rosanna, who said her farewells and left the shop.

Upon her absence, Rhoda eyed Nellie closely. "Please don't even ask me," Nellie blurted.

"Well, aren't *you* peeved," Rhoda shot back.

Nellie sighed. "I 'spect Mamma has pulled the last of my bread from the oven by now. I'll be back in a bit." Heading out the door, she decided to take the longed-for detour to the meadow, not caring for the moment that doing so might make Rhoda late for her job. *Oh, how I do wish Dat would allow Mamma to mind the store again.*

Lifting her skirt, Nellie ran through the nearby pastureland, all the way out to the vast meadow on the easternmost side of her father's land. *Let Rhoda see what it's like to be inconvenienced for once,* she thought. Her eldest sister had never been one to offer a helping hand—not without Dat's encouragement. Rhoda frequently didn't come home for supper, let alone help to prepare it, and she'd slip out of the house and be gone all day when her sisters and Mamma needed help getting the house ready for Preaching service when their turn to host came around. And if the bakery shop needed a thorough cleaning, Rhoda usually made herself scarce then, too.

No matter Rhoda's tendency to selfishness, Nellie didn't see her getting in over her head the way Suzy had with her English friends. For one, Rhoda didn't seem to have any suitors. No, as far as she knew, Rhoda was getting mighty close to being passed over by the young men in the district—twenty-one was nearly past courting age. Even without a beau, she ought to take baptismal instruction next year and join church.

Someone else hadn't joined church yet, either, although he was much younger than Rhoda. Caleb was holding off, which was interesting, especially the way he'd talked last Sunday. Why hadn't he planned to take the baptismal vow with the rest of the candidates in a few weeks? The day would surely come when she would be doing the same thing herself.

She shivered happily at the memory of speaking with Caleb yesterday. After months of waiting, *she* would be the girl to win Caleb's heart. Or so she hoped.

She couldn't help but smile as she strolled into the woods, suddenly realizing she was farther from home than she'd intended. She relished the idea of having this time to herself and wandered onward, taking her time . . . breathing in the fresh, clean air, and observing the pretty patterns the filtered sunlight made on the grassy floor below. She whispered Suzy's name, wondering if the dead could hear what you spoke out into the air. *The Lord does . . . Uncle Bishop says so.* Yet if that was the case, why then were none of the prayers offered by the People spoken aloud? Only the bishop or their preachers ever prayed out loud, and then only at Preaching service.

Her mind wandered back to Suzy, who had so often walked this very way with her. How had she sneaked away to the world without confiding in Nellie, when Suzy had so long had a habit of blurting out things better left unsaid? Until her sister's Rumschpringe, Nellie and Suzy had faithfully confided everything in each other. Yet in the last year of her life, Suzy had seemed to turn more to her diary than the anxious ears of her sister.

The diary . . .

Never one to sneak a peek before, Nellie had avoided doing so as Suzy had grown increasingly secretive, keeping her thoughts hidden in her side of the dresser.

A single page was all Nellie had allowed herself the day after Suzy drowned, snapping the diary shut upon reading the words *What have I done to myself? Honestly, I'm in over my head.*

Nellie Mae tensed at the thought of Suzy possibly about to abandon her Plain life, on the verge of embracing the world.

Did she die for curiosity's sake?

Nellie would never forget the lengthy admonition the bishop had given at Suzy's funeral. Uncle Bishop had sounded a clarion call to the young people that it was time to "consider the consequences" of dying without having joined church. Nellie had been terrified to think her own dear sister had died too soon.

Not wanting to submit her parents to further heartache, Nellie had decided to bury the diary and Suzy's many secrets—the evidence spelled out in Suzy's own hand. Her sister's guarded words and long absences, as well as her deliberate resistance to Preaching services in her final months, were burden enough. Yet it appeared that burying Suzy's diary was not enough to protect the family's reputation. Nellie had noticed strange looks from some of the more gossipy members of the grapevine, particularly Susannah Lapp and two of her girl cousins.

The diary's gone forever, she thought, remembering the moonless night she'd buried it, unable to bring herself to burn it as Suzy had directed. As she pondered having tearfully dug the hole and tenderly set the plastic-wrapped diary into the ground, she realized she wasn't sure she could locate its hiding place.

For a moment she regretted burying it at all. Being able to hold Suzy's precious journal—the final words her sister had ever written—might have brought some comfort now.

Why didn't I stash it in the house instead?

She pushed away any lingering second thoughts. *Good riddance . . . a life gone awry should be forgotten. For our sake . . . and for Suzy's.*

Sitting on a fallen tree branch, Nellie bent to tug on the hem of the black apron that covered her feet, her hands now resting flat on the tops of her work shoes. She'd noticed the way the large branch partially blocked the pathway home, overgrown as the faint trail had become.

Birds flew low overhead, the sound of their wings haunting her as she recalled the many times she and Suzy had tramped through these woods. Suzy knew every bird by its color and song, delighting even old-timers with her knowledge. Often they'd watched deer, hiding quietly in the brush and nearly holding their breath so they wouldn't startle them. Suzy had decided a deer's favorite meal consisted of clover flowers or berries from a juniper tree, but never herbs or herbal flowers.

Ach, how Suzy enjoyed nature! Every sound, every sight made Nellie Mae think of her.

When she could contain her sadness no longer, Nellie sobbed into her hands, muting the sound of her broken heart.

CHAPTER 9

Wiping away tears, Nellie Mae stopped at the quiet house to collect the remaining loaves of bread and returned to the shop.

"Where were you?" Rhoda snapped. She'd obviously been fretting.

"I'm sorry, Rhoda," Nellie apologized. "I needed some time away . . . I should've asked."

Rhoda clucked her tongue and turned to fairly fly out the door without another word.

I've done myself no favors with her, Nellie thought sadly.

She noticed a few stray graham cracker crumbs on one of the shelves of the display case and brushed them into her hand. Rhoda didn't keep things the tidy way Nellie liked them, but Nellie recognized it was foolish to expect her sister to see things the same way she did. After all, it wasn't Rhoda's name on the sign outside.

Moving now to inspect the cookie shelves, she counted how many dozen of each kind were left for the day. Plenty of chocolate gobs remained. Some folks called them whoopie pies because children often declared "Whoopie!" when they first tasted the sugary-chocolate concoctions. Nellie smiled, thinking back to her earliest recollection of having enjoyed her grandmother's version. The fat chocolate sandwich cookies were made with cake batter and held together by a thick layer of tempting creamy frosting.

She turned and straightened the floral wall calendar, wishing the shop was less sparsely furnished. Nellie hoped to convince Dat to build or purchase some chairs and tables to set up by the window like she'd seen at other small shops. Certainly there was ample room. She liked the idea of making it possible for those customers who wished to, to linger and visit, perhaps over a cup of tea or coffee.

She had a clear picture in her mind of the way she wanted things to look and be. Apart from these changes, the place was pretty well just as she desired it—well organized, neat, and—except for the crumbs that had escaped Rhoda's attention—clean.

Leave it to me to care 'bout stray crumbs, Nellie thought wryly.

The bell jingled on the shop door, and she looked up to see Rebekah Yoder coming in, all smiles.

"Hullo, Nellie Mae!" Normally ever so prim in a dark green dress and long black shawl, Caleb's older sister was today a sight to behold: A raspberry-colored oven burn marked her graceful forehead, though she didn't seem self-conscious about it. Rebekah's had become a familiar face in the neighborhood in the past few years, since taking a job as a mother's helper to an Amish family a half a mile away. Nan especially had benefited from seeing Rebekah more often. Too bad Nan was home nursing a cold today.

"Nice to see you, Rebekah," Nellie said. "What can I get you?"

Rebekah glanced down at the fringes on her shawl and picked at them a moment before lifting her gaze. "Mamma ran out of time and needs four dozen dinner rolls for a gathering this very evening."

"Four dozen, you say? I can fill that order," Nellie said quickly.

She nodded. "My parents are planning to go over to Preacher Manny's place."

Nellie thought nothing of it, but as she began to bag up the soft white rolls, she wondered if this wasn't yet another meeting about the recent upset in their community—and with Uncle Bishop and his wife gone, too. Were men now allowing their wives to put in their say on the matter?

Rebekah smiled and brushed her hand against the burn on her face as she reached for the rolls. "Denki, Nellie." For a long moment she stood there, gazing at Nellie—almost staring.

Nellie wondered if Rebekah noticed her swollen eyes and abruptly turned to the old-fashioned cash register. "Anything more? Pies? Cookies, maybe?"

"Just the rolls."

Rebekah was beaming now as she handed her a crisp five-dollar bill. "Will you be goin' to Singing next weekend?"

Nellie Mae felt the air go clean out of her. Did Rebekah suspect Caleb was pursuing her? She felt at a loss for words and was actually glad the cash register jammed right then.

"Ach, but there's somethin' wrong with this machine. . . . I need to go and ask Nan." With that, she excused herself, leaving Rebekah standing there without her change.

Nellie hurried toward the house in search of Nan, who always knew how to fix the finicky machine.

When she found her sister in bed sound asleep, her dark hair strewn over her pillow, Nellie didn't have the heart to waken her. It was obvious Nan was in no condition to help today.

Nellie quickly returned to the bakery shop, but she discovered that Rebekah had already gone, leaving behind a note.

Nellie Mae,
   Put the difference on Mamma's credit, if you don't mind. See you next Saturday!
                                        Fondly,
                                        Rebekah

Fondly? Nellie laughed.

Surely Caleb's closest-in-age sister knew something of his interest in Nellie, if not his written invitation. She found this quite curious, since dating and courtship were done in complete secret, up until an engaged couple was "published" after Preaching service. At that time the father of the bride-to-be stood up and extended a wedding invitation to all the membership.

Whatever Rebekah's knowledge, Nellie realized she was smiling as she worked with the cash register, which miraculously fixed itself after a few minutes.

Nellie noticed the dwindling batch of chocolate chip cookies and made a mental note to bake more of that kind tomorrow morning.

Wonder if Caleb likes chocolate chip? She giggled, her heart fairly singing now as she glanced again at Rebekah's brief note.

Fondly, indeed!

Caleb worked alongside Ephram Fisher, building a much-needed woodshed. They had been at it since sunup.

What was I thinking, putting a bug in Rebekah's ear? he thought.

Frustrated with himself, Caleb took care not to exert too much force as he pounded each nail. Typically he was in control of his emotions and would not let his annoyance at his own stupidity get in the way of his work. But he felt guilty at having sent his sister over to see Nellie when Rebekah had stopped by after lunch to give several jars of strawberry preserves to Maryann. He'd happened upon the two women discussing his mother's lack of dinner rolls and sent Rebekah to Nellie's to purchase some.

He had merely hoped Rebekah might find a tactful moment to bring up deceased Suzy to Nellie, if the bakery shop wasn't populated with customers. The mysterious circumstances surrounding Suzy's drowning troubled Caleb, who had decided to hold off on his growing interest in Nellie after learning of her sister's death. Whom his family spent time with mattered a great deal to Caleb's father—reputation was everything. Caleb had meant to appease his Daed by finding out the truth about Suzy, along with the rest of Reuben Fisher's family. He'd supposed that Rebekah's friend Nan would have been able to divulge the important information he sought, but it was reasonably clear from Rebekah's subtle prodding that Nan knew precious little about the day of Suzy's fatal accident. Maybe Nellie would reveal more to Rebekah. He only knew he thought it unwise to do the asking himself.

He patted the pocket containing Nellie's letter, glad Rebekah had intercepted the day's mail and thought to bring him the much-anticipated reply. His heart beat more rapidly to think Nellie had said yes, but the problem of his father remained.

Guess one can't blame him. Can't be too careful during these troublesome times when so many are speakin' out against our heritage. These beliefs had defined them for hundreds of years.

Ephram's wife brought out a jug of water. They stopped to take a swig, and Maryann fidgeted as if something urgent was on her mind. When they had drunk their fill, Maryann took back the jug, studying Ephram.

"What is it, Maryann?" asked Ephram.

"Word has it there's a meeting over at Preacher Manny's tonight. Both sides of the debate are comin'."

"That's enough."

"Marrieds are welcome."

"Well, *we* won't be goin'!" Ephram fairly snapped.

The strong response to Maryann's remark startled Caleb. Ephram had always struck him as rather fixed in his opinions, but before now, he'd always seemed fair. Why this sharp tone with his wife? Was Ephram privy to something? Or was it simply that he preferred his wife keep herself out of such discussions?

Ephram was quiet as they finished laying the last few boards on the inside of the building, nailing them into place. The woodshed complete, Ephram gave him a slap of appreciation on the back, and Caleb headed to the barn. He led out his fine horse and hitched it up to the black open carriage his father had purchased for him last year.

Caleb thought again of Nellie's little sister. What was the truth about Suzy? With rumors still flying, he considered the more pressing question to him: *What's the truth about Nellie Mae?*

He had been lectured more than a few times regarding the importance of "marryin' proper." According to Daed, the apple rarely fell far from the tree. "You're tying the knot with a family, not just the daughter . . . marrying into their reputation. We Yoders won't be linked to wickedness."

For sure and for certain, if Daed had any inkling of his interest in Nellie Mae, he'd be taking him aside and warning him but good. Evidently Reuben Fisher hadn't been able to rein in his youngest girl. Was Nellie Mae born of the same foolishness?

CHAPTER 10

Rhoda and Nan's room was furnished much the same as Nellie's, yet something seemed different about it as she and Rhoda sat talking after supper Wednesday evening. Nan was downstairs, seemingly eager to be out of her room now that she was feeling better, and Rhoda had perched square in the middle of the bed, her feet tucked under her. Loose strands of golden hair poked from beneath her head covering. Nellie sat across the room on the old cane chair beside the window, unable to put her finger on what she sensed. "Something seems amiss here."

Rhoda chuckled and removed her glasses. "Nothing's changed, sister. Or were you noticing my new necklace? See it over there?"

Nellie spotted the long yellow-beaded necklace draped on one end of the mirror. She rose and went to look. "Has Mamma seen it?" Even as she touched it, running her fingers over the firm roundness of the beads, the necklace wasn't the only thing different.

"Mamma poked her head in and frowned."

Nellie gazed at the delicate loveliness of the necklace. *Worldly, for sure. Where did Rhoda get it?*

Here was more evidence that Rhoda's working for En-glischers was clearly a mistake, just as Dat had said from the start.

Stepping back, Nellie noted the attractive way Rhoda had looped it over part of the dresser. *Perty as can be.*

She glanced at her sister. "Oh, Rhoda, you're not . . ." She paused.

"I'm not what?"

"Thinkin' of goin' down the path of . . . ?" Nellie stopped, refusing to say Suzy's name. "What I mean is, you're not thinking of goin' fancy, are ya?"

Rhoda's pretty green eyes shone. "Last thing on my mind."

"Why the necklace, then?"

Rhoda's face flushed. "I s'pose hanging it keeps me from wearin' it. Just for show, that's all."

Nellie looked all around the room, still trying to deter-mine what she felt. She went and sat again. "Did you spray something sweet in here?"

"Earlier this mornin'." Rhoda pointed her nose in the air and sniffed. "I guess I do kinda smell it yet."

"Perfume?"

She nodded, grinning. "Want some? I can get you the same thing . . . if you'd like."

Nellie couldn't deny the sweet scent was ever so tempt-ing. "Honestly, that's too strong for me if it lasts all day. I'll stick with my lilac fragrance."

"Suit yourself." Rhoda smoothed her dress, shifting her legs beneath her. "I ran into Susannah Lapp on the way home from work today."

"Oh?" The mention of Susannah's name annoyed Nellie.

"She was full of gossip, more so than usual—said a whole group of folk came to the house last night. Men and their wives, of all things."

Nellie nodded, looking Rhoda square in the face. "I heard from Rebekah Yoder there was a similar meeting the night before at Preacher Manny's. What do you think's goin' on?"

Rhoda reached up to undo her Kapp. Then she began removing the bobby pins, her butter-blond hair cascading down over her shoulders, past her waist. "Seems more folks are demanding tractors and other modern conveniences—enough to form a fairly large group. The meeting at the deacon's was pretty one-sided, as I understand it."

"Which side?"

"Which do ya suppose?" Rhoda shook her hair free. "'Twas the side of the Old Ways . . . as we are now. But the other meeting, the one you mentioned, was open to people from both sides of the issue."

Rhoda surely seemed to be the one in the know.

"Any idea why Dat and Mamma didn't go?" Nellie asked.

Rhoda picked up the hem of her apron and fingered the edge. "I s'pose because they're homebodies . . . like you, Nellie Mae." Her sister gave her a teasing grin.

Nellie sighed. The fact she had only to walk a few steps to work must make her an oddity in Rhoda's eyes. "I daresay there's maybe another reason."

"What's that?" asked Rhoda.

"Dat's ever so settled with the way things are."

Like Caleb's family. The thought comforted Nellie. No matter how many folk betrayed their tradition, her family—and Caleb's—would stand solid and true.

"Sure seems that way," Rhoda said. "But change is coming, and you never know what might happen."

Nellie wanted to tell Rhoda what she knew about the bishop's trip—and how upset Aunt Anna had seemed—but she held her peace. It wasn't her place to say what she presumed, and it was bad enough to hear of two meetings happening behind their backs. If Rhoda didn't already know about Uncle Bishop, the grapevine would tell her soon enough.

Nellie Mae settled into her room for the night. She considered writing to her cousins, as the circle letter she'd been expecting had come in the afternoon's mail full of news about who was published to be married last week after Preaching in Bird-in-Hand—Treva had written of the candidates for baptism, as well. Nellie always enjoyed collecting news to add to the letter before sending it along to yet another cousin down in Paradise. The ever-expanding letter would journey on to several others before Treva returned it to Nellie again in another ten days or so. A weekly journal of sorts, circle letters were one of the things Nellie most looked forward to.

This time she had been dismayed to hear from Treva about a group in Bird-in-Hand talking of getting cars and tractors. "Whatever's happening among our people sounds as contagious as the flu," she whispered to herself as she slipped into bed.

Thinking of what she might write back, she deemed it unwise to share the little she knew about the unrest here in Honeybrook. *Maybe I'll wait and reply when things die down a bit.*

She felt somewhat guilty at the prospect of holding up the circle letter—it was no fun when others dawdled—but she wasn't in the mood to write about the ordinary things of her life. And was it really anybody's business what was going on here among the church brethren? Her greatest concern was that such gossip might simply fan the flames of discontent.

If only Rosanna lived nearer. It would have been a relief to talk plainly with her friend, but it was too late in the day for that. Since Elias had found him and Rosanna a nicer house to rent, across from Ephram's, she'd seen less and less of her. At moments like this, she could see how mighty nice it would be to be able to pick up a telephone and call her dearest friend.

Quickly, she dismissed the thought. While some bishops did permit families to install a phone for the purpose of medical emergencies, Nellie could not imagine Uncle Bishop allowing one. No, he and Preachers Lapp and Manny embraced the Old Order as much as any ministers she knew.

Bet Susannah Lapp hasn't ever wished for a phone, Nellie thought. Considering her rival now, Nellie wondered if she dared to flirt a little with Caleb this Saturday night. Unlike most boys who simply invited a girl during the Singing, Caleb had played it safe, planning ahead where Nellie was to meet him afterward. This way no one would likely see them together as a couple. Surely there was a reason for Caleb's desire for such unusual secrecy.

But Nellie wouldn't allow herself to fret over the details of their first date. She could trust Caleb Yoder to know what he was doing, couldn't she? Still, she wondered if his reason had anything to do with Suzy.

———

Thursday evening Rosanna's cousin Kate came striding into the utility porch at the back of the house. With a short knock and a soft "yoo-hoo," she appeared in the kitchen, an enormous smile on her round face. She looked much bigger than last visit, Rosanna thought, trying not to stare at Kate's protruding stomach.

"How are you feelin', cousin?" she asked, quickly offering her a chair.

"Oh, not too bad, really."

"Would ya care for something to drink? A tall glass of fresh milk, maybe? Whatever you'd like."

Kate waved her off as she lowered herself into the chair. A refreshment seemed to be the furthest thing from her mind. "Truth is, Rosanna, I've come to talk about the baby." She fixed her gaze on the table before them. "John and I've been talkin', and *we* think it would be a smart idea to let our baby—yours, really—know who his parents are. Or if it's a girl . . ." Her voice trailed off, and she brought her eyes up to meet Rosanna's.

Rosanna felt her stomach knot up, but she forced a smile. "Why, sure, I think that's fine."

Kate fanned herself, seeming quite relieved. "It's not that we want to have much say-so in his or her life. It's just . . . we think it would be nice for the baby's brothers and sisters to know him, too."

Again Rosanna nodded. "I have no problem with that, Kate. Doubt Elias will, either."

"Well, that's mighty good to know."

"You sure I can't get you something to wet your whistle? You look all in."

Kate's eyes glistened. "Oh, I don't know . . . maybe, jah."

"Well, what's a-matter? You all right?"

Kate nodded bravely, giving a weak smile. "One minute I have such get-up-and-go, and the next, I fizzle out mighty quick. Can't say I've ever felt quite like this with my other babies."

"Ach, maybe you shouldn't have come all this way alone." Rosanna glanced out the window, noting the gray family buggy parked outside. "You want someone to ride back with you?"

"No, no, I'll be fine in a few minutes." Kate breathed in slowly.

Rosanna couldn't help but wonder if Kate's now rosy cheeks had to do with the realization the baby growing within her would know the parents who gave him life. It was a reasonable request.

Elias will surely think so, too.

"The midwife says the baby may be due sooner than we thought," Kate commented as Rosanna poured her some warm peppermint tea.

"Before Christmas would be ever so nice."

"Might be closer to the middle of December, seems."

"Ah, right during wedding season, then," Rosanna said.

"Jah, and what a busy one this will be." Kate went on to say that several nieces and two nephews on both sides of John's and her family were rumored to be getting hitched come late November or early December.

"More couples means more babies." Rosanna smiled. "We'll all be in good company, raisin' our little ones."

The People grew their communities through large families. Ten to fifteen children were not uncommon.

Kate agreed, a knowing look in her eye. "Just think, you'll soon have yourself a wee one to call your own."

Rosanna reached out to touch her cousin's hand, ever so thankful for Kate's generosity, yet hoping her cousin was truly comfortable with the whole idea.

Nellie Mae sat in the corner of the kitchen, behind the table closest to the wall, trying to suppress her envy as she watched Rhoda and Nan sitting on the large rag rug in the center of the room, playing a cozy game of checkers.

I'm always the third wheel anymore, she thought.

That Rhoda and Nan had each other was certain, and just now as Nellie watched them smile furtively before moving their checkers, she truly felt she had no one. *Not even to play checkers with.*

Neither sister had made any effort to reach out to her in her time of loss, though they, too, were in mourning for Suzy.

Redirecting her thoughts, she decided now was as good a time as any to add to the circle letter. No sense inconveniencing those waiting by putting it off. After doing so, she shuffled through her stationery and chose a soft yellow sheet, intending to also write a more personal letter to Treva.

Dear Cousin Treva,

Greetings from Beaver Dam Road . . . and Cousin Nellie Mae.

Have you been out walking much this autumn? I can't resist the nice weather. I'm sure yours is quite similar, although Dat says you can never tell around here. Just look at how odd it was that all our sweet corn—and our neighbors'—was stunted, but yours wasn't. Still strange, I daresay.

It was such fun to hear of the poetry you're reading. I, too, like Emily Dickinson's poems, if they're not too sad.

There is enough sorrow without having to read about it, seems to me. My sister Rhoda is reading Pilgrim's Progress and when she's through, I plan to read it, as well. Dat says he read it when he was a teen, so I know he'll approve.

Business is as busy as ever at the bakery shop. It would be awful nice if you and your sisters could come over and see it for yourself sometime. Rhoda and Nan would enjoy seeing you, and while Mamma has recently been in need of some solitude—understandable, considering—she'd no doubt be glad for your company, too.

Lately I've been experimenting with a new cookie recipe, but I haven't put it out in the display case just yet. I want to make sure it's good and tasty first. I haven't decided what to call it, either, but it's chock-full of red, green, and yellow peanut chocolate candies. Mamma says I could call them cheer-you-up cookies because of all the colors. What do you think of that?

The Sunday after next we're having Preaching service at Ephram's, so we'll go over there and help Maryann clean out her corners come Friday. It will be good to have some more time with her and her family again.

I hope you'll write again soon.

Your cousin and friend,
Nellie Mae Fisher

There was so much more Nellie could have written. Next time maybe things would have calmed down to the point she wouldn't have to mention a word about the private "tractor meetings" . . . or that it seemed their bishop had flown the coop.

CHAPTER 11

When Nellie spotted Iva Beiler at Singing in a bright cranberry-colored cape dress without even an apron over it, she immediately thought of strawberries and homemade ice cream. Where on earth had Iva gotten the bold, nearly red fabric? Surely not at the yard goods store they all frequented. Was she hoping to catch Caleb's attention?

The sweetness of a lowland musk pervaded the area in the barn just below the haymow. A slight haze of dust hung in the air from the good sweeping the barn floor had doubtless received earlier.

Nellie Mae was glad for the large turnout. *Lots of youth from other districts.* She saw many new faces but not the face she most wanted to see. She certainly didn't want to appear to be looking for Caleb or anyone in particular. That was the way to do things, she'd learned from coming along with Rhoda and Nan for a full year now. A few months back, Rhoda had announced she'd gotten her fill of these gatherings and quit coming. Nan, on the other hand, seemed to live for them, her blue eyes shining like boy-magnets.

Nellie chose to sit with some of the other girls at the far end of the length of narrow wooden tables, content to be where she was. Again, there was no sign of Caleb among the boys on the other side of the tables. Nellie reminded herself there was no need to worry: Caleb was *her* date this night. Oh, the way he'd looked at her last Lord's Day—the inviting twinkle in his hazel eyes, eyes that looked into hers as if he'd been searching for her his whole life.

When at last she saw Caleb across the room, Nellie Mae's heart skipped a beat. He came toward her, finding a place across the table only a short way down from her. In that same moment, Nellie spotted Susannah Lapp, whose eyes fleetingly met hers. One glance of understanding and they saw in each other the potential rivals they were.

Briefly looking once more at Caleb, Nellie remembered sitting with her three sisters in the schoolyard one spring years ago, watching the boys play baseball during afternoon recess. Caleb had been up to bat, and instead of swinging and fooling around at home base like most of the boys did to show off, he had leaned forward with the bat, licking his lips as he awaited the pitch.

Crack! On the very first pitch, the bat had slapped the ball, sending it high into the air, over the top of the boys' outhouse and clear out past the white picket fence into the pastureland beyond. She remembered squealing as Caleb ran around to all the bases, his right foot stamping hard on each one as he flew by, headed for home. Never once had he looked over his shoulder at the outfielder, who was still hunting for the ball. Nellie had pressed her hand over her mouth to stifle her glee, so pleased he'd made the home run.

Presently he grinned across the table at her and then wiped the smile off his face fast. There were oodles more songs before they could talk to each other, assuming Caleb would even want to. The way he'd written to her, planning for her to wait elsewhere for him to pick her up, made her think he

106

might not seek her out here at all, not in front of others. All of that was just fine with her, as long as he appeared later in his buggy to pick her up.

Suddenly feeling a bit shy, Nellie Mae decided to mingle with some of her girl cousins and her sister Nan, far removed from the table where they always sat to sing the usual songs. Surprisingly, someone had brought along a guitar. Instruments were not usually allowed, at least at the Singings meant only for their church district. Was all the fuss about pushing the limits of the Ordnung filtering into the Singings, too?

Dozens of boys gathered around the fellow, and Nellie longed to press in and see the fingers working the strings that made such lovely music. For sure and for certain, something was quite different about this gathering—even though it was much too early in the evening, girls and boys were already pairing off. Some had gone high into the haymow to sit and dangle their feet over the sides, holding hands and laughing.

Her heart beat faster as she wondered if Caleb might sit that close to her tonight in his buggy. While she'd ridden next to several different boys on other nights, none of them had affected her the way Caleb did even now, from the other side of the room.

"Nellie Mae." She turned to see him smiling down at her. "Let's go walkin'."

She nodded, following him, but he slowed to let her walk beside him toward the barn doors, instead of behind like some boys preferred.

"Such a moon." He glanced at her, smiling more freely now as they stepped into the privacy of twilight.

She wanted to say something memorable, but the right words didn't come. It wasn't that she was too timid to speak; she simply wanted every word to count.

"Did you see that guitarist?" he asked. "Came all the way up from Georgetown. My older brother knows of him. Says he's trouble."

"No doubt. Uncle Bishop's gone a few days, and this?" There, she'd said something worthwhile, or so she hoped.

Caleb stopped, his back to the full moon. She couldn't make out his expression in the shadow. "Bishop Joseph's gone? But where?"

Her heart sank. "You didn't know? I figured your father or one of the other menfolk must be helpin' with his livestock." She went on. "Aunt Anna was in the shop Monday to purchase some sweets for their trip. They're out visitin' her relatives in Iowa," she said, telling what little she knew.

Caleb stood silhouetted against the blazing white moon, taller than she'd ever remembered. And silent.

"They're in need of some rest, is all," she offered.

"Well, I hope they have a right good time." He leaned toward her and reached for her hand.

The warm thrill of his touch caught her by surprise, rooting her feet to the soil. She wondered how her hand felt to him—probably all sweaty from nerves, even in this nippy weather—but so far he hadn't let go.

The unmistakable sound of lively guitar music came from across the barnyard.

"My father says it's best to run away from evil, not move toward it."

Caleb surely meant the guitar player in the barn, not their holding hands. Nellie smiled, mighty glad for the shadow cast on them as he led her through the thick willow grove, far from the barn and the devil's music. She wouldn't admit to having been drawn to the pleasing sound . . . wouldn't think of saying anything to make him stop walking with her, his thumb stroking her hand, his arm brushing against hers. She needed to be able to think clearly, to be alert and on her guard all the rest of their time together tonight. No matter her attraction to Caleb, Nellie Mae would not disappoint her mamma by behaving recklessly.

"We'll walk over to that white stake—see it?—then we'll head back," he said, pointing.

"Jah, fine." She had to smile. How confident her voice sounded, nearly fooling even herself.

With the house good and quiet—Betsy busy with her embroidery and the girls all out for the evening—Reuben settled down with two Bibles, the old German family one and the English one. He much preferred sitting in the front room near the open door, but now that fall was in the air, he found himself enjoying the warmth and comfort of Betsy's kitchen.

"Betsy," he said, glancing over at his wife, who sat within the golden ring of light coming from the gas lamp he'd hung over the table.

She looked up from her work. "Jah?"

"I'll be reading the Scriptures now."

She nodded.

She has no inkling what I have in mind. . . .

This night he would read the whole of chapter three in the Gospel of John. Reuben had been downright curious about the passage ever since his visit to Cousin Jonathan's. According to his shunned relative, there was something important—even powerful—to be learned from this section of Scripture. Others too.

He felt a glimmer of guilt as he thumbed through the unfamiliar pages, one mingled with a hint of boldness. Truth be told, he had felt peeved ever since Preacher Manny had laid into him for no understandable cause. Manny knew precisely where he stood on things. Why treat him so?

With all the commotion already going on, what could it hurt for Reuben to read where he wished to in Scripture? He wanted Betsy to hear this, too, halfheartedly though it might well be.

For that reason, he began in English—he would read the same chapter to himself in German later. " 'There was a man of the Pharisees, named Nicodemus, a ruler of the Jews. The same came to Jesus by night, and said unto him, Rabbi, we know that thou art a teacher come from God: for no man can do these miracles that thou doest, except God be with him.' "

He paused, glancing over at Betsy. *Her mind's wandering, for sure.*

He continued. " 'Jesus answered . . . Verily, verily, I say unto thee, except a man be born again, he cannot see the kingdom of God.' "

Right there, that's what Cousin Jonathan talked about: being born again.

Reuben hadn't believed these words were written at all the way his wayward cousin had stated them, yet they were right here before his eyes. Had Betsy heard what he'd just read?

He went on to the next verse, then the next, eager to see what else Scripture had to say. Was this what Jonathan meant by "hungering after the Word of God"? He shrugged off the memory. Leave it to outspoken Jonathan to say such things. Better for Reuben to do as he was told, to do things the way the People had always done them. Better he should listen to the bishop . . . and close the Good Book right now.

Listen and submit.

But when all was said and done, who was the final authority? Was it God and His Word? Or the bishop and the ministerial brethren?

Reuben struggled with all he had been taught . . . the unique way the Lord God identified the men to lead the People . . . the ordination process by the drawing of lots. All of it.

Can I trust what I know . . . what has always been?

His eyes followed the outline of his wife's ample shape across the room. Her body sagged with exhaustion and grief. Neither of them was getting any younger. Had they missed something altogether important, as Jonathan had suggested? In daring to consider this, was Reuben opening himself up to what was not allowed, letting worldliness creep in? And if he were to memorize these verses, what then? *Would* they spring to life in him as Jonathan had insisted they would?

Puh! He was just offended enough by Preacher Manny's rebuke that he forged ahead. " 'That which is born of the flesh is flesh; and that which is born of the Spirit is spirit. Marvel not that I said unto thee, Ye must be born again.' "

The air seemed to leave him, and he found himself gasping. He read on, silently now. Jesus seemed genuinely surprised that Nicodemus did not know the vital things of which he spoke.

Reuben reread the same verses. Neither had he known the truths Nicodemus had missed. Reuben realized at that moment that somehow he had been kept from the truth due to tradition—following carefully, cautiously, what his forefathers had always done. Never, ever wavering.

If I have told you earthly things, and ye believe not, how shall ye believe, if I tell you of heavenly things?

There it was again. He was as bad off as this Nicodemus fellow. He had not known this at all.

. . . that whosoever believeth in him should not perish, but have everlasting life.

Stunned, Reuben looked at the verse again. Was it truly written so clearly? Yes, he'd made no mistake in the reading. Yet his people did not believe a person could have the assurance of salvation. You had to wait till the Judgment Day to know whether you were heaven bound.

He thought of Suzy and trembled at the thought of her life being snuffed out. He'd lost many nights of sleep over his youngest's death, tormented by the knowledge she had died before making her life vows to the church. Not a soul knew of his dire concern. Not even Betsy, dear woman. He could not consider adding his worries to her own heavy burden of sadness.

He opened his German Bible, the ancient, large book where births and deaths of his ancestors over the generations were recorded. Where he had printed Suzy's date of death with a shaking hand.

Reuben studied each verse from one through fifteen, comparing them to what he'd read in the English version as he balanced both holy books on his knees.

"No wonder some folk want to study on their own, without the bishop present," he muttered.

"What's that you say?" Betsy's question broke into his thoughts.

He stared at her, almost not seeing her at first, so caught up was he in what he'd read.

"The Lord says I will have everlasting life . . . if I but believe." He closed the Bibles and rose from his favorite chair to go stand by the back door, looking out through the summer porch to the pastureland beyond the yard and the small outbuildings.

"Reuben, are you all right, dear?"

He heard his wife's voice, but the haze in his mind was so thick he felt nearly helpless to respond. Not now, while this arrow of light was piercing his soul.

" 'That which is born of the Spirit is spirit,' " he whispered, suddenly realizing his actions must be quite perplexing to Betsy. He was behaving strangely, just as she had in the days immediately after their Suzy drowned.

Would his darling daughter burn in hell for her sins as the church taught?

To keep his own pain and fear at a manageable level, he knew he must give Suzy's death and her eternal reward up to the Lord God. Not only once, but again and again for all the remainder of his days.

Maybe this was why his Betsy was so taken with little Emma. Like many of their other grandchildren, James's only daughter had become their sunshine in the midst of deepest sorrow. Surely the Good Lord knew they needed some light in their darkness of loss.

The Good Lord Jesus . . .

Reuben reached for his kerchief and wiped his eyes; then he pushed open the door and headed out into the night without even bothering to pull on his work coat. Out, into the most radiant night he'd witnessed in years.

Chapter 12

The moon was a luminous round flare. Below Nellie's feet, small and unseen creatures doubtless scurried in the brush as she peeked through the thicket of trees and shrubs, waiting for Caleb to arrive in his courting carriage. She could still feel his hand over hers as it had been all during their long walk earlier. Really they had talked of little beneath the sky and the willows. The memory stirred in her and she could scarcely wait to see him again.

Will he hold my hand again?

What might it be like to bake his favorite pie or cake . . . serve it to him sitting and smiling at the head of the table? How would she feel knowing he was out digging up, then marketing, their own potatoes, his tobacco crop already cut and stored in the shed, ahead of the frost?

She mused on what their daily chores would be as husband and wife. But no, this was merely their first date; she couldn't be sure if there would be more. All the same, her thoughts turned to the future, pleasant *what if*s filling her mind while dozens of buggies hurried past her hiding place near the road.

She thought of Nan, who'd asked repeatedly if she was all right, since there was no young man in sight to see Nellie home. Nan, as always, had an invitation to ride long into the night. *I'll walk a bit,* she'd told Nan, not wanting to say more. And, oh, had she walked. A good, long way to this secluded spot previously chosen by Caleb.

Looking up, she could tell the moon had moved only slightly, judging the time by its slide across the sky. Surely Caleb would be along soon.

She reached into her dress pocket, where she kept Suzy's Kapp strings. Some might frown on her decision to snip and cherish the strings, but Nellie took comfort in having these tangible reminders of her sister. These small pieces of Suzy were one way in which the memory of her short life lived on. Little by little now, Nellie found her great sadness was slowly subsiding as she turned toward the good things life had yet to offer. At first, in the days and weeks after Suzy died, she had wished to simply dissolve into the moonlight, disappearing like dew evaporates in the heat of the blazing sun.

Truly she had much to live for . . . much to do before it was her turn to cross the wide Jordan.

She heard a horse and buggy coming, slowing now, and shifted forward to peer through the branches. Surely this was Caleb, yet she must play along with his strange game and be certain before making herself known.

Scanning the overgrown area along the roadside, Caleb reined in the horse, standing now to look for Nellie. It was obvious she'd kept herself from view. *Wunnerbaar-gut,* he thought.

In spite of himself, he had started the evening scrutinizing her, but the more he observed, the more he genuinely liked Nellie. It had been difficult to tear himself away from her to go their separate ways after the Singing, as had been his plan.

Even so, he knew it was best to be as discreet as possible, at least until he knew whether he wanted to pursue her. After tonight, once he determined whether there was anything of Suzy in her, he would know what he wanted to do.

Still holding the reins, he halted the horse and lingered without moving. How long before Nellie would emerge from the darkness? Was she here . . . nearby?

Finally, impatient to see her again, Caleb leaped down from the carriage and walked toward the thickest area, where he assumed she was hiding.

On a night so well lit by the moon, he could see nearly everything. The blue-black outline of the elm and oak branches and, if he wasn't mistaken, the shadow of a girl, her head tilted in expectation.

"Nellie?" he said softly.

The girl said nothing.

Was it Nellie standing there?

"It's Caleb," he said more urgently, stepping forward.

Still the girl he could plainly see did not reply.

Then he heard it . . . a small giggle.

He rushed toward the bushes and found himself face-to-face with her, pulling her near before he realized what he was doing. She laughed happily in his arms. "I daresay you're a tease," he whispered.

"And you're not?" She squirmed out of his grasp and stepped back.

He laughed heartily, and his horse whinnied and stomped. "Well, we'd better hurry . . . or we might be walkin' tonight."

He reached for her hand and they scurried toward the black open buggy, all shined up to beat the band, though she might not notice in the darkness. He steadied the horse, glad he'd studded the harness with lots of silver buttons.

117

They caught the moonlight just now as Nellie sprang into the carriage, her face beaming.

Reuben took his time outside, moving along the perimeter of the meadow, the moon illuminating his every step. He had no idea how to pray on his own, to voice his thoughts to the Holy One of Israel. Sure, he'd said all the rote prayers he'd learned as a boy, but he had never cracked open the door of his heart and let God hear what was inside. If the God of Isaac and Jacob had appointed His Son to speak so frankly to a Jewish ruler, what would He be saying to the People today?

Ach, what would He say to me?

Reuben could not shake the remarkable things he'd discovered this evening. To think they'd been there, unmistakably plain, all this time. "Yet I never knew," he murmured.

He had the greatest urge to seek out Cousin Jonathan and tell him about this. Just what *had* happened, anyway? Could he even put his finger on it?

"Jah . . . I believe the words of Jesus, the Christ." He lifted his head toward the sky. "O Lord God, almighty One, I believe in your Son as my Savior. May I have the promise of eternal life your friend Nicodemus received?"

As sure as he was Reuben Fisher, he embraced the dawning within his soul. He raised his hands out before him, palms open, fingers spread wide. "Born again . . . by the spirit of the true and living God."

He knelt down in the dirt, asking the Lord God and heavenly Father to receive him into the kingdom. As he did, he pictured Nicodemus doing the same.

He bowed his head low and breathed in the stillness around him, unsure of himself, hoping no one but almighty God was witnessing his gesture of contrition and faith.

In time, he rose and headed toward the house, feeling the need to tell someone. He couldn't begin to describe what he'd experienced out there in the field alone with God. However, he must be careful how he explained it, for if he were to use the wrong words, he could be ousted and shunned like his cousin.

No matter the risk, he must share this with his beloved Betsy. But by the time he opened the door to the kitchen, it appeared he was too late; Betsy had evidently abandoned her embroidery to retire for the night. "Well, now, I s'pose there's tomorrow," he said, disappointed.

Eyeing the Good Book, Reuben went to it and sat down again, opening its pages. Never did he want to forget the splendid words he'd read, so he began to memorize the sayings of his Savior, beginning with the first verse of chapter three.

Haven't our preachers ever read and pondered this chapter? Hasn't the bishop?

———

Nellie's mamma might have been surprised to know Caleb could hold Nellie's hand and sit smack-dab next to her in his right-fancy courting buggy without attempting to cross any other romantic lines. They'd been riding under the glow of the most beautiful moon she'd ever seen for two hours, yet he had not so much as slipped his arm around her.

Mamma would like this boy, she thought, trying not to smile too broadly.

"You cold, Nellie Mae?" He leaned near.

How could she be cold under several lap robes and with a handsome fellow sitting next to her? "I'm fine," she answered.

"You sure?"

She nodded, wondering if he hoped she might be chilly. By the twinkle in his eye, she was certain she'd guessed right.

They rode without talking for a long stretch, and then he surprised her by mentioning Suzy. "I know it's too late, but I'd like to offer my sympathy."

"It's been terribly hard . . . to say the least." Her throat closed up, and she hoped he wouldn't say more.

"It must be, considerin' the rumors, jah?"

She stiffened. "What do you mean?"

He shrugged awkwardly. "I've heard some talk about . . . well, how she drowned and all."

What on earth?

Her breath came in little catches.

"Some of the People were worried 'bout the company she was keeping."

Surely he'd also heard the sanitized version of Suzy's life that Dat and Mamma had offered. "Her company—you know them?"

Caleb turned his head to look at her. "You haven't heard what's bein' said, Nellie Mae?"

All of a sudden she didn't like his tone. She let go of his hand. "Why are you askin'?"

He seemed to force a smile. "I've wondered, is all."

She let the silence take over. He had no right to question her so; he scarcely knew her.

"What was Suzy like, really?" Caleb seemed to be changing the course of the conversation a bit.

"She was everything you saw." Nellie felt compelled to defend her sister. "I loved her ever so much. She was kind and loving. . . ." She hesitated, realizing that what she wanted to say was more a fib than anything.

Frustrated and fighting the familiar sadness, she began again. "The rumors you've mentioned, well, they're false. Suzy was a good girl." The lie slipped out.

He leaned his head against hers. "I'm sorry, Nellie. Of course they're not true. If you say it, then I know so. I shouldn't have—"

"No, no, it's all right." But it wasn't and she held her breath, trying not to cry. She wanted him to take her home right quick.

"I'm awful sorry," he said, going on to say that his sisters thought a lot of all her sisters, including Suzy. "They talked often of all four of yous."

She sniffled and nodded.

"Sometime, Nellie Mae . . . when you feel you can trust me, can we talk about this again?"

Instead of speaking her mind, she kept her eyes on the lap blankets that covered her folded hands. "I'd rather not," she admitted at last.

"All right, then. Suit yourself," she heard him say as he moved to put some distance between them.

So much for Caleb asking me out again.

Furious at herself for letting him push her into a corner, she wondered if his curiosity was the reason he'd wanted her to go riding in the first place. She hoped not, yet she wasn't naïve.

Have I been duped?

CHAPTER 13

"I'll be seein' you, Nellie Mae. . . ."

Caleb's final words echoed in her ears as Nellie lay in bed. Sleep did not come easily. She'd slipped into the house, noticing two Bibles side by side on the kitchen table. She'd wondered about that as she made her way up the steps as quietly as she could, even holding her breath, wishing to make herself lighter on the stairs.

Poking her head into her sisters' room, she had seen Nan was not home and in bed as Rhoda was. This had made her feel better about coming in past two o'clock. Some girls stayed out till nearly dawn, and she'd heard of couples who pulled off to the side of a deserted road, or in a covered bridge, stopping to neck rather than talk. She couldn't help but wonder if Nan was involved in such behavior even now with her beau. Perhaps Nan was close to becoming engaged and published by the minister. If so, all the better, especially if the fellow was whom Nellie suspected: David Stoltzfus, the blacksmith's apprentice.

As for the slumbering Rhoda, Nellie figured she was going to be a *maidel*, which was just fine if that's what the Lord God willed. From what she could tell, Rhoda didn't seem too put out at the prospect.

Tired, she stretched her left hand out to the spot where Suzy had always slept. For as long as she remembered, they'd shared this room—plenty of other things, too, including secrets. Not *all*, though, she thought sorrowfully.

"I still miss you something terrible, Suzy." Nellie pressed her hand firmly into the mattress—never before had she felt this cold in bed. A tremor went up her back, and she supposed she wouldn't feel so chilled if Caleb hadn't probed so hard about her departed sister.

Despite how things had soured, they'd managed to make small talk later, the evening not a complete letdown. Caleb had even asked her to ride with him again next Sunday. Her anger not yet forgotten, she'd thought momentarily of turning him down, except that the young folks were to gather at a Singing for their own district, which sounded ever so fun. She felt a twinge of sadness at the thought there would likely be no guitar players this time.

Presently she wasn't as upset anymore as simply feeling guilty for not having been plainspoken with Caleb. What would he think if he knew the things she suspected of Suzy? The rumor mill had hastened to convict her sister of many sins. But really, what did anyone know for sure?

Reliving Caleb's earlier comments, she felt even colder. Had the ugly truth managed to surface, even though she'd buried Suzy's diary?

Shaking her head, she defended Suzy in her mind. Whatever rumors Caleb had heard, they couldn't all be true. Maybe *none* of them were. Oh, how she hoped it were so. . . .

Breathing deeply, Nellie Mae slid her hand back toward the warmth of her own body and clasped both hands in a solemn pose for her rote prayers. When she'd finished, a new sense of resolve welled up in her. *I'll let Suzy prove her innocence.* First thing tomorrow, she would head into the woods, even before helping Mamma with breakfast.

Nellie pondered the risk—Suzy's account of her last six months might offer something helpful, or it might present secrets better left unknown.

Is digging up the diary a good idea? Will I regret reading it?

She rolled over and tried to rest, glad tomorrow was an "off" Sunday—no three-hour Preaching service to sit through. It would be a short night and she despised dragging all day, consumed by thoughts of slumber. There would be plenty of visiting to do tomorrow, too, as the family made their rounds to all her married brothers and their families, starting with Ephram. Then on to Jeremiah and Thomas's place; the twins shared a large divided farmhouse with one side for each brother and his wife and family. Next they'd travel up the road a piece to James's, finishing their day of visits at Benjamin's.

Before Sunday became too busy, Nellie Mae hoped to dig up Suzy's diary and bring it home where it belonged, to the sweet haven of their room, safe at last from the elements of the far-off woods. Somehow, she would prove to herself that she had spoken the truth to Caleb.

Nellie recalled the meadow twinkling with lightning bugs and the sound of crickets filling her ears the deep summer day Suzy had urged her to burn her diary should anything happen to her. At first Nellie had been bewildered. *"What on earth do ya mean?"* she had said at the outlandish request.

"Ach, you know, if I should die young or something," Suzy had replied with a shrug.

Now Nellie thought it odd, wondering if Suzy had been given a forewarning of her own death. Nellie had heard of such things, but she'd never put much stock in them.

Reluctantly Nellie had given her word to her sister, never thinking she'd have occasion to follow through with it.

Staring at the ceiling now, she considered the trek into the woods three months ago and realized she might not remember exactly where she'd hidden Suzy's diary. No particular landmarks came to mind. As distressed as she had been at the time, it was no wonder. Certainly she'd failed to imagine then that she might someday wish to retrieve the journal.

Suddenly Nellie feared Suzy's last words might remain as lost to her as Suzy was.

Getting out of bed, she went to the window and looked out at the land to the west, awash in moonlight. Would she lose a whole night of sleep over Suzy and Caleb, both?

She sighed, staring at the sky. Was Caleb glad they'd gotten better acquainted? Were his toes curled up in anticipation of next Sunday's date, as hers were right now? She laughed at the notion. Caleb was a brawny farmer. If his toes were curling, they were working their way into muddy work boots.

She closed her weary eyes, the moon's light upon her face. *Lord willing, I'll remember where I buried the truth of Suzy's last days.*

The same fervency that had motivated her to conceal the diary propelled her now to find and read her sister's words. For her own sake, Nellie must discover all there was to know.

Even in the gray tint of their semi-darkened room, Betsy could sense something amiss. Reuben was walking up and down the hallway, pacing as though he was either worried sick or too keyed up to relax. Was it good news he contemplated? Or something worrisome? She never could quite tell with Reuben, because normally he concealed his emotions so well.

Just then he entered their room to sit on the chair, moving his hands and looking as if he were praying. Betsy leaned up, unable to sleep much herself. She pushed her loose hair back, the weight of it spilling over one shoulder and her white cotton nightgown.

"You're awful twitchy, dear."

At first he did not respond, but when he did, he kept his face toward the window, its green shade pulled high. "I didn't mean to wake you."

"Oh, you know me . . . a light sleeper, no matter what."

He stood, coming to the bed and placing one hand on the footboard. "Something wonderful-*gut's* happened, Betsy."

"Oh?"

He nodded his head, moving around to her side of the bed. He reached for her hand, clasping it in both of his. "It's too good to keep to myself." His eyes fairly shone in the dimly lit room.

"I know what we've been missin', love." He leaned down and kissed her cheek, then her lips, lingering there, his fervor so pleasing. "All these years, really."

"Oh, Reuben . . . what is it?" She reached up and linked her arms around his neck.

He kissed her again, leaning into her. "Well, to put it simply . . . I've been born anew."

Alarmed, she felt herself go stiff. She'd heard the passages he had read to her following supper, unmistakably different from the Psalms or Proverbs or other passages from the Old Testament he usually chose. "Best not admit that to anyone else, Reuben."

He pulled her close. "Ach, I'm ever so happy! We must know this salvation together."

She could feel his joy in the strength of his arms, the way his head tipped toward hers, the way he held her so tightly, yet tenderly.

"I want to read all of the Gospel of John with you—I myself have been up reading it through this night." Reuben released her, but his breath was on her face and he held both her hands, bending down to kiss one.

"Can it wait till morning?" She chuckled, taken with his enthusiasm.

"First thing," he said, going around the bed and climbing in next to her. "How fitting that we have the whole day to ourselves."

Betsy didn't know if he meant they would read the Bible instead of visiting their sons and families. Truly, she wanted to hug darling Emma once again! But she also sensed something was mighty different about her husband, talking as openly and excitedly as he was. What would it hurt for her to know more, too?

———

Nellie blinked and slowly awakened, briefly confused. When she was fully alert, she realized from the position of the moon that it was but an hour or so before dawn.

In the cold dimness of her room, she brushed her hair and twisted the sides into a low, thick bun behind her head. She then dressed quickly, choosing her gray choring dress and oldest black apron.

Momentarily poking her head out her bedroom door, she determined the hallway was empty before slipping out and down the stairs, quiet as a feather, as she often did mornings when she arose well before dawn to begin her baking.

She hurried to the summer porch, where Mamma kept their long woolen shawls and heavier coats for work and dress. Sitting on the wooden bench her father had made specifically for donning shoes, she pulled on her work boots and wondered how cold it would be with the sun not rising for another hour. She would do well to bundle up—and quickly, too. "Time's a-wastin'," she told herself, stepping outside into the predawn light.

As she did so she heard muted conversation coming from the road. She turned to see a young woman waving at a black open buggy. Right away Nellie assumed it was Nan bidding her beau a fond good-bye. She pitied her sister for having been out in this nippy weather all the night long—pitied her and envied her, both.

A split second's delay and Nan would see her, and then what would Nellie say? *I'm going digging for Suzy's diary . . . want to come along?*

She turned to head for the barn, but Nan was already calling to her. "Nellie . . . wait!"

"Hullo" was all she could muster when her sister drew near. "You're getting in kinda . . . well, *early* in the morning, jah?"

Nan nodded, touching both hands to her face. "I'm nearly froze." She looked at Nellie Mae. "What on earth are *you* doing just comin' home?"

This was her out if she chose to be deceitful. But Nellie knew better. "Oh, I've been home a good long time already."

"Oh?" Nan eyed her.

"I got in late, but not as late as you." She had no idea what else to say. She surely wasn't going to stand here and chat, not when she needed to move along.

"So you walked all the way home, then . . . after the Singing?"

"No . . ."

"Ah, so you met up with someone." Nan was quick.

Nellie changed the subject, just as any sensible Amish girl might. At this moment, she was particularly thankful for the secretive nature of their dating rituals. "Well, if you hurry, you'll have an hour's rest, at least."

"Jah, 'spect so." Nan suddenly looked all in.

"You all right?" Gently, Nellie touched her sister's arm.

But Nan merely turned away. "I best be getting some sleep." With that she headed for the back door.

Nellie made her way to the barn and selected a shovel that was not too large to lug through the meadow and over to the woods. She hoped Nan wouldn't mention to either Rhoda or Mamma having seen her out here so early. Likely it wouldn't matter to Dat if she was out wandering in the dark, as he was known to do such things, too.

Grabbing the shovel, she spotted a small flashlight and snatched it up, as well. She headed out the back way, through the barnyard, to avoid being caught. She cut across the dewy pastureland, veering north to the treed area, where she tried to recall her steps last June, after Suzy's passing.

She crept along cautiously, aware how easy it would be to stumble in the murkiness. Darkness had never affected her before Suzy's death, but now she felt unusually conscious of the lonely nocturnal hours. She shivered, longing for the warmth of Mamma's kitchen.

In any case, she needed to be back in the house and cleaned up before the rest of the family awoke, ready to go visiting. She enjoyed their no-Preaching Sundays when they went around to each other's homes. Truth be known, here lately, as much as she honored and respected their Plain tradition, Nellie Mae was becoming weary of the church services.

Shining her flashlight around the thicket, she had a sudden notion that she might have dreamed she'd hidden Suzy's journal. Had she been too caught up with grief, only imagining she'd come here?

But no, she recalled carrying the diary beneath her petticoats in a makeshift pouch, created out of quilting scraps. She'd felt she must, at all costs, do her best to respect at least something of Suzy's request. Maybe she had done so, far too well.

Pointing the flashlight at a row of bushes, she sighed. "I can remember endless recipes, but I can't remember where I put Suzy's diary?" *How can this be?*

Chapter 14

Before the sun peeked over the eastern ridge, Reuben was up and lighting the tall gas lantern on the dresser. Without a word, he headed downstairs and brought up the King James Bible to read aloud. Betsy lingered in bed, a bit droopy, as she often was at this early hour.

She watched him, the way his eyes were intent upon the words he presently read to her. The lines around his mouth seemed softer in the flickering light, and he removed his glasses partway through the chapter to wipe his eyes.

He looked at her from across the room, tears welling up again. "To think what God's Son did for us—taking our punishment." He covered his mouth for a moment, his emotion apparently too great for words. "Oh, Betsy . . . I want you to share this joy, too . . . this most blessed salvation."

The expression on his face was nearly as convincing as the Scriptures he read, for she had never, ever seen Reuben weep—not at the funeral for Suzy, nor the burial, where they had laid their precious daughter to rest in the People's cemetery. No, Reuben was not one to shed tears at all.

"May I read to you every mornin', love?" he asked, coming around to her side of the bed.

"In secret?"

He sighed and placed his glasses on the bedside table. "Well, I guess that's what I mean. Jah, for now."

For now?

"What about evening prayers? Will you be readin' from this chapter then, too . . . in front of the girls?"

He closed the Bible. "I'll think on that," he said softly. "My prayer is that each of our family will come to know the Savior, as I have."

"Know Him?"

"Jah, love." His face was against hers. "We'll study His ways together."

She sat up, snuggling against him, her head on his chest. "We won't be found out in time?"

"I'm trustin' the Lord God for our future, Betsy. It's His doing, so we must heed the command not to worry." He held her near, as he often did of a morning. But today there was more urgency in the way his arms wrapped around her, as if his embrace alone might convince her to join him in his newfound belief.

If she were honest, she would admit to her husband, dear man that he was, that she was floundering terribly in a mire of sorrow. Perhaps Reuben's keen interest in Scripture—in passages forbidden and otherwise—might be exactly what the Good Lord had in mind for her during this time. If trustworthy Reuben was willing to swim against the current sure to come, certainly it was a good thing for her to consider, as well.

"Let me read the passage for myself." She reached for the book, glad he'd brought up the King James Bible.

"Here, I'll show ya where to start." He thumbed through the pages.

"Denki," she whispered.

"No need to thank me." He turned his face toward the ceiling and closed his eyes. What looked to be a heavenly light shone across her dear one's face. Betsy felt as if she'd seen a glimpse of heaven . . . where she secretly hoped with all of her heart that darling Suzy resided.

Nellie Mae propped the flashlight in the crook of a nearby tree, shining it down at the spot in the ground, her third attempt near the base of the tree she suspected sheltered Suzy's secrets.

How many holes must I dig?

She stopped briefly to catch her breath but then she pressed on, burrowing deep into the soil with the shovel. There had been only a single frost thus far, so the ground was yielding enough. She kept working the spot until she was certain the diary was not to be found there.

She straightened and wiped her face with a hankie, glad she'd remembered to slip it into her pocket; surely her face must be smudged. She stopped to adjust the flashlight and push the shovel into the earth, creating yet another hole.

Daybreak came and Nellie stopped to watch the sun peep over the horizon, its golden light pouring over rolling hills. Despite her frustration, she drank in the sight, surrounded as she was by trees and all of nature. Normally she would be up to her wrists in dough at this hour, too intent on her work to greet the day.

Fondly she recalled now the scent of wildflowers around her feet in early summer. Suzy had commented on the colorful variety when she and Nellie had come walking up here in early June. They'd gone even farther to find the area where as young girls they had planted their favorite red columbine—from the buttercup family—to brighten the spot and attract hummingbirds. Year after year, the five-petaled scarlet flowers had propagated rapidly amid the sun-dappled area.

As a child, Suzy would often return home with a fistful of tiny blossoms, bluebells and columbine mostly. Placing them on the decorative plate on their dresser, instead of in a vase of water like their English neighbors might, she wished for them to dry as they were. *In their perty little dresses,* as she would say. Unfortunately the flowers had never dried the way Suzy had anticipated, but had rather wilted and withered. Yet she'd continued to pick them and take them home, always hoping that one day they might dry *just so.*

The pale blue plate with its floral rim now lay empty on the oak dresser, and Nellie wished for some bluebells to pick in memory of her sister, but the chill of autumn had snatched them away.

She turned her attention back to her search, more concerned than ever about her inability to locate the diary's hiding place.

Why didn't I mark the spot?

Frustrated with herself, she stopped her search and returned to the house. *I won't despair,* she told herself. *Somehow . . . I will remember!*

Back at the house, there was nary a sound. But as she climbed the steps, she overheard her father's voice as he read aloud from the Good Book. Odd as that was, Nellie didn't dare linger at the landing to listen. Instead she hurried to her room, removed her Kapp, and shook out her hair, surprised at the tiny twigs and even the small leaf that fell from her long tresses. Brushing her hair vigorously, she wound it back into the formal bun and pinned her head covering back on. Then she slipped into a better dress for their visiting day.

Heading downstairs again, she briefly visited the washroom to clean the morning's grime from her face. Reassured that no one would now guess at her morning's activities from merely looking at her, she began to lay out the cold cereal, fruit, and juices—there was no cooking or baking to be done on the Lord's Day. It was for that reason Nellie found herself having to do so much catching up early Monday mornings.

She began to slice bananas to top off their cereal and heard laughter, followed by what sounded like weeping. *Mamma?* Instantly she felt heartsick, wishing something could be done to help her mother get through this awful sorrowful time.

Nellie was glad Dat was with her. Her father was more tender with Mamma these days, especially when that sad and faraway look was evident in her mother's eyes. A haunting, troubled look, to be sure.

"Maybe it will help her to be out and about," she said, anticipating today's visits.

———

After Dat offered the final silent prayer following breakfast, Mamma announced they would not be leaving the house till after the noon meal. No word of explanation was given for this clear departure from their off-Sunday routine.

Nellie Mae did not allow her disappointment to show. Still, it was hard to push aside thoughts of the excitement they typically enjoyed on a day like this. So once the kitchen had been cleared, she went upstairs to ask Rhoda and Nan, now settled in their room, if they wanted to go walking. Without a second thought, Rhoda shook her head, her glasses perched almost at the end of her nose as she studied her crocheting book. Nan yawned and said, "Some other time, Nellie Mae," before climbing forlornly onto their bed.

Nellie dragged her feet back to her room, downcast. She closed her door and sat on the bed, wondering if she might have opportunity to look for the diary another day when there was more time. *Some sun would be helpful, too,* she murmured to herself. Truly, she didn't know when she could get away again, what with her duties at the bakery shop. She knew she should feel guilty for having tramped through the woods, shovel in hand, exerting herself on the Lord's Day, when even sewing and needlework were forbidden. Just now, this rule seemed petty, and she was amazed at her own feelings. How long had she harbored apathy?

She yawned, feeling the effects of precious little sleep. Even so, the hours spent with Caleb were worth any amount of lost rest. She hoped he was like her own father, always so loving and attentive to Mamma.

I want a husband like that.

She propped herself up with several bed pillows, taking from her oak bedside table the weekly newspaper, *The Budget,* which focused on Plain communities. She selected the pages featuring the goings-on in Kalona, Iowa, curious if the journal-style columns might shed some light on what Uncle Bishop and Aunt Anna could be doing there.

Lorena Miller, an Amish scribe from that area, began her column by mentioning the rain, wind, and falling temperatures . . . with frost predicted. She also listed the visitors attending a recent worship service—a Jonas and Fannie Hershberger and the Earl Beechys, all from out of town. Nellie didn't recognize any of those last names.

Lorena also wrote of nightly revival meetings.

Were Uncle Bishop and Aunt Anna aware of such gatherings? Word had it there were similar lively meetings held on Friday and Saturday nights here locally at the Tel Hai tabernacle, an open-air building not far from the road. The place could really draw a crowd, or so she'd heard.

Scanning the paper further, she noticed the first line of a column from Mt. Hope, Ohio. *Best not to tiptoe around what you're yearning for, eyeing it, longing for it . . . or you'll miss your life ahead,* it read.

She wondered if she might not be doing the same thing, marking time while she waited for Caleb. She'd let him see her prickly side—a mistake, probably. Of course, if he had eyes in his head and ears, too, he surely knew she'd always respectfully spoken her mind at school and other places where he'd encountered her.

Sighing, she was too tired to rehash what he might think of her refusal to discuss Suzy's death. Despite their shaky beginnings, he seemed to like her well enough to want more of her company.

A week away . . . an eternity.

Closing the paper, she folded it neatly, still considering the Iowa revival meetings. Who attended such gatherings? And from what did people need to be revived?

She rose and poked her head into the hallway, listening. No voices came from her parents' bedroom, so maybe they'd finished their discussion.

Already weary of being stuck at home, Nellie closed the door and leaned back against it. Why weren't they heading off to visit her brothers and families as they always did before the noon meal? Wouldn't Maryann be putting out cold cuts in expectation?

Too tired to ponder further, she returned to the made bed and lay down to rest on this most disappointing Lord's Day.

"You're quite taken with the Good Book, ain't so, Reuben?" whispered Betsy as they sat on their bedroom loveseat.

Her husband held the Bible reverently on his lap, and she noticed how he caressed it, his big hands moving slowly over the leather. "More than ever before, jah."

She sat, enjoying his presence as always. She couldn't remember their ever lingering this way on any day of the week, let alone a no-Preaching Sunday.

"This book has come alive to me, Betsy." His eyes welled up with tears. "I can't explain it . . . but its words have given me something right here"—he placed his hand on his chest—"something I've needed my whole life."

Moved by his response, she nodded, squeezing his hand. Yet she did not understand what was happening to her strong husband.

He reached for his kerchief. "I wasn't even searchin' for this . . . at least I didn't know it." He wept again openly.

"Ach, Reuben, are you all right?"

He nodded. "Never better, dear one. It's like the Lord God himself came lookin' for me."

And found you, thought Betsy.

Chapter 15

James's roomy clapboard house was the third stop on their regular route every other Sunday, and Nellie was overjoyed to see cute little Emma again, late in the afternoon though it was. It seemed Mamma was even happier than usual to see her granddaughter as the girl came running straight to her, wrapping her chubby arms tightly around Mamma's knees.

"Oh, my dear child, I missed you so!" Mamma stooped down to kiss the top of Emma's blond head.

Emma's brothers—one older and two younger—Benny, Jimmy, and Matty—ran to greet their Dawdi Reuben, who hugged them quickly and patted toddler Matty on the head. "Ach, look at yous. You've grown in just one week," he said as all of them jabbered at once in Dutch.

As promised, Emma readily showed her dolly to Nellie and her sisters, though Rhoda and Nan sat a bit aloof over in the corner of the front room. Emma told them the handkerchief doll had been one of Suzy's many creations, her eyes bright as she described her dolly's pretend adventures.

Rhoda perked up some during Emma's telling. But Nan, however, continued in a dismal mood.

Problems with her beau? Nellie wondered. Or was Nan peeved about having to stay put so long at home this morning?

But Emma's antics would not permit Nellie to wonder long.

The girl crawled up on her Mammi's lap. "I have me a secret," Emma whispered, leaning close.

Mamma listened and then pulled back and played at clapping her hand over her mouth. "My goodness, that's just wonderful-gut!"

Rhoda got up to move to a chair closer to Mamma. Removing her shoes, she tucked one pudgy leg under her, perching there like a pumpkin about to roll off. Nan stayed where she and Rhoda had initially sat, appearing almost unaware of the goings-on around her.

As for Nellie, she was mighty curious about Emma's so-called secret, especially when the child slid off Mamma's lap and hurried upstairs. In short order, she was back, carrying a small block of a potholder, three-fourths finished.

"See, Mammi? It's crocheted . . . Mamma taught me how, this very week."

Martha smiled, bobbing her head to confirm it. She sat on her father's old hickory rocker with twenty-month-old Matty sprawled on her lap. "I daresay all I did was show her a few loops and she kept on goin'," Martha said, blue eyes sparkling. "Not to boast a'tall, but she's got a knack."

"Is that right?" Mamma inspected the potholder with its green, blue, and purple strands of variegated yarn, oohing and aahing as she made over Emma's creation. "It's awful perty. Really, 'tis. Maybe you can make a whole bunch of them to give as Christmas presents."

Emma smiled her crooked smile and touched Mamma's arm. "I'll make one for *you,* Mammi Elizabeth."

"I'd like that very much," said Mamma, acting startled upon hearing her formal name.

" 'Cept it won't be a secret now," Emma lisped.

To this, Mamma reached over and cupped Emma's chin with her hand. "You're quite the chatterbox today, ain't so?"

Rhoda laughed softly.

Martha attempted to redirect Mamma's attention away from Emma to towheaded Matty, who was pulling on the hair of one of Emma's ragdolls on Martha's lap. In spite of Matty's adorable grin, Nellie saw it was all Mamma could do to keep her eyes off Emma.

After a while they all sat down together and enjoyed some of Martha's delicious baby pearl tapioca and chocolate chip cookies. Mamma, Martha, and Nellie were clearing the table when Emma tugged on Mamma's skirt and looked up at her. "Aunt Suzy really ain't comin' back ever?"

A frown quickly appeared on Mamma's face. She glanced nervously at Martha.

But there was no time to talk things over, not with Emma within earshot. Mamma smiled ever so kindly. "Our dear Suzy's gone forever, jah. . . ." Her lip trembled and she turned slightly so Emma wouldn't see.

Rhoda quickly diverted Emma's attention, taking her into the smaller sitting room near the front room. Nellie and Nan stayed close to Mamma, comforting her by getting her some hot tea and having her sit at the table awhile.

Later on their drive to the last visit of the day—Benjamin and Ida's place—Nellie couldn't help but notice again how considerate Dat was of Mamma, asking her if she was all right. Nellie wondered if Emma's question had grieved Dat, too . . . knowing full well that even if it had, he would never speak of it.

———

After she'd completed her baking and helped her sisters and Mamma hang out the wash early Monday morning, Nellie took herself off to the bakery shop. She waited on more English customers than usual, or so it seemed. She didn't mind, as long as they didn't stare, which did happen occasionally—Rosanna observed the same thing, tending her roadside vegetable stand. Nellie preferred the regular Englischers, who were more accustomed to the Plain way she and Nan dressed.

Rhoda had already headed on foot to work at the Kraybills'. So bubbly was she that Nellie wondered if something had happened between yesterday afternoon's visits and this morning.

Nan, on the other hand, remained as *schlimm*—sad—as Nellie had ever seen her. With Rhoda gone for the whole day, Nellie wondered if maybe she might get a chance to hear what was up.

But Nan was slow to assist at the bakery shop, not arriving until midafternoon. By then the place was too swamped with customers for any sisterly talk.

About that time, Rebekah Yoder showed up. "Dat's been draggin' his feet about puttin' down our old buggy mare," she said, seemingly in the mood to chat. "Every time anyone's mentioned it, he's said, 'Ach, there's one more mile in her. A good-natured horse like that's determined to die in the harness.' Anyway, this mornin' he hitched her up and took off to town, going by way of the one-lane bridge on Beaver Dam Road." Rebekah paused for a breath, appearing eager to tell the whole story.

"What happened?" Nellie asked.

The other customers leaned in to listen.

"Well, if the horse didn't collapse right in the middle of the road!"

"That's just awful."

"It was sad, of course, but kind of funny, too, accordin' to Dat." Rebekah shook her head. "There was a long, long line behind Dat's buggy—a whole bunch of buggies, and a good many cars, too. Amish farmers and English drivers both were jumpin' out and askin' what a dead horse was doin' on the road."

"Well, *was* she dead?" asked Nellie.

"Apparently not. A large truck somehow'd got off course and onto the narrow road. When it gave a few loud blasts from its air horn, ach, if the horse didn't leap up on all fours, and they were off again." Rebekah giggled before composing herself, and Nellie laughed, assuming that was the end of the story.

"Turns out Ol' Dolly let out a final shudder on the way home and fell down dead in the middle of the turn lane on Route 322. Poor thing. Probably a heart attack, Dat says."

"Oh, Rebekah . . . what a fright for your father."

"Jah, it was." She sighed. "But he told me he had nobody to blame but himself."

"Good thing no one got hurt."

"Or killed," Rebekah added. " 'Cept the horse, of course."

The cluster of customers began chattering at that, but Rebekah's story had gotten only a halfhearted crinkle of a smile from Nan.

———

As they closed the shop for the day, Nan took issue with Nellie. "I daresay you overreacted to Rebekah's storytellin'."

"You think so?"

Nan nodded. "Nothin' funny 'bout what she was saying."

"Well, it struck *me* that way."

Nan folded her arms. "You seemed terribly pleased to see Rebekah today. What with the hearsay . . ." She flashed a teasing grin. "I think you must like her brother an awful lot, that's what."

"You don't know that."

"Well, Benjamin's brother-in-law told Becky Glick that he saw what looked to be you and Caleb over in some bushes after Singing, of all things!"

Nellie was stunned. She stopped to stare at her sister. Caleb *had* hugged her in the thicket, but only momentarily. Old Joe Glick's granddaughter—Susannah Lapp's best friend—had made too much of an innocent gesture. Oh, how she despised the grapevine!

"Benjamin's brother-in-law knows nothin' at all, and neither do you," Nellie spouted.

"Well, you did meet up with a boy after Singing. Don't say ya didn't."

"My lips are sealed."

"Jah, and so is your fate."

"You have no idea what you're babblin' about, Nan!" she hollered back.

Face red, Nan ran off to the house, slamming the back door.

As much as Nellie wanted to ignore her sister's cutting words, she could not stop thinking about the possibility Susannah had one of Nellie's own brother's kin spying on her. *Susannah must be afraid she's going to lose her chance with Caleb. That's what!*

Nellie followed her sister's lead and went inside, where the smell of one of Mamma's best hot dishes almost cheered her, turkey casserole being a favorite. She hurried to help both Nan and Mamma get the table set and all the serving dishes on the table, trying not to pay Nan any further mind.

Nellie was surprised at the feast, which included baked beans, buttered carrots, and cut corn in addition to a gelatin salad and homemade muffins. Nellie looked at her mother and was heartened to see a healthy blush on her cheeks. *Is she finally feeling better?*

When Dat came in from getting the mules into the barn, he washed up quickly. Rubbing his hands together, he went to get the Good Book down from the tall cupboard at the far end of the kitchen. "We'll be havin' some Scripture reading right after the meal." He took his seat at the head.

Nan and Rhoda exchanged glances as Nan filled the last of the water glasses. She sat down next to Nellie, across from Mamma, who sat in her place to their father's right.

"Let's bow our heads," Dat said. "Our heavenly Father, we ask for your blessings on this food, which we are ever so grateful for . . . just as we are for your dear Son, our Savior, the Lord Jesus Christ. Amen." Instead of praying silently, he had blessed the food aloud.

Nellie had never heard such praying, let alone at the table. She looked first at Mamma, who was beaming at Dat nearly like a schoolgirl. Then she looked at her father, who was getting on with the business of eating, reaching now for the large spoon stuck in the casserole dish.

What on earth was that? Nellie wondered the whole way through the meal.

After they'd finished, Dat resumed his prayerful mood and bowed his head, offering the usual *silent* blessing this time.

Half Amish prayer . . . half not?

Nellie rose to clear the table with Nan's help, telling Mamma and Rhoda to stay seated. As she worked, putting away food and scraping clean the plates while Nan got the water ready for washing, she kept trying to sort out what had just occurred. She'd heard her father pray aloud with her own ears, addressing God as he would someone he knew well.

When at last the kitchen was clean, Dat asked her and her sisters to come and sit at the table, a departure from their usual evening Bible reading, when they were allowed to sit wherever they wished, perhaps even playing checkers or doing something else while he read. Not this night. Dat asked them to listen carefully as he read from passages in the Gospel of John she'd never heard in her life.

The Scriptures told of a man whose name was unfamiliar to her: Nicodemus. Full of questions, he was. *Just as I've been since Suzy passed away,* Nellie thought. She liked this new story from the same old Bible Dat had read from since they were born.

He paused and rested his gaze briefly on them before going on to the next verse. " 'He that believeth on the Son hath everlasting life: and he that believeth not the Son shall not see life; but the wrath of God abideth on him.' "

Nellie found herself fighting back tears. She reached into her pocket and squeezed Suzy's Kapp strings, wanting to ask her father to read the verse again. If only poor Suzy had the everlasting life promised to those who believed on the Son. Was the wrath of God abiding on her?

Not wanting to draw attention to her state of mind, Nellie Mae headed upstairs and closed her door as soon as Dat excused them. She longed to be free of the guilt she carried in her heart, but she had no way of knowing if that was possible.

Her legs felt too weak to hold her, so she knelt beside her bed for the first time ever. Because she didn't know what to say to the Lord God and heavenly Father, so tongue-tied and ashamed was she, Nellie merely wept.

———

Dat began to make a routine out of reading from the New Testament following breakfast and again after supper. By week's end, he had read them the entire book of John. Nellie had especially enjoyed the story about the woman who'd come for well water and left with something better, her soul satisfied. *The Lord's abundant water . . . life-giving.*

How tantalizing it seemed. Evidently Mamma thought so, too, for Nellie Mae found her reading on her own, right where Dat had placed his long blue bookmark. As relieved as Nellie was to see the rosy glow returning to Mamma's countenance after all these depressing weeks, she was hesitant to discuss this with her mother.

Gladdened, yet perplexed, Nellie prepared for her second date with Caleb, taking extra care in twisting the sides of her hair back into the hair bun, smooth as can be. She scrubbed her face and chose her crispest, whitest Kapp. Then, waiting till dusk, she slipped out of the house, presumably unnoticed. Nellie was sure Mamma and Nan knew she was going out, but which boy she was seeing was anyone's guess.

Nellie made her way down the road to meet Caleb, wishing Nan hadn't seemed so put out this week at having to help a lot in the shop—peeved at everything, really. "That might change soon with Mamma starting to feel better again," she whispered to herself, eager for the day when her mother would be up to returning to the bakery shop.

———

Caleb had not asked Nellie to wait tonight at any particular spot along Beaver Dam Road, so she made her way near the grassy shoulder, conscious of the somber stillness of every tree. The sky was awash with thin clouds. How fragile they seemed . . . like the way she felt, realizing her words had the power to kill or build her friendship with Caleb.

I best be biting my tongue this time.

She glanced down at her plum-colored dress and fresh black apron, all ironed for the evening. Her black shoes were well polished, too, as if for Preaching.

An open buggy passed by just then, and a few minutes later, another. Each time she kept her head down so as not to be recognized. She did not care for any more gossipy accounts of her doings from Nan.

Niemols—never again!

She puffed in disgust at the audacity of the deacon's daughter, taking the underhanded route by persuading her friend to spy on Nellie—or so she assumed. Of all the nerve; it was exactly like Susannah to behave so. All the same she was not about to allow her aggravation to spoil the evening. She wondered if it would be only a few hours at the Singing, then some riding, and home again. Or would he keep her out all the night long like Nan's beau?

She could only imagine what Caleb had planned. Most of all, she hoped he would not press her anymore about Suzy. She might not be able to restrain her frustration tonight. She would do all she could to keep him talking about more pleasant things.

Spotting his courting buggy, Nellie Mae put on a big smile and waved. His hand went high into the air in a grand return wave, and her heart took flight.

Goodness' sakes . . . I'm done for!

CHAPTER 16

Betsy felt overjoyed to have some time to herself. Reuben had left the house to hitch up the horse and carriage to run an errand over at Ephram's. That gave her plenty of opportunity to read, what with Nellie out with a beau and Rhoda still not back from the Kraybills'. Nan was out taking a walk, or so she'd said.

" 'Who coverest thyself with light as with a garment: who stretchest out the heavens like a curtain. . . . ' " Betsy read where the page had fallen open, which happened to be the Psalms. *Bishop approved,* she thought, and glad of it.

She was compelled to read the entire psalm, curiously taking a close look at God's description of himself as being "clothed with honour and majesty." But it was the reference to light that fascinated her most.

Closing her eyes, Betsy imagined what a covering of light would look like—the heavenly Father's garment, full of goodness and love. She kept her eyes squeezed shut, taking in the picture she saw in her mind's eye.

The Lord God of light and love sent His Son to us . . . for a reason. How happy, even joyful that thought made her husband. Betsy'd never thought of the Scriptures the way Reuben had recently described them.

Life-giving.

She read further, wondering what had prompted Reuben to want to read the Good Book so often . . . and for such long stretches at a time. How had he come upon the chapter he'd read to her last Saturday? Had he purposely searched out new sections to read?

She honestly didn't understand his desire for what he called truth. Their heritage held her fast. Wasn't the truth to be had in the lessons of their forefathers—in their Ordnung?

Opening her eyes, she read the next verse and the next, until she had read the entire chapter—all thirty-five verses. Captivated, she went back, now reading aloud. Pondering each sentence, she felt the urge to move on to Psalm 105, except Nan came running into the house, sniffling.

"Sorry, Mamma . . . I, uh, need to be alone." Nan hurried out of the kitchen and up the stairs.

Ach . . . troubles with a boy, likely.

She would wait a bit, then head up to see if Nan wanted to talk as she sometimes did, although that daughter would hem and haw and never come right out and say what was bothering her. Oh, but Betsy knew. She well remembered her own courting days. All the pain of them . . . and the joy, too.

Returning to the Scripture, she read Psalm 105 through twice, and having done so, she felt torn—both with gladness and an alarming feeling that she had somehow sinned.

Reuben dreaded stopping by Ephram's tonight, scarcely knowing how to conceal his elation at the change in his soul. It had taken him over in the oddest way, making him feel almost like a boy and as light as grain on the threshing floor. The Good News had nothing to do with a set of rules. It was a love story . . . between God and the human race.

He'd reached the point of wanting each of his sons to know this same jubilation that he had already begun to reveal in part to his daughters. Betsy knew all, of course, and he'd already set to praying unceasingly for her to come to the light, just as he had. Clear out of the blue, nearly knocking him between the eyes.

Yet he had not sought it, much like the handful of ministerial brethren back two decades ago whose spiritual eyes were also opened upon reading Scripture. Like him, they had not pursued this path, as it were . . . having believed all along that truth was literally their tradition. Till a week ago Reuben had failed to grasp that this could have occurred without any conscious effort on their part. Would his sons now view him in the same puzzled way?

With some degree of apprehension, Reuben returned sundry tools to Ephram's barn, hoping to avoid seeing his son just yet.

Closing the barn door, Reuben glanced back at the house. Ephram was moving toward him carrying a lantern and his walking stick, his sturdy shoulders seemingly bearing a load that made him old before his time. "Hullo, son!" he called.

"Daed . . . you didn't have to make a special trip over here, and after dark yet."

Reuben waved off the comment. "A nice night, so I saw no reason not to. Besides, tomorrow's goin' to be awful busy."

Ephram leaned on his walking stick. "Someone else dropped by unexpectedly this afternoon."

He waited for Ephram to say more. "Who might that be?"

"A right fancy fella wearin' a tie—Mr. Snavely, he said he was." Ephram pulled a white business card out of his pocket. "Gave me this . . . said I should look him up."

Reuben peered at the card in the lantern's light, noticing the image of a tractor.

"He said something else, too."

Reuben didn't like the way Ephram was frowning. "What's that?"

"He stopped by your place, too . . . talked to Mamm."

This was the first he'd heard of it.

"Mamm didn't mention anything?"

"Nary a word." Reuben chuckled. "You know your mother. She only tells me what she wants me to hear."

Ephram nodded toward the house. "Our women . . ."

Yet Reuben didn't know what to think of this. Betsy had talked with a tractor salesman? How long ago? "I doubt Mr. Snavely got very far talkin' over such things with your mother."

Ephram pushed on his stick again, digging it down, like a stake. "To be frank, Dat, I'll have nothin' at all to do with them tractor folk." He raised his lantern. "If you understand my meaning."

That he did. And good for Ephram. In fact, Reuben would've been right there with him, standing firm in the Old Ways, had he not read the Gospel of John . . . and so many other eye-opening passages, too. For sure and for certain, he'd be taking Ephram's side if heaven hadn't opened the eyes of his understanding about the Ordnung. If it was wrong on some things, who was to say it wasn't wrong on others, too?

"Well, don't know 'bout you, but I'd best be getting home. The air's turnin' chilly," Reuben said, heading toward his horse and buggy.

"So long, Dat."

Reuben stepped into his buggy, anxious to return to Betsy—and to the Good Book. *Jah, eternal life. Such a wonderful-good gift.*

In time, at exactly the right moment, he'd have a sit-down with Ephram.

Caleb had a big talk going, and Nellie was delighted to listen. He was telling her about the hayride next Sunday night after the Singing. "There'll be plenty of goodies to eat and lots of group games and whatnot. Will you go along, Nellie?"

She smiled, knowing the night was young yet. She nodded her head, forgetting he couldn't see her response; nightfall was so complete. Then when she realized he was waiting for an answer, she quickly asked, "Where will it be?"

"Over at the stone house near Mill Road. The deacon's sister's place."

Susannah's aunt!

She groaned inwardly. Would she never escape that girl's scrutiny?

"Sure, I'll go," she replied, nearly grinning at herself.

He surprised her by reaching for her hand. "I'd like to be the one to take you home following . . . all right?"

Why was he asking her so far ahead? Why not pair up at the actual gathering, as was their way? Oh, the flickers of excitement every time he touched her hand!

"Sounds just fine."

From the moment she'd stepped into Caleb's open buggy tonight, she had felt a sense of rightness, as if somehow she was supposed to spend the evening with him. Supposed to enjoy the starry night and the whispers of the dark trees. Something within her urged: *Trust your heart. . . .*

"When do you think you'll join church, Nellie?" The question startled her.

Well, he certainly didn't leave any stone unturned, this boy. Caleb leaned close for a moment, like he wanted her to know he, too, was contemplating making his life vow.

"I haven't thought much 'bout it." That was the truth. "Why're you askin'?"

"Have you considered it?"

"Not yet."

He paused. "Do you plan to put it off?"

"Just bein' honest. It's still early in my Rumschpringe . . . same as it is for you."

He was chuckling now, and she didn't know what to make of it.

"You're laughing at me?" she said.

"A little."

"What for?"

"You're so easy to kid, Nellie." He squeezed her hand. *He thinks I'm gullible. . . .*

"When do *you* plan on joining?" She was stepping out of bounds slightly. A girl scarcely ever asked this of a boy, since being baptized into the church was usually followed by a wedding the next month. But he'd put her on the spot, so why not?

"I'll join a year from now—next fall," he stated.

"You know this for sure?"

"Why put off what I plan to do anyway?"

She frowned, glad he couldn't see her expression. No streetlights shone here as they did near the main highway. These back roads he was taking her on were perfect for obscuring facial responses.

Caleb continued. "I'll start baptismal instruction when the time comes. When Deacon Lapp offers classes next summer."

Susannah's father . . .

The silence that followed was one Nellie Mae didn't feel worthy to fill—just as she didn't know how she could possibly kneel before the Lord God and the congregation of the People and say all the things required. Not with all the shame she carried around in her soul.

"We could take the classes together," he suggested.

With all of her heart, she wanted to say yes. *Sure, Caleb, I'll do that with you . . . and I'll be your sweetheart-girl, too.*

"Nellie?" He turned and was mighty close. "I'm askin' you."

The tears came too suddenly to stop them. Wasn't this the very thing she'd wanted . . . for Caleb to show how much he cared?

"Aw, you're cryin'." He reached around her, holding the reins with one hand. "Nellie . . . honey . . . whatever's wrong?"

She couldn't speak, though she wanted to. He must've understood, for he didn't press her further, instead letting her cry on his shoulder, her face against his black woolen coat.

Then almost before she realized it, the horse was pulling the buggy off the road, beneath a towering old tree. He waited for the horse to come to a halt before resting the reins on his knees.

Turning to her, Caleb cupped her face in his hands. "Listen, Nellie . . . you take your time, ya hear? Making the kneeling vow is the most holy thing you'll ever do. The most important, too. No one can tell you when you're ready."

Oh, I might fall too hard for him if he doesn't quit talking like this. She felt the warmth of his breath on her face—his intense, yet tender nearness. She thought he might want to kiss her if only to cheer her up.

Slowly, though, he moved back, his eyes still on her. "We mustn't . . ." He stopped short of saying what she knew he meant.

He likes me more than a bushel and a peck, she thought. Yet as happy as that knowledge made her feel, she had some figuring out to do before she could fully commit to taking the baptismal vow.

In every way, Caleb Yoder seemed to know precisely what he wanted.

Chapter 17

Betsy had made several attempts to draw Nan out, to no avail. Her poor daughter merely shook her head, expression gloomy. Truth be told, Nan looked to be pouting, sitting there in her corner of her bedroom.

Somewhat mystified, Betsy studied this pretty girl who was typically full of life. Her delicate features were enhanced by the lovely blue of her big eyes—a striking contrast to her dark brown hair. She'd often thought them a fine combination of Reuben's deep brown hair and her own blue eyes. Nan's looks were the kind to readily attract a boy's attention . . . though it appeared not enough to keep it.

"Looks like you'd rather sit here alone, then?" she said, her final try.

Nan nodded unconvincingly, tears welling up.

Betsy went and stood near her, slipping her arm around Nan's slim shoulders. "You can trust me with whatever's bothering you, dear."

Nan's lower lip quivered. "It just ain't fair, that's all."

Leaning her head atop her daughter's for a moment, Betsy stroked her back, trying to soothe her. "Jah, life may seem ever so unfair at times, no doubting that." She well knew there was no sense in discussing grievances, and she would not inquire about the boy who'd ditched her forlorn Nan. Doing so would hush her girl right up. Why, she'd been much the same way around her own mother, after once being jilted.

Nan sobbed into her hands as though she'd lost nearly everything she'd ever cared about. "Oh, Mamma, I loved this boy . . . I did."

Silently Betsy pulled Nan into her arms.

"And he didn't love me, not like he said." More sniffling.

Better to find out now. Yet she wouldn't dare say such a thing.

She held Nan for a good long time, offering her presence, which, as she remembered when she'd experienced her heartbreak, was all she'd needed from her own mamma.

At long last, when Nan's tears were brushed away and her nose red with the blowing, her daughter surprised her by revealing her beau's change of heart, *after* proposing marriage.

Dishonorable, Betsy decided then and there, battling her ire.

But there was more. Another girl had caught the boy's eye . . . the deacon's niece, as Nan described her. "She took my dear beau away."

"Ain't much dear 'bout him, I daresay."

"Oh, but he was, Mamma. He *was.*"

She couldn't bear to see Nan this way, distressed over the worst of the bunch, for sure. Time for Betsy to share something of her own Rumschpringe days.

"Joshua was my first beau ever," she began, hoping to get Nan's mind off her obvious melancholy. "He was everything I thought I wanted and much, much more. . . ."

Their parents were downright strict about when Joshua and Elizabeth could do their courting—Sunday night Singings only. Betsy was "awful young," or so her mother thought initially, pleading with her father that just because Betsy'd turned sixteen, the expected age to begin courting, she wasn't ready to be dating yet. But tradition won out over her mother's insistence, and her father permitted her to start going to the various youth activities, where she met Joshua Stoltzfus, the best-looking boy in the whole church district.

They dated for nearly six months, marking each and every month's anniversary with intense emotion and promises of love. But, alas, when a new family moved into the area, renting a farmhouse from Englischers that was already wired for electricity, Joshua offered to help uninstall it. While doing so, he met and fell in love with the second of their six daughters.

"In the end, though, I was ever so glad it happened that-away," Betsy admitted.

"Why, Mamma?" Nan said.

"Well, think of it . . . what if Josh hadn't gotten his swivel neck straightened out before we got married? What then?"

Nan blinked her weepy eyes. "I s'pose, for one thing, I would never have been born."

Betsy chuckled. "You can say that again." She sighed at the memory. "I lost track of Joshua and his family some years after they moved to the Finger Lakes area of New York to help some of their elderly relatives. I heard later that he and his wife never had any children at all."

"Oh, I'm so glad you didn't end up with that boy," Nan was saying, a peek of a smile appearing. "You would have been unhappy all of your days without all of us, Mamma."

"'Tis true." She kissed Nan's forehead. "I say, be glad this beau of yours left when he did. Count your blessings, dear. All right?"

Nan was nodding. "When you put it that way, jah, I can see things . . . for what they are." She brushed away a solitary tear. "Or were."

"That's my girl." Betsy patted Nan's hand and went to stand in the doorway.

Smiling, Nan replied, "It was good of you to dredge up your past like that for me."

"Ach, our little secret. How's that?"

Nan's smile was complete this time. "Jah, our secret."

With that, Betsy made her way down the hall to Nellie's room. There, she leaned on the doorjamb, thinking now of Suzy and her Rumschpringe. Her mind still played tricks on her at times, because if she hadn't known better, she would have thought she'd just seen Suzy hurrying down the hall and into this very room . . . her waist-length hair, the color of corn silk, floating behind her.

But she's gone for good, she reminded herself, moving to the antique dresser and staring down at the small blue plate, remembering the notes Suzy and Nellie had left for each other there. *Roses are red, violets are blue, wildflowers are best, and so are you!* Suzy had once written to Nellie.

Going and sitting on Suzy's side of the bed, she felt glad to be able to help Nan through her heartache. *If only the brethren would agree to push back the Rumschpringe till the youth were older . . . some of this heartache might well be avoided.*

Betsy wanted to protect all of her girls for as long as possible. Nearly all the women her age said the same about their daughters. So it was. Most had grown up by experiencing both the heartbreak and the delight of dating. Sadly, there was very little in between.

Caleb felt sure he was lost, though he'd traveled this way at least once before. But no, he must have blocked out the memory of *that* night completely. He wouldn't let the chuckle that came just then escape his lips, however, for neither did he want to dwell on that particular date, nor did he wish to explain to Nellie Mae why he was suddenly so amused. Now this girl sitting next to him was as sweet as the cherry pie she baked. She was much too good to lose—he sensed it as clearly as he knew he'd taken a wrong turn somewhere several miles back.

He'd known the horse fences and expanse of cornfields along the road back yonder. But nothing at all looked familiar now, although it was difficult to see much in the murky night, what with the moon hiding behind a thick covering of high clouds. Even so, he had earlier recognized Preacher Manny's house and Preacher Lapp's spread of land, too . . . and Bishop Joseph's, evidently gone out west for some peace of mind. It was no wonder the bishop had a hankering for time away. According to the grapevine, several meetings a week were happening, the dissenters taking advantage of the bishop's absence.

A pair of ring-necked pheasants scuttled along the low-lying brush, across the roadside gully. Caleb steadied the reins and watched as the twosome began to rise almost vertically, a loud whirring in their wings. He was now certain he did not recognize a single landmark, though he knew by the stars he was heading east, away from Nellie's father's house. The farther away they went, the longer it would take to return. He was mighty content to ride onward with Nellie snuggled next to him, close enough for him to feel the warmth of her arm on his, their hands intertwined beneath the heavy lap robe.

"Have you ever thought you knew where you were headin' only to find out you really had no idea?" he asked her.

"Well, you could take that two ways." She sat up straight, releasing her hand from his and stretching a bit.

"I don't have the slightest notion where we are."

She laughed softly. Her gentle laughter was like the rippling music in the mill creek near where he'd met her on their first date, the destination he'd contemplated taking her yet tonight. It seemed to suggest she almost enjoyed the prospect of wandering together.

He felt emboldened. "Jah, I admit it—we're lost."

"We could go back and try to find where it was we lost our way."

He chuckled. "But how's that any fun? Don't you want to keep going and find out where we're headed . . . eventually?"

"If you've got all night, I s'pose."

"All the time in the world."

They both laughed at that and he leaned against her arm, wishing her hand was available now. He decided to wait till later, at the millstream, to hold her hand again . . . assuming they ever found their way back. And if they didn't, well, they'd simply ride all the way to Delaware. They'd bump into a major highway somewhere along the way.

The thought of riding aimlessly into the night with Nellie to talk to was as delicious a thought as his mother's schnitz pie. How was it he had missed her all this time? It was as if he'd just met Nellie, even though they had grown up in the same community.

He had courted several girls for short periods of time over the past year. Only one had he deemed worthy to take to the lovely, secluded setting behind the mill, but in the end even she had been too eager for words of love, and he had held back, more hesitant as time went by.

Nellie, for her part, was unpredictable, sometimes warm toward him and other times almost distant, as if she were testing the waters. Even so, conversation between them generally came easily, which again was a change from the other girls he had courted. He'd been quick to discover he had not loved any of them. Caleb was waiting for the girl with the missing puzzle piece that matched his heart perfectly. Was Nellie that girl? To think she'd been here all along, awaiting his notice.

"Are you warm enough?" he asked. The bricks he'd heated before heading over to Beaver Dam Road to fetch Nellie had not held their warmth as he'd hoped. But maybe that had more to do with the strength of the cold and not the short time the bricks had been in the fire.

"I'm fine, Caleb. How 'bout you?"

"My toes are a smidgen cold, that's all," he said. *So are my hands*, he thought, reaching for his gloves tucked under the seat and putting them on. He would be practical, as he usually was. *Practicality reigns*, his father had always said in regard to women, though his father had courted and married a girl far different from Nellie. *His choice . . . we all choose.*

Seeing a cluster of lights up ahead, he decided to turn soon, and coming upon an extra-wide intersection, he maneuvered the horse into the fan-shaped turn, mindful not to tip over the buggy—something he'd done upon first receiving it from his father. *Won't make that mistake twice.*

Now they were heading northwest. Caleb directed his horse to gallop, speeding up the ride. He didn't want Nellie to be too tired before they stopped at the spot he'd chosen . . .

if they found it. The question was how she would respond to what he had in mind.

Had it not been for her sister's untimely death, Nellie might be more outgoing, perhaps. He understood her grief, for it had not been too many years since his young nephew had fallen to his death inside a silo. Weeks had passed before Caleb could begin to think of much beyond Henry's accident.

We can't wish our loved ones back. Suzy's early death was God's plan for her, he thought. The same went for young Henry.

Caleb had decided not to bring up Suzy at all tonight— not unless Nellie herself happened to. So far, that seemed unlikely, especially since he suspected her tears earlier were related to that sister.

He reached to open his glove compartment, removing a tin box containing more than a half dozen cookies, fresh this afternoon from his mother's oven. "Would you like a treat? Mamm's peanut butter cookies."

She accepted one. "Your mother must enjoy bakin', too."

"It would seem so. Every time I head into the kitchen, she's opening the oven door, pushing something in or taking something out."

"Sounds like me in the early morning. Of course, my customers like having a variety of choices. I keep a running list of their favorites."

He was engrossed by Nellie's talk of baking and running a business on her father's property.

"Have you ever run out of pastries?"

"Sometimes, if a customer places an unusually large order, but I generally don't run low till late in the afternoon."

"So you estimate everything that will sell in one day's time, then?"

"Oh sure. But the best part of the work is all the fun I have talkin' with customers."

"How many are English?" Secretly he wondered how comfortable she was with worldly folk.

"Well, there are the regulars from up and down the road. Whenever they have company or folks droppin' by, they bring them over and go hog wild in my shop."

He loved the way she expressed herself so clearly. Nothing timid about Nellie, and she was not only interesting, but ever so appealing to look at, too. Apprehension reared its head, and Caleb could hear Daed's words now—should Daed ever put two and two together and realize his youngest was seeing Suzy Fisher's sister. *You're courtin' Nellie Mae, sister to that lost soul? Ach, Caleb, use your head . . . don't let me down. We're Yoder men, staunch followers of das Alt Gebrauch—the Old Ways.*

He hoped the rumors about Suzy would blow over before his father could speak such harsh words to him. Anxious to get his mind on more pleasant things, he asked Nellie, "What's your favorite cookie?"

"To eat or to bake?"

"There's a difference?"

"Why, sure. I enjoy baking lots of cookies, especially my thin sand tarts, but I much prefer biting into a thicker cookie."

"Jah, substance in a cookie's a fine trait." He offered another peanut butter cookie from his stash. *Come to think of it, substance aptly describes Nellie, too.*

"What's *your* favorite, Caleb?"

"Chocolate chip first and peanut butter second."

She let out a giggle.

"What's so funny?"

"You." She was still laughing.

"Let's see . . . I'm funny because I answered your question?"

"No, because you're so thorough." She smiled at him. "You're quite funny."

"No one's ever said that before."

"It's a very nice thing, believe me."

"If you say so, it must be." He would not restrain himself any longer. He slipped his arm around her. "*You're* ever so good, Nellie Mae."

She briefly leaned her head on his shoulder.

"We're no longer lost, I see," he said, recognizing a sign-post now. "Would you like to walk awhile?"

"I wore extra socks, just in case."

"So did I," he admitted, finding it encouraging that she'd planned to be out with him a long time on this, their second date of what he hoped would be many.

CHAPTER 18

When Reuben confronted her, Betsy was reluctant to acknowledge that a sales representative had dropped by ten days ago. "The man was here but a few minutes," she reassured him.

"When were you goin' to tell me?"

"Wasn't . . . I s'pose."

He shook his head and smiled at her. "Well, ain't you the case?"

"What did Ephram tell you, anyways?" She was curious, having heard a bit of gossip from her daughters-in-law at a recent quilting. According to Martha, there was a growing group among them who favored using tractors.

Reuben scratched his long beard. "Ephram's not at all interested in fancy farm equipment, if that's what you're worried about."

"Not worried, no. Just wonderin'." She finished brushing her hip-length hair, noticing in her small dresser mirror the streaks of gray intermingled with the flaxen . . . and the ever-widening middle part. Goodness, she had been pulling a comb down that part for nigh unto forty-eight years now, next birthday come July. "I am awful tired," she said.

"Before you sleep, let me pray for you," Reuben said.

"Whatever for?"

He inhaled slowly, his eyes solemn. "Aw, now."

She felt immediately sorry and stretched out her hand. "Reuben . . ."

"That's all right, love. I'll be prayin' for ya on my own."

She knew he would, because she'd awakened in the night to him kneeling at the bed, hands folded, lips moving in the lantern light. Not wanting to disturb him, she'd tiptoed around him, heading down to their one and only indoor bathroom. It was as if Reuben took the verse to "pray without ceasing" literally.

Truly, Betsy didn't know how to view what was happening. It seemed all encompassing—either he had his nose in the Good Book or his nose pressed into his hands as he prayed. Highly unusual, she was ever so sure. She guessed if she contemplated God's Word long enough, she might give herself over to it, too, and get herself into the hot water her husband surely was headed for. For now she felt too drained of energy to walk such a road herself.

With talk of Reuben's parents moving as soon as next month into the Dawdi Haus next door, Reuben would have more than his share of work to tend to. *And less time for reading and praying. . . .* Doubtless his father would intervene, as well, if Noah Fisher realized what Reuben was daily studying.

Her husband *had* become ever so considerate since memorizing Scripture, doting on her now more than ever. There was no question Reuben's devotion for his God had filled him to the point it was spilling over to her.

Just so the brethren don't come round asking questions once he starts sharing Scriptures with our sons. . . .

She thought of Rhoda, Nan, and Nellie, having observed their reactions to the twice-daily readings and their father's expressive table blessing before the meal. None of them had said anything, but if it continued, Nellie would likely be saying something—and not any too kindly, knowing that one.

Betsy pushed her pillow beneath her head, seeking a comfortable position. Nellie was out with a beau again tonight, she was quite sure. Looking over at Reuben, still leaning against the side of the bed in prayer, she wondered if she ought to ask him to remember both Nan and Nellie in beseeching the Lord God and heavenly Father this night. One for a shattered heart . . . the other for strength for whatever was to come.

The long ravine toward the old gristmill—now a knittery—was nearly too dark to walk through. Nellie picked her way over the uneven ground near the bank of the mill-race, glad for Caleb's foresight in bringing a flashlight. So far she was enjoying herself, yet in her happiness she felt a touch of sadness, too.

Regardless of time's passage, she struggled some with the notion of enjoying herself at all. Nellie contemplated the peculiar feeling, wondering why she felt guilty to be getting on with her life. Was this a common thing for people who'd lost loved ones?

Neither Rhoda nor Nan had voiced any such thing. But now Mamma . . . she might understand.

Nellie wanted to fully delight in Caleb's attention; he had long been the boy she'd dreamed of. There were times when she felt completely at home with him. At other times, she felt less relaxed with him than with other boys. Was she bracing herself for future questions about Suzy? More likely she was nervous about the lie she'd told him. If, indeed, it was a lie, which she must find out somehow.

She breathed in the cold air and held it. *Enough of that thinking.* Then, letting the air *whoosh* back out, she wanted to pinch herself. Was it too good to be true the way Caleb looked at her? Would she ever awaken from this wonderful-good dream?

When he pointed his flashlight to shine directly on her path, Nellie Mae was brought out of her reverie. Oh, how she wanted this night to last and last. Such a romantic setting, one Caleb must have picked just for her.

He laughed softly. "It's so beautiful—private, too. My sisters and brothers and I sometimes ice skate on the pond, over yonder." He asked where she and her sisters liked to skate, and she mentioned the pond not far from their house. He nodded and said, "I'd like to bring you back here when it's sunny. I think you'll come to like this place as much as I do."

She wouldn't ponder whether he'd brought other girls walking here in this secluded area. Not when he was seemingly quite content to be with her now.

He reached for her hand and once again she thrilled to his touch. *Will this always excite me so?* Careful to guide her and keep her from slipping, Caleb shone his flashlight as a guiding beacon.

Soon they came upon a lively stream and stopped to listen to its murmuring as it spilled over rocks, making its way south below them. Nellie wished for a moon—the surrounding trees and shrubs suddenly seemed ominous and too black. She shivered, fearful.

"What is it, Nellie?"

"I . . . uh, it's awful dark out . . . is all."

They were deep in a dense covering of trees, the stream nearly at their feet. "I'm here with you. Don't be afraid."

She held tightly to his hand. "Honestly, I was never scared of the dark . . . well, before . . ."

"Before Suzy drowned?" His question came without warning.

She looked up at him, overwhelmed, and shrugged, afraid another discussion about Suzy might begin.

"I can see why you'd feel thataway." He led her toward the millstream, making no further comments about Suzy to her surprise and relief.

Then he leaned down to place the flashlight on the ground, pointing it toward the water. Straightening, he turned to her, a smile on his face. "I want to ask you something, Nellie."

She held her breath.

"Will you be my girl? Will you go for steady with me?"

All during their lengthy ride tonight, she'd considered what it would be like to be without Caleb, as before . . . her heartfelt longing to know him. She did not want to return to those days.

"Will you, Nellie Mae?"

Only one answer formed on her lips. "Jah, Caleb . . . I will."

He leaned forward and planted a kiss on her cheek, then let out a whoop and a holler.

She laughed out loud, his delight mingling with her own.

All the way back to the horse and buggy and on the long ride home, too, she considered that she knew for the first time what Mamma had meant. *You'll know when the right boy comes along. . . .*

Nellie Mae's heart sang and her toes wiggled as the buggy flew through the wee hours. Caleb Yoder was going to court her, and in due time, she would become his bride. Nothing could possibly stand in their way.

CHAPTER 19

Nellie sensed an air of anticipation in Mary Glick's house on Thursday morning. The place was abuzz with chatter and delicious treats as she, Mamma, and Nan arrived for the quilting bee, eager to stitch together a wedding-ring quilt for a new bride-to-be. Though the girl wasn't related to Nellie, she was one of Rosanna's many first cousins, and Nellie looked forward to seeing her dearest friend here today, too.

Standing in the tidy kitchen to warm her hands near the stove, Nellie overheard Susannah Lapp's mother talking about their bishop. "He's under the weather out there in Kalona. I daresay he and Anna've been gone a mite too long, jah?"

"Sure seems so" came the reply. "Next thing he'll be stuck out there, being ill 'n' all."

Susannah's mother sighed loudly. "Time he gets home again."

Uncle Bishop must surely be perturbed to have to remain so far away, Nellie thought. *Or is he lingering on purpose?* She moved away, lest she give in to the temptation to eavesdrop—a fault she disliked in others.

Mary Glick's front room was filled with a large quilting frame and twelve chairs set up around it. There were six piles of fabric stacked on the wooden settee, neatly folded and sorted by color. "Looks like there's another quilt in the plannin', too," Nellie remarked to Nan, who was more pleasant and cheery today than she had been in a good while.

"Wonder when they'll start doing the piecework." Nan inspected the brightest colors, choosing a bold plum color and holding it up. "What would I look like in a dress made out of this shade of purple?" She held it under her chin. "What do you think?"

The image of Iva Beiler at the last Singing flickered through Nellie's mind. "Why, it'd look plain worldly, wouldn't it?"

"Amishwomen in Holmes County wear cape dresses of this color," Nan said. "And even brighter colors, too."

"How do ya know?"

"From my circle letter."

Nellie found it odd that Nan should write to someone so far away. "Who in your letters is from there?"

"No one." Nan was still fingering the radiant fabric as if she was coveting it. "One of my friends in Paradise seems to know all about the doings out in Berlin and Sugar Creek. That's all."

Nellie nodded. Funny how the grapevine worked—it had a way of piping in the tartest hearsay . . . and the sweetest. But the words coming from right behind her now were more surprising than sour or syrupy.

"I've just found out the most exciting news," Kate Beiler's mother, Rachel Stoltzfus, was saying. "My daughter Kate is carrying twins."

"Ach, really?" said her friend.

Rachel was beaming. "Who would've thought?"

"Twins?" Nellie murmured, eyeing Rachel. Was Kate's mother aware of the arrangement her daughter had made with Rosanna?

Nellie Mae couldn't help but think now of Kate's having shown early. And here lately she'd looked as if the baby was coming any day instead of close to Christmas. Nellie craned her neck, looking for Rosanna, who still had not arrived. When Nellie asked, neither Nan nor Mamma had seen her.

The fact Rachel had ceased talking about the babies and did not say a peep about Kate and Rosanna's agreement made Nellie wonder if Rachel knew anything more.

Has Kate informed her mamma?

Soon they all sat down, and Nellie saved a spot for Rosanna, who, according to her mother, was most definitely on her way. A small scrap of somewhat mismatched fabric was peeking out between two others right in front of Nellie. Only a few of the older women kept this tradition alive; Mary, for one, liked to have a slight imperfection in every quilt.

When a full hour passed with no sign of Rosanna, Nellie presumed she wouldn't be coming after all.

Is she home sewing up double of everything? Or is she so stunned about twins, she'd rather stay put? Nellie truly hoped Rosanna was all right.

As much as she was fond of babies, she couldn't begin to imagine what it would mean to care for two newborns at once. Of course Mamma knew all about that, having had Thomas and Jeremiah first off.

She wondered what Rosanna would do with twins instead of a single baby. Kate, too—would she change her mind? Surely she wouldn't split up the babies between the two families. Even so, Nellie had heard of such a thing—parents who couldn't provide for their triplet babies dividing them among the mother's other siblings.

Raising them like cousins.

Nellie tried her best to focus on making the tiny quilting stitches expected of her, but her hand shook as she contemplated dear Rosanna's possible response to such news.

If she even knows yet. . . .

Rosanna listened with both ears, unable to edge in a word as Kate sat across the kitchen table, eyes glistening. "Listen," she finally managed to slip in, "I'll take all the wee babes you want to give."

Kate's eyes grew wide and solemn. "Honestly?" She brushed away her tears. "You have no idea what you're sayin', Rosanna."

"Oh, but I do." Rosanna knew she could care for twins. In all truth, she'd care for as many as God saw fit to give her. "I'm ever so glad you stopped by, cousin. You almost missed me."

"Jah, there's a quilting, and I'm sorry to keep you from it."

"No worry."

Rosanna noticed how Kate cradled her stomach. How must it feel to carry two babies?

"All right, then," said Kate. "It's settled."

They went on to talk of booties and blankets and all the many items of clothing the little ones would be needing. Rosanna mentioned having made one afghan so far; there was ample yarn to make another. "I have plenty of time to get ready, Kate. Don't fret."

Kate sighed, looking toward the window. "I don't know what John will say . . . if they're both boys."

"You haven't discussed that with your husband?"

"Oh jah. He just hasn't decided what we oughta do, well, 'bout you and Elias getting both of them."

Rosanna felt as if the wind had been knocked out of her. *What's Kate saying?*

"I know what we talked about, but—"

"Well, I just don't understand," Rosanna interrupted, terribly confused. Her cousin seemed befuddled. Was this unique to expectant mothers or had the news of twins somehow addled her? She couldn't recall Kate behaving like this before—wavering back and forth. No, Kate had always been one to make up her mind and stick to it.

"We'll talk it over more, John and I." Kate rose slowly and headed for the door.

Rosanna choked down her emotions and followed her waddling cousin out the back door and down the walkway. "Take good care now, ya hear?"

Kate nodded.

"Come over anytime."

"I'll visit again . . . help you sew up some baby clothes." Kate waved, a half smile on her face.

"That'd be fine." Rosanna's heart sank as she wondered how many more times Kate would second-guess her offer.

Reuben never even heard Preacher Manny open the barn door and step inside. He was busy pitching hay to the mules when he looked up and saw the preacher there.

"Well, you almost scared the wits out of me," Reuben said, trying not to let on how jolting it was.

"I called out to you more than once. Didn't ya hear me?"

"No." Then Reuben noticed that Preacher Manny seemed more shaken than he was gruff—as white as if he'd had himself a nightmare.

179

"Reuben . . . I don't know who to tell this to," Manny began.

Leaning on his pitchfork, Reuben observed a twitch in Manny's jaw. "What's a-matter, Preacher? You got troubles with your hay crimper again?"

"Naw, ain't that." Manny grimaced, rubbing the back of his neck.

"You got yourself some pain? I say get your wife to rub that hot oil on your back and shoulders again."

Manny removed his felt hat. His bangs were smashed flat against his forehead, and he seemed terribly restless, even troubled. "It's not a pain in my neck, though it could turn out to be."

"You all right?"

"In a bit of a quandary, really." He hemmed and hawed. Looking at Reuben, he asked, "Is there someplace we can go and talk?"

"Well, I—"

"I want to speak as a cousin and a friend . . . leavin' the preacher part behind for now."

Reuben was immediately concerned. He hoped this wasn't more talk about which farm equipment to allow in their Ordnung next month when they would vote on additions and such. By the look of Manny's sober expression, Reuben couldn't begin to guess what was up unless it was something of that magnitude. "Why, sure . . . let's walk out to the woods a ways." He poked his hayfork down into the loose pile.

"No need callin' attention, jah?" Manny added quickly, falling in step.

As they walked, Manny explained that he had begun regularly reading the Good Book, poring over it, as it were.

He hesitated before adding, "I don't know any other way to say this, but a light's turned on in me."

Reuben felt a shiver of recognition . . . and excitement. Emboldened, he asked, "Where were you readin', Manny?"

He turned and looked hard at Reuben. "You mean to say you ain't goin' to ask me what I was doin' reading and studying thataway?"

"Nope." Reuben was itching to tell his relative what he himself had done, hoping that maybe Manny had also uncovered some previously unknown kernels of truth.

A smile spread across the older man's face. "Well, now, Reuben Fisher, what're you sayin' to me?"

"Just that I believe I understand, Preacher . . . er . . . cousin." He took a gulp of a breath. "You see, I know exactly what you mean by that light goin' on."

Manny stopped walking. "Ach, can it be?" His words came slow and solemn. He was nearly gawking now as he looked Reuben over but good.

Reuben couldn't keep his grin in check.

"Well, then, you must be saved, too. Ain't ya?"

Reuben wanted to fess up with everything in him, though he knew there would be no turning back. "Jah, and I read the whole book of John, mind you. Ever look closely at chapter three?" He didn't know why, but he was whispering now, when he wanted to holler it out.

Manny blinked his big eyes. "I believe God directed me to talk to you, Reuben. Jah, I believe He did."

Reuben listened, comprehending. "I'm mighty glad ya did."

"I, too, read that chapter . . . and then the entire Gospel of John." Manny was grinning himself.

Reuben clasped his arm. "It's so good to know we're brothers in this."

Then Manny began to tell about his most recent circle letter, which shared that a half dozen preachers across the country—"including out in Ohio, too"—believed the eyes of their understanding had been opened. "All in a short space of time."

"Really? Must be some sort of awakening, then."

Manny's face lit up. "Bishops are havin' dreams of the Lord with outstretched hands, showing them His pierced hands and feet. 'For you I died so that you might have eternal life,' He's telling them. Others are being drawn to the Scripture, devouring it like starving men."

Reuben nodded. "That's me."

"What about us havin' a Bible study? For anyone who'd like to attend."

"Well, I don't have to tell ya what the bishop will say."

"Bishop's gone . . . and may not be back for some time is what I hear."

Reuben still felt they should make an attempt to get a sanctioned gathering. "Whether or not we have his blessing is one thing—"

"We'll never get it, Reuben."

"You goin' to write him and ask permission, or should I?"

Manny shook his head. "It's a waste of time for me to try."

Reuben could see where this was going. "Well, since Joseph's my elder brother, I s'pose . . ."

Manny nodded, smiling. "Jah, that's just what I was thinking."

He's mighty glad to be off the hook, thought Reuben, wondering how to explain to Bishop Joseph their desire to study Scripture.

Chapter 20

Nellie struggled with a feeling of distress all that next Friday morning after the quilting as she pondered the goings-on in the house. What had caused her father to develop his strange obsession with the Bible? They read twice each day as a family now, but then Dat spent several more hours reading and studying on his own, hurrying through his chores to do so.

Peculiar . . . and worrisome.

She wanted to talk with Mamma about both that and Dat's fancy praying, but she couldn't bring herself to raise the topic. Oddly, her mother seemed to be in compliance. Mamma was known for often speaking up, yet in such a gentle way that Dat could never scold her for being less than meek.

She recalled the night Dat had first read from John to them—how vulnerable she'd felt kneeling at her bed, weeping into her hands. It was impossible to forget her longing at that moment . . . how she'd wished for the Lord God to soothe, even mend, her guilty heart. Like a young child in need of loving help.

Nellie forced her thoughts back to taking note of the varieties of muffins, whole wheat rolls, and cupcakes already dwindling fast this morning. She began to count the dozens of cookies.

Hearing a car pull into the lane, she looked up to see a group of five women enter the shop. "We saw your cute little sign out front," said one.

"Hope you don't mind if we come in," said another.

"Make yourselves at home," Nellie Mae replied.

"Do you sell to non-Amish?" a third woman asked, the tallest and youngest-looking of the bunch.

"Everyone's welcome," said Nellie.

A redheaded woman who looked to be in her thirties was the first to order, requesting a half dozen of Nellie's morning glory muffins. The Englischer got to talking about recipes with her three friends while Nellie filled the order.

"Will that be all for you today?" Nellie asked.

She raised her eyes to Nellie's. "Actually, I was wondering where I might get my hands on some authentic recipes."

Nellie smiled. "Well, if it's Amish recipes you're after, I have plenty in my noggin." She tapped at her temple. "What would you like—hot dishes, baked goods . . . desserts?"

The woman brightened. "A general question first—do you use shortening or butter for your cakes and sweet breads?"

"Well, that depends on what we have on hand," Nellie answered. "There are times when I use lard, too."

The redhead was now eyeing the sticky buns, tapping on the glass counter with her long pink fingernails. "And do you use store-bought flour or grind your own?"

"Oh, either's fine," Nellie said. "We don't mind going to the grocery store for things, but we like to make do with food off the land." She paused to determine their interest before continuing. "Each family puts up about a thousand jars of vegetables, fruit, and preserves every year at the harvest."

"What about your delightful language?" the oldest-looking woman in the group asked. "Is there any way to learn it?"

Nellie shrugged. "Outsiders call it Pennsylvania Dutch, but it's not Dutch at all. It's a folk rendering of German—not written anywhere that I know of."

"Not even your Bible?" one piped up.

"Ach, that's in either High German or English." Nellie felt like a pincushion all of a sudden. Surely these were the most openly curious Englischers she'd ever met.

"Would you mind if I asked about your faith?" the youngest-looking woman said.

My what?

Nellie felt trapped. She'd never had such a conversation, and she wished with all her heart Nan would hurry up and come running.

"Or are your . . . uh, ways based on—"

"Pamela, no . . . that's not what you want to say." A previously silent woman was talking as though Nellie weren't standing right there.

"Aw, don't mind her," the first woman said to Nellie, linking her arm through Pamela's.

Nellie stared past the Englischers, looking out the window. *Where are you, Nan, when I need you?*

"I'm sorry," Pamela said. "I didn't mean to embarrass you, miss."

Nellie tried to think of something to say or do to change the subject, but nothing came. Finally she said, "Well, jah, we have our beliefs . . . our ways, passed down from generation to generation." Nellie figured Dat might have had a more suitable answer. Or would his interest in soaking up the long sentences in the Good Book make his answers to Englischers too free?

How soon before his fondness for Scripture reaches the wrong person's ears? She clenched her jaw, hoping Caleb's father might never, ever hear of it.

"Really . . . I want to apologize." It was the redhead again. "We didn't mean to be rude."

Nellie forced a smile. "Not to worry." She accepted the money for the muffins, thankful for a working cash register today. "Is there anything else I can do for you?" she managed to say. "A written recipe, perhaps?"

The redhead nodded, and Nellie began to write down the ingredients and instructions for her sweet bread—a coffee cake recipe from her great-grandmother.

The women thanked her repeatedly, and then the others took turns ordering cookies and other goodies. When they'd paid and made their way back to their fancy red car, Nellie sighed with relief.

Not much time later, she noticed Dawdi and Mammi Fisher entering the drive in their enclosed family buggy. She assumed they wanted to talk with Mamma about getting settled into the Dawdi Haus—leaving behind the farmhouse over on Plank Road, where they'd lived since Dat received this house after marrying Mamma. Nellie was looking forward to having her father's parents closer, especially Mammi Hannah, known for her stories about their family and its doings through the years. All the Fisher women would benefit from having Mammi living under the same roof, so to speak—especially Mamma.

But Nellie's present concern was finding time to rescue Suzy's diary from the woodland soil before winter's onset. Almost two weeks had gone by since she had first made her search, and thus far no other opportunity to look had presented itself. Her responsibility to run the bakery shop and always be on hand for her customers left her with virtually no time of her own. That, coupled with the frustration of not remembering the diary's exact location, worried her.

Will I ever find it?

Nellie Mae glanced up to see the crimson red car creeping back up the driveway. Pamela stepped out, returning to the shop. "I nearly forgot—do you have shoofly pie?" she asked.

"Sure." Nellie picked up one of the two pies remaining and showed it off as if it were one of her offspring. "We make the wet-bottom kind here," she said.

"Sounds perfect." Then Pamela asked, seeming a bit shy, "Would you happen to know the ingredients offhand?"

"I'm happy to jot them down for you." Nellie waited for the woman to pull out a tablet from her small brown pocketbook.

"It's ever so easy, really," Nellie told her after writing the recipe. "Nothing more than eggs, corn syrup, baking soda, and boiling water for the filling. Do you make quite a lot from scratch?" she asked.

"I can hardly stay out of my kitchen." The Englischer laughed and motioned toward the wet-bottom shoofly pie. "I'll purchase that one, please."

Nellie placed it in a white box and taped the lid shut. "Anything else?"

"That'll do it. Thanks!"

"Enjoy the pie," Nellie called, happy that her supply was dwindling. She would need to get up extra early to make sure she had plenty of choices for customers tomorrow.

So, no trip to the woods for at least another day.

Pamela paused at the door, and Nellie had to smile. *Now what?*

"Do you happen to know where we can get a buggy ride?" the woman asked.

Nellie thought about that, fairly sure they were expecting to pay for the experience. "Can't say I know of anyone."

The woman's disappointment momentarily registered before her expression brightened again. "Well, thanks anyway. Have a nice day!"

"Same to you!" Nellie said. Only when Pamela was on her way did Nellie allow her pent-up laughter to escape. *Goodness, such a curious sort!*

———

When Nan had finished her indoor chores, she carried the mail out to Nellie. "Here's a letter for you, sister," she said. Nellie noted it was the circle letter she'd been expecting from Cousin Treva.

"Did you get one, too?" asked Nellie, thinking a letter would further improve Nan's frame of mind.

Nan shook her head, eyes downcast. "I don't 'spect to, neither."

"Aw, Nan . . . I'm sorry. Really, I am."

"You don't have to be sorry. It's my *dumm* fault."

Nellie's heart went out to her sister. "I'm a good listener, ain't so?"

"Well, maybe you are. Still, I don't want to talk 'bout it." Unexpectedly Nan turned and departed for the house.

When will she ever let me in?

Then Nellie realized Nan must've misunderstood, thinking she was asking about her former beau. *And now I've peeved her. . . .*

Nellie stepped back behind the counter. Since there were no customers, she opened the envelope and pulled out the six handwritten pages.

Dear Cousins,

Hello from New Holland! I hope you are all doing well. We've been canning up a storm here, and some are already doing a lot of quilting for the wedding season.

Something more's happening over here, too, and not the usual goings-on. I can't begin to explain it, but there are groups of folk getting together on no-Preaching Sundays for a sort of Sunday school. A handful of people are even having Bible studies of an evening—or so my sister says. She's been going rather regularly. So far, the bishops don't seem to mind. Either that or they don't know yet.

"Oh, but they will," Nellie muttered to herself. It was impossible to keep something like this quiet.

She read on, finding it interesting that a number of others were as preoccupied with the Good Book as her father.

When she'd finished the first letter, she was reluctant to move on to the others and Cousin Treva's. She felt as though she might be ill as she sat down to let all this sift into her mind.

What's it mean?

Surely her father wasn't caught up in this gathering storm, was he?

She hoped not. It wasn't for the sake of the People she felt that way—a selfish motive ruled her entirely. She must shield her deepening relationship with Caleb with every ounce she had.

Heading out of her shop, Nellie Mae stood outside and breathed in the brisk autumn air. A scuttle of wind came up then and she shivered, wishing she'd slipped on her woolen shawl. She watched the leaves swirl at her feet and sensed an ominous feeling much like the one Dat had expressed when the corn quit growing nearly overnight.

In the distance a long V-shaped pattern of Canada geese dotted the sky. She had always wondered what sort of coded messages they sent to each other to create such precise flight formations. Did every bird know exactly where to fly in the lineup? Did the Lord God direct them from on high? If it *was* a divine thing, did that same Creator God care about the course of her life? And Dat's?

She shuddered to think what might befall their family if either Nan or Rhoda began talking about Scripture to friends or cousins, locally and otherwise. No worry of Mamma saying anything. And, of course, Nellie sure wouldn't think of sharing about her father's odd behavior, not even with dearest Rosanna.

No, the brethren must never know. . . .

Chapter 21

Nellie found it excruciating to sit in the cluster of girls during Sunday night's hayride. Surrounded by so many—Susannah Lapp and Becky Glick included—Nellie was able to catch only an occasional glance from Caleb. She pretended not to care that they were separated for the long and bumpy ride, preferring to think ahead to their time together later.

Susannah was awful *bapplich*—chatty—as she eyed the bunched-up boys on their end of the hay wagon. No doubt she sought Caleb's attention. A few minutes later, Susannah actually dared to call over her shoulder, "Ain't that right, Caleb Yoder?" before bursting into a rainbow smile directed at him.

Nan, too, was smiling to beat the band, which was surprising because she had been withdrawn and nearly sullen again since Friday. Nellie couldn't begin to fathom what had put the sunshine on Nan's face, but the clouds were surely gone tonight as she whispered with Caleb's sister Rebekah. So caught up were they in private talk, it was impossible for Nellie to speak with her own sister.

Taking a quick survey of the boys, Nellie wondered if Nan was over her former beau and already sweet on someone new. Knowing Nan, though, that seemed unlikely. Nan was not known to be fickle, but she hadn't weathered well the storm of splitting up—twice it had happened already. Yet, given time, Nan would surely find another suitor in their crowd. Certainly there was no shortage of boys, and Nan had plenty of admirers among them.

The night was nippy with a damp breeze. Some of the girls were shivering even though they sat shoulder to shoulder, while the boys were talkative and, in some cases, louder than usual.

With Nan talking with Rebekah, and Susannah the obvious center of attention, encircled as she was by a dozen or so other girls, Nellie felt somewhat alone. Knowing it was simply for now, she rather enjoyed it, relishing the thought of her upcoming buggy ride with Caleb.

Looking at the stars, she began to count them silently. The fainter ones at first, all across the expanse of sky, then the more brilliant ones—intense white sprinkles against the black backdrop of space.

Quite relaxed at present, she leaned against a soft mound of hay, lost in the enormity of the sky above. She felt small and insignificant and remembered one late summertime night when she and Suzy had slipped out of the house. They'd gone into the meadow, trying to find the exact middle of the field, where they lay in the thickest patch of sweet clover. On the verge of adolescence, they began to count stars, soaking up the serenity of the night. Suzy lost count after two hundred or so, but Nellie reached four hundred, maybe because her eyesight was sharper than her sister's.

Sighing now, Nellie adjusted her head covering, making sure it hadn't gone cockeyed or gotten stuck with hay. That had happened to her once before on one of her first hayrides last fall, a time when she'd had no real interest in any of the boys on board. Tonight, though, it was hard not to think of

Caleb, whose furtive glances delighted her heart and made her think foolish, romantic thoughts.

Nellie tried to keep her smile in check. What *was* it about Caleb—his whole face appeared to light up when he looked at her.

She and Suzy had occasionally talked about their opinions on boys and love. Nellie remembered one particular afternoon right after the New Year, six months before Suzy died. The two of them had closed themselves away on a dismal and cold afternoon, cozy and comfortable under the old quilts piled on their bed.

Suzy'd had a room-spinning headache, including nausea. Nellie could hardly tend the bakery shop, hating the thought of Suzy sick and all alone. Finally she'd pleaded with Mamma to let her spend some time with Suzy, promising not to catch whatever it was her sister had.

As she'd slipped under the quilts beside Suzy, her sister had moaned, opening her eyes. "Ach, now I won't be able to meet my friends tonight," Suzy had whispered. "Not with this awful headache."

"Meet who?" Nellie had wondered if she meant a group of more progressive Amish youth.

Suzy squeezed her eyes shut against the pain. "Oh, Nellie, I've gotta tell you something . . . my greatest secret."

Bracing herself, Nellie covered her head with the top quilt, but Suzy promptly sighed and changed her mind. "Maybe I'd better be tellin' my diary instead."

"Ach," Nellie said, emerging from the quilt covering, "I'm listening, honest I am."

By then, though, Suzy seemed put out. She went silent on her, a far cry from the way she usually behaved, always chattering and living to the full, pushing the light at both ends of the day.

To think such an energetic, jovial girl had died at dusk, her lungs filling up with lake water at the moment of sunset. Had Nellie kept Suzy from boating that day, Suzy would still be alive and sitting right here beside her, leaning back in the hay, saying she'd given up on counting stars.

Oh, Suzy . . . will I soon know your great secret? The whole truth about you?

Breathing in the splendor of the night, Nellie thought back again to the night she'd buried the diary. Suddenly she recalled a detail she'd forgotten.

There had been a honeysuckle bush sending out a glorious, sweet aroma nearby. Its scent had registered even as the fading sunlight had made blurry prisms of her tears.

Pushing her hands into the straw, she sat straight up, her mouth gaping open. She might have said something right out into the cold air had she not remembered she was riding with thirty or more teenagers on the hay wagon.

I know where I buried Suzy's journal!

Caleb sat in the far corner of the hay wagon, as close to the edge as he could get, dangling his legs as the road passed beneath his feet. He'd worn his older brother's shoes, embarrassed of his own, so thin were the soles. His father had asked him to make do for yet another month, "till the snow flies," and he'd agreed. Where Daed was concerned, he was agreeable to a fault.

The rumble of the wagon wheels shot right into his hips, but Caleb didn't mind. He was used to the jolts of wagons and farm equipment . . . of life in general. But now things were going to be mighty different—here he turned to cast a fleeting look at his darling. Already Nellie Mae was precisely that to him. As soon as they turned eighteen next year, he would love and cherish her till death. Then he would claim the land that was rightfully his, and his parents, who were ready to be free of the toils of farming, could move into the larger Dawdi Haus, while Mamm's parents would move to the smaller built-on addition. He and Nellie would enjoy life together as husband and wife in the big farmhouse, smack-dab in the middle of the two older generations. There he would do his best to ease her sorrow and brighten her day, and they would live and love and create their family as the Good Lord saw fit.

Caleb twisted a piece of straw between his thumb and pointer finger, staring at it, then sliding it between his teeth. He looked out across the field, aware of the silence beyond. Somewhere out in the dimming twilight was a stillness he longed for. Here on the rowdy wagon there was no place to be alone with his girl. He yearned to have Nellie in his arms, but lest his passion get the best of him, he must refrain. His older brother had not heeded that inner warning and was forced to marry before he was ready, premature fatherhood thrust upon him. The family secret had been well kept, and it had served as a powerful warning to Caleb and his siblings. To be sure, there were honorable and less than honorable boys among them . . . even riding now on this wagon. The same thing was certain of the girls.

Suzy Fisher came again to mind, but he dismissed her immediately. Nellie had assured him Suzy was innocent of the sins attributed to her by the rumor mill.

Caleb removed his felt hat and ran his hand through his hair. Courtship, as he saw it, was training ground for the union of man and woman under God. Regardless of the tales of Suzy's Rumschpringe—whatever the whole of it—he loved Nellie.

Caleb tossed his piece of hay straight out as he'd pitched paper airplanes at classmates in the one-room schoolhouse over on Churchtown Road, where students were both English and Amish. The worldly and the set-apart learning together.

He sighed. The reputation of his future bride and her family was utterly vital, at least to his father.

Right or wrong, Nellie's my girl, he thought. *I'll worry about Daed later.*

———

Caleb was more talkative than usual this evening, and Nellie was intrigued by his stories of horses, especially his mention of Amish selling some breeds to racetracks down in Florida. "Can ya imagine such a thing?" he asked, appearing to stifle a laugh. "You wouldn't think of paying money to see one of those races, would ya?"

"More sensible ways to spend money, seems to me."

He nodded. "Jah. Yet there *are* Plain folk who deal in that. Daed says it's wrong."

"I s'pose mine would say the same." As closely connected to the world of horses as Dat was, Nellie'd never heard her father speak of this. To many of the men his age, horse races meant one thing: a big waste of money. Betting and gambling were of the devil.

They headed straight for the millstream behind the old stone millhouse, going to sit on a wrought-iron bench not too far from the creek bank. "It's so perty here," she said, still feeling a bit awkward at first when alone with Caleb. Even though she longed to talk and laugh with him, the initial moments together took some getting used to, particularly after the hubbub of a youth gathering. They wanted to be near each other so badly but were both trying to balance that desire with propriety.

"Our place, jah?" He slipped his arm around her.

She nodded, glad to lean her head on his shoulder.

Caleb talked of the weather, wondering if there would be any much-needed rain before winter's snows. Then he brought up the hog-butchering frolic the Saturday afternoon after next at his uncle's house. "'Tis over near Cains, a little south of here. Several families are donating meat to the ministerial brethren. I'm goin' to help hang the large hams and shoulders. Are you goin'?"

She sat up straighter. "Um . . . s'pose I could."

"What, Nellie? You don't like watchin' the slaughtering?"

She cringed. "It's the smell I can't abide."

He chuckled, "Well, some of my brothers will cut out the intestines and wash them so that *you* can stuff 'em and make sausage." He was clearly amused.

"I wouldn't mind helpin' grind meat, maybe. But better get someone else to stuff the sausage."

He laughed softly. "I don't know too many Plain folk who are squeamish 'bout that."

She had to laugh, too. "Guess I'm better suited to workin' with flours and spices and such." She looked at him; even by the dim light of the moon, his eyes seemed to twinkle.

"Mind if we walk a bit?"

She agreed and he reached for her hand as they strolled through the black trees along the creek bank, their feet making soft padding sounds on the soil.

Hours later, after Caleb's fond *"Gut Nacht!"* at the end of her lane, Nellie felt almost too tired to put one foot in front of the other—they'd walked and talked that much. But deep within, where Mamma said the soul of a person resided, she was skipping with delight. Caleb had been ever so thoughtful again, making it known he wanted her by his side for all the upcoming youth get-togethers. She had herself a true beau.

One who will never break my heart. Not like Nan's.

She thought again of Nan and how happy she had been tonight. Was it because of Rebekah's friendship? Between Rebekah and Rhoda, Nan had her share of confidantes. Nellie wished her older sisters might sometimes include her, in spite of the age difference. Now that Rosanna was preparing for a baby—*twins!*—Nellie felt even more alone. Of course, she had Caleb, but it was a completely different sort of sharing than one did with a sister or a girlfriend.

Noticing a light in her parents' bedroom, she was stunned to think her father was still up reading. With that in mind, she crept all the way back around the barn, lest she cause a racket and send her father outside.

There, just inside and hanging on the high hook, Nellie Mae spotted Dat's lantern, essential for her late-night task. Tomorrow's duties would start in a few hours, with all the extra baking required after their Lord's Day and the washing to be hung out on the line.

No time to waste . . .

CHAPTER 22

Reuben had started writing the letter to the bishop more times than he cared to count, the crumpled-up pages of lined paper lying like popcorn balls on the bedroom floor. Remarkably, Betsy had slept through it, dear wife that she was.

I'm putting my family in jeopardy, he thought. *We'll be lumped in with those wanting tractors!*

Going to the window, Reuben stretched his arms. Was he doing the right thing by writing to the weary man of God? Word had it his brother had fallen ill out in Iowa. *What kind of man am I, putting this on him, too?*

Certainly in the eyes of the Lord he was doing right by requesting the Bible studies. Pleasing God was Reuben's focus now. He would gladly give all he had to follow Him.

My aging parents are coming to live in a house with their soon-to-be shunned son. He swallowed hard, blinking back the tears that threatened his sight. How had Cousin Jonathan and his family survived thus far? His sons, all farmers, held as firmly as their father to their newfound belief. Yet Jonathan's parents and grandparents were strongly opposed, as staunch in tradition as most older relatives were expected to be. Still, when a man chose to wholly follow the Lord, as Jonathan had, the family often followed close behind. Reuben had seen this before among the People.

He had much to ponder. Going out in the hallway to pace the floor from one end of the long corridor and back, he could hear daughter Rhoda snoring softly as he moved past her room. Nellie Mae, on the other hand, didn't seem to have returned from the evening's event. Evidently she was still with a beau.

He smiled, recalling his own courtship of dear Betsy. Like a sunrise, she'd appeared in his life. He still remembered the pleasure of seeing her eyes light up for him that first time.

I'm a blessed man, Lord. And I ask you this night for yet another blessing. . . .

Without intending to cause a ruckus, Reuben planned to sit down with his father and lay out what he'd learned about salvation by grace. After nearly a lifetime of believing you worked your way to heaven, Reuben now knew the Bible's position on the matter. Naturally there would be plenty of room for the Plain way of doing things, so well ingrained now, but Betsy and the girls, at least, must accept the whole of the gospel, too. He prayed it would be soon.

What his Daed might say would make no difference to Reuben's path, but his father would have a choice to make: His parents could reside here in the Dawdi Haus as expected, or they might prefer to live with one of Reuben's other siblings who would remain in this church district, after the dust settled.

What will my sons choose to follow? What of their wives and children?

He thought again of young Emma, so much like their Suzy at that age. Would she grow up to know the Savior? Would any of his precious grandchildren?

These questions occupied his mind, taunting Reuben as he wore out the rug.

It was pointless to try to sleep after nearly an hour of staring at the window in his room, watching for the first hint of dawn. Any rest eluded Caleb. So he rose, dressed, and went on foot a ways, traveling a mile or so east. He had to walk off his pent-up energy, though he would be dog-tired at first light. Time to put his interest in Nellie Mae into some logical perspective. Yet how could he hope to accomplish that by walking to her house and standing out in the trees along the road? Caleb looked up at the many windows under the eaves, wondering which one belonged to her. In order to shine his flashlight on the right window, he must know . . . should the day come to ask Nellie Mae to marry him.

He knew there were young people in other church districts farther north who practiced bed courtship—*Bundel*. Here it was frowned upon, although he'd heard enough stories to know some of the older folk had practiced bundling—grandparents and the like. Some of them were now the same outspoken elders who were trying to hold the line against tractors and other worldly pressures.

What *was* acceptable for an engaged couple was a visit to the girl's bedroom, where, in most cases, she had a small couch in the far corner. He'd never seen a girl's room, except his sisters' at home. Most likely, Nellie's was especially neat, just as she was. It would smell mighty nice, too, no doubt.

Nellie had confided in him earlier tonight that she and Suzy had shared nearly everything as sisters, including their room. This revelation had him even more curious than before. That and another offhand comment from one of Susannah Lapp's friends.

He hoped Nellie Mae was quite certain about her sister's behavior. Suzy was even mentioned in passing among the local boys.

Truth be told, Caleb was attracted to Reuben Fisher's third daughter like a parched man to cold spring water. Not only was he fond of Nellie, he wanted to shorten the time between their dates. He wished the seasons would fly, too, bringing next year's baptismal Sunday around right quick—and, not long after that, his and Nellie's wedding day, Lord willing. He could envision Nellie baking her delicious pastries in his own mother's kitchen, greeting him with her endearing smile, and holding their little ones someday, too.

I'll write her a letter, Caleb decided, knowing his father would advise him to slow down—and right quick.

The tree stump made an ideal lampstand. Lowering the heavy lantern onto it, Nellie was glad for the wide swath of light the oil lamp provided. The right honeysuckle bush had been relatively easy to locate, thanks to the ancient stump next to it. The pyramid-shaped sweetgum tree, its leaves showing traces of the purple-red it soon would be, was the other familiar landmark.

As she dug, Nellie thought of Caleb, wondering what he would think of her up here doing man's work. He might be impressed at her strength, though she was not even half as strong as any of her five brothers. *Course, he'd be mighty curious 'bout what I'm up to.*

She kept reliving their date. How would she possibly wait another whole week before laying eyes on him? She wondered if it would be too forward to write a note—make a little card for him, maybe. Yet if she let herself express the things she was eager to say, she might embarrass herself.

No, best not to pick up a pen at all.

Nellie's shovel bumped into the dirt-caked plastic she'd wrapped around the diary. Quickly she leaned down to retrieve it from its earthy hiding place. Gently brushing away the soil, she unwrapped the book and wiped it with the hem of her apron.

She clung to the journal, relieved to see it remained in good condition. "Suzy . . . oh, dear sister. What people are saying 'bout you."

A sudden fear welled up as she contemplated what might be revealed within these pages. Suzy had recorded her honest thoughts, surely never thinking someone other than herself would be reading them, even someone who loved her dearly. Nellie was the sole protector of Suzy's intimate reflections . . . of her dreams. Perhaps of her sins, too. Here between the hard covers of her sister's journal was the disclosure of what had pulled a good Amish girl toward the world.

Dare I read it?

Still gripping the diary, Nellie reached for the lantern, suddenly aware of the dancing shadows, the way the light, adequate for digging, now played insufficiently against the darkness . . . the predawn gloom. She lowered her hand and shivered as uncontrollably as she had at hearing that Suzy's life had been snuffed out. Hugging the diary, she felt grateful for its recovery and somehow closer to her dead sister. Then, making a pouch from her apron, she carefully tied the book into the fabric. Reaching again for the lantern, Nellie Mae slung the shovel over her shoulder before picking her way through the woods, the fatigue of having been up all night—and the weight of what she might soon discover—creeping into her bones.

The attic extended the entire length of the house. Given that Betsy hadn't mounted the creaky steps in months, she decided to organize a bit, her other morning work caught up for a while.

Time to chase away some dust bunnies.

Reuben was out training his new colts, giving them commands on the track behind the barn, and the girls were working in the bakery shop or, as was the case with Rhoda, for their English neighbors. So Betsy headed to the attic to redd up, hoping to locate several older quilts that might prove useful with Reuben's parents coming to live there. Of course, her mother-in-law, Hannah, would bring a good many quilts of her own, but with the cold of winter on its way, one could never have too many.

Mammi Fisher's multicolored antique quilts were of exceptional quality, especially the sixteen-patch quilt, with its bold reds, purples, and deep blues, handed down from the 1880s on the Fisher side—Reuben's grandmother's handiwork. Suzy had once spent several days with Mammi Hannah taking in the stories behind the quilts, the quilting frolics, and the womenfolk who had gathered to make them.

Betsy had not forgotten the bright-eyed wonder on Suzy's face upon returning home. "I saw me some wonderful-gut stitchin', Mamma!"

Suzy . . . my little quilter.

She gave in to her tears, there on the narrow attic steps. She leaned her head on the wooden railing, sobbing. More recently she had not allowed herself to be overtaken with grief, although her husband likely thought otherwise. Why else would he continue to be so worried as to steer her clear of the bakery shop, where she might break down at hearing condolences offered by loyal customers? More than likely that was why Reuben had put the nix on her helping Nellie.

Drying her eyes with her apron, Betsy made her way to the landing and into the large attic room. She laid down her feather duster and surveyed the place. Over in the far corner, she spotted the old family trunk and lifted the lid wide. She peered into the depths of her collection of heirloom quilts, astonished to see an envelope with *To Mamma* printed on it in Suzy's hand.

"My, my, what's this?" She reached for the envelope, and for a moment she merely held it. "For goodness' sakes," she whispered, choking down more tears.

Looking on the back, she saw that her youngest had written, *Just another little note from me to you. Love, Suzy.*

"Was she planning to give this to me and forgot where she hid it?" Betsy said into the dim light.

It made no sense . . . unless Suzy had placed yet another note somewhere—something she'd enjoyed doing. Still, why would Suzy leave it in the quilt collection, as though hoping Betsy might find it?

She couldn't bring herself to open it, and she set the envelope aside while selecting two large quilts for winter, deciding she would ask Reuben to take them downstairs later. She then began straightening stacked boxes, making sure the lids were fastened tight. Several old chests needed dusting and she took care of that right quick, also tackling the cobwebs near the dormer windows.

When she was satisfied things were more orderly, she returned to the quilt trunk. Eyeing Suzy's note, she stood there, overwhelmed at this unexpected gesture of love. She felt a strange chill, as if she might be coming down with something. One of Suzy's favorite places to play as a child, besides outdoors, had been this very spot high in the house. Betsy sighed, remembering the way her youngest had liked to hide here with a book or some needlework. Or her diary.

Even as young as five, Suzy could be found up here chattering to her faceless dolls, all of them lined up on a trunk or chest, making each speak by changing the sound of her own voice.

Betsy stared at the envelope, lip quivering now, thinking of all the evenings sixteen-year-old Suzy had left the supper table ever so quick. *Why'd you go and run off like that? I scarcely ever knew where you were.*

She thought of Rhoda, who went off now quite as often herself. Same thing seemed to be happening with her, only Betsy knew where she was most of the time—at least she thought so.

"Ach, go on, open it," Betsy told herself. She needed a dose of courage this minute, despite yearning to hear Suzy's voice in the words she'd written.

When did she pen this?

Betsy reached for the envelope and opened it.

Dear Mamma,
    Look under the bottom quilt in this trunk to find a surprise . . . an early birthday present.
                   Lots of love,
                   Suzy

Betsy smiled. "What's she got under there?" she muttered, leaning down to lift one quilt out after another. She smelled it even before she'd spotted the small purple pillow, its seams handsewn with tiny, even stitches. Betsy realized it was one of Suzy's special sachet pillows filled with lavender, marjoram, and crushed cloves. Suzy had named her clever creation a "headache pillow," something she had kindly made for several sisters-in-law during their pregnancies. *And also this one, for me. . . .*

Kneeling before the wooden trunk, Betsy pressed her nose into the face-sized pillow and wept. *Suzy was always doing such thoughtful things. Our little darling.*

After a time, Betsy rose and began to replace each hand-made quilt, mindful to keep them wrapped in heavy tissue paper for protection. Then, closing the lid, she sat down, staring first at the lovely pillow, and then at the note.

A verse she'd secretly memorized came to mind. *For God sent not his Son into the world to condemn the world; but that the world through him might be saved.*

The meaning was ever so clear—the Lord would not have condemned Suzy to hell if she had belonged to Him.

If . . .

Sitting there, she recalled other verses Reuben had requested that she read, verses he himself was committing to memory. She had carefully done so, often many times over. She was deeply sad—sorry even—about the way she'd lived so long in the dark, thinking the hard work she did for her family and community might give her a better chance of heaven someday.

I could only hope before . . . now I can know.

"But, oh, dear Suzy. . . ." She sighed, wishing the Lord God had brought this spiritual light to her Reuben before that dreadful June day. She was torn, not knowing what to think about all of it—or much of anything she'd been taught.

Bowing her head, Betsy prayed, "O Lord, I want to be counted as your child." She pressed Suzy's note against her heart. "Take my sins far from me. I want to follow your Son, Jesus, no matter what it means for Reuben and me. Or for our family."

Just please let me see Suzy again . . . someday.

CHAPTER 23

From the moment Rosanna arrived at Maryann Fisher's house, she felt on edge. Both the Fisher toddlers were crying—wailing, really—and dishes were piled high in the sink. She didn't know why she was so *naerfich* today. She assumed it had started with Cousin Kate's visit Thursday—all the talk of the twins and Kate's seeming reticence. It had permeated Rosanna's dreams since. Didn't every mother long for twins? Elias was excited about the possibility of sons. Of course, there was the unspoken concern, for him, that Kate's babies might turn out to be daughters. Every Amishman wanted boys, and as many as possible, but Rosanna secretly longed for a little girl.

Now that she was here, she reached for sniffling Katie, attempting to soothe her cries, swabbing the runny nose with her own embroidered hankie, making sure she did not wipe the child's tender nose on the side with stitching. "There, there, honey-girl," she whispered, rubbing the curve of her lower back and feeling the small spine.

One day I'll do the same to quiet my own children. . . .

"You're so good to help," Maryann said from across the table, balancing even smaller Becky on her right knee, jiggling her up and down as she rolled out dough for three

209

pie crusts. "As soon as I get these pies in the oven, I'll sit and chat."

"Oh, I don't mean to take up your time," Rosanna said quickly. "I'm simply here for a bootie pattern, if you have one."

"You must be knittin' some for your cousin Kate's wee ones, jah?"

Rosanna nodded, feeling peculiar not telling Maryann the full reason for why she wanted the patterns.

Nellie's sister-in-law's face was a rosy pink now, and perspiration was evident on her forehead. Her disheveled light brown hair looked as if it needed a good washing. Even a solid brushing would help.

Will I look this schtruwwlich *as a mamma?* Rosanna wondered, recalling how admiring her husband was of her. She would not want to dampen Elias's enthusiasm, so to speak. It would take some doing, but she hoped to remain attractive for her darling even with twin babies to care for.

Maryann placed the dough in three pie plates and pinched the sides all around. She glanced up at Rosanna, her countenance serious. "I'm worried 'bout our bishop," she said softly. "Imagine the good man being so sick so far away and all."

"He's still under the weather?"

"Jah, word is he's too ill to travel."

Rosanna noticed the angst in Maryann's eyes. "I hadn't realized 'twas that serious."

"So I'm told . . . but I don't know much. Only what Ephram says."

Rosanna was not very fond of Nellie Mae's staid big brother. "How'd he hear?"

Maryann frowned. "Well, I really shouldn't say."

Rosanna nodded without prodding further. She understood that tone and look.

Maryann put Becky down to play with her sister and some empty spools for thread. She slid the pies into the belly of the cookstove. "Now, then, you're here for some bootie patterns?"

"Jah." But as Maryann hurried out of the room, leaving her with Becky and Katie, Rosanna suddenly felt concerned. She had an irresistible desire to ask the Lord God to help their bishop, older man that he was. Some of Elias's friends in another church had made such prayers, and she thought it a wonderful-good idea to beseech the Lord for protection and care. And, in this case, for the bishop's healing.

So she bowed her head and prayed silently, trusting their heavenly Father to hear and answer. When she was done, the little girls were still sitting near her feet, babbling and laughing, draping the strung-together spools on each other's arms.

Rosanna daydreamed, wondering what her life might be like in two short months. As a mother, she was ever so sure she would be praying daily for her children, just as she had for the bishop. Even if secretly.

Slipping the loop of the rope over the colt's sleek neck, Reuben led it around the training track. Glancing up, he noticed that one of the martin birdhouses high on a post near the back of the house was listing to one side. He'd have to fix that before spring.

As a boy Reuben had helped his father build many a martin birdhouse; the six-sided "apartment style" was the most popular among their family and neighbors. They'd given them away as gifts, although Reuben knew some Amish who built them for profit nowadays. His father had also placed several such birdhouses strategically around this very house to keep unwanted insects at bay. The whole family had watched the male martins with their blue-black feathers—gleaming almost purple in full sunlight—arrive in the spring, followed later by the gray, pale-bellied females.

Reuben's favorite thing as a curious child was to watch all the tiny beaks poke out of the many holes on the birdhouses he'd helped make. What fun it was to see the new hatchlings eventually fly away.

Once, he and his father had banded a new bird to calculate its lifespan. They'd observed the same bird return for seven consecutive years, which his father had thought might be something of a record. Since that time, Reuben had read of purple martins living to be even nine or ten years old.

Nine or ten years old . . . about the age Suzy was when she helped me build several birdhouses. "Course, that was before she decided she liked boys better than birds," he said ruefully.

Reuben clucked to the colt and watched as it picked up its gait, the memory of working beside his daughter giving him pause. It had been too long since he'd shared the tradition of making birdhouses with a child. He'd tinkered with the idea of making an extra-large birdhouse with his grandson Benny, James's oldest. Perhaps after the harvest and the wedding season there would be time.

An ambitious project for a six-year-old, but doable with some help.

If his parents decided to go ahead with moving back to their original home place, he might just include his aging father in the birdhouse-making task. And if James joined them to help saw or sand or paint, there would be four generations of Fishers working side by side.

Coming full circle.

Leading the colt around the track a final time, Reuben contemplated the coming Lord's Day, which might be the last peaceful one they'd have around here. Preacher Manny had informed him last night that Bishop Joseph was seriously ill and that Reuben should refrain from writing to ask permission to hold Bible studies until their leader was better. Reuben felt stricken at the news, because he'd already sent the request to the bishop, inviting him and others of the ministerial brethren to join with Manny and himself. Reuben had figured there was no reason to exclude anyone, even though he doubted they would participate. On the contrary, they'd be appalled to think one of the preachers was involved, as well as Reuben, a member in good standing.

"The timing is in God's hands," Manny had said, taking the news of Reuben's letter well.

Manny must think my request could worsen my brother's health, Reuben thought now. *How sick is Joseph?*

He stared at the side of the barn a stone's throw from the training track, noticing a few places where the sun had beaten hard on the west side. He would see to it that either Ephram or one of the twins got it painted and right quick. It wouldn't do to go into winter with any of the siding peeling, what with the harsh weather the almanac forecasted. While they were at it, one of his sons could right the birdhouse, too. He wasn't quite as spry as he used to be on a ladder.

It came to him that his sons might not be as ready to help as in the past once they heard of their father's newfound belief. *This great salvation has the power to unite or divide us all. . . .*

Reuben began to pray as he led the colt, asking the Lord to protect his close-knit family. "Bring all of them safely within the fold of your grace." He sighed, mopping his brow with his hand. "And may we not lose another one for eternity, O God." His voice thickened as he thought again of Suzy.

Inhaling deeply now, he added a prayer for the bishop, both for renewed health . . . and for an understanding heart.

Betsy and Nan chopped piles of carrots, celery, new potatoes, and onions to make a beef stew for the noon meal. "How's Nellie Mae doin' out there today?" Betsy asked, glancing out the window at the bakery shop.

Nan shrugged. "Lots of customers for the middle of the week, I'd say."

"More than usual?"

"Seems so." Nan scooped up a handful of carrot chunks and dropped them into the black kettle. "Must be autumn's in the air."

"Jah, the tourists flock in from all over, seems."

"Some from as far away as London, Rhoda says."

Rhoda knows of this? Betsy felt somewhat surprised that Rhoda should be privy to the comings and goings of such fancy people. "Your sister hears these things from the Englischers she works for?"

Nan blushed, nodding. "Jah . . . and Nellie and I both hear a-plenty from the shop's English customers, too, Mamma."

Betsy straightened. "Ach, I'm afraid of that."

Nan left the counter and went to the sink, washing her hands quickly. Her daughter often put a quick end to conversation whenever Betsy came close to touching on anything to do with Rhoda and her work outside the home. More and more young Plain women were eager to make money, cleaning for Englischers or working as nannies, but Betsy had a mother's concern that permitting such things endangered the Old Ways. Betsy wanted to ask Nan if she, too, was thinking along the lines of getting a job, but she didn't feel up to hearing the potential reply. What would be would naturally come; there wasn't much stopping the young people once they got something in their heads.

At least Nan seems mighty interested in good Amish boys, Betsy reassured herself. She had higher hopes in that regard for Nan's future than Rhoda's. At least, she *had.* Now she honestly didn't know how this daughter was doing.

"I don't think you have a lot to worry 'bout where Rhoda's concerned," Nan said suddenly, interrupting her thoughts.

"Why do you say that?"

" 'Cause I believe I know her."

"She's not too taken by the world; is that what you mean?"

"Not like Suzy was. . . ." Nan's eyes grew wide and she covered her mouth. "Ach, Mamma, I'm ever so sorry. I didn't mean to bring up Suzy. Truly I didn't."

Betsy had wept enough for one day. She turned to head for the sink to wash her hands, hoping Nan hadn't seen her tears spring up.

"Nellie's sufferin' something awful, too . . . over, well, you know." Nan's voice quivered.

Betsy nodded her head, the lump in her throat nearly bursting. "We'll all suffer for a long, long time, I daresay."

Nan sighed. "You and Nellie most of all."

Betsy leaned her head on Nan's shoulder as her daughter placed a gentle hand on her back. "Nellie's got to be in terrible pain, really." She didn't go on to say what she was thinking. Fact was, the two girls had been inseparable from the time Nellie had first attempted to hold her sister—Nellie had been nearly a baby herself at eleven months old. The pair had been much like twins, being so close in age.

"Honestly . . . I think Nellie's reading something of Suzy's," Nan whispered.

"Oh?"

"Jah, I wouldn't be surprised if it's her diary." Nan looked sheepish.

"You're sure?"

"Jah, looked like Suzy's little diary to me." Nan moved to the counter again to chop the last of the potatoes.

Startled, Betsy considered whether Nan knew what she was talking about. Pushing the thought aside, Betsy dried her hands and set to working again. "Time you got back out and helped your sister," she said at last.

Nan chuckled. She finished quickly with the potatoes and hurried over to the sink to clean up once again.

Betsy was glad to have the stew ready to go onto the fire. "Thank you, Nan. I love all my girls . . . ever so much."

Nan smiled. "I know you do, Mamma. I know." With that she was off to assist at Nellie's Simple Sweets.

That one sure knows how to get me stirred up, Betsy thought, wondering again whether what Nan said was true. She'd known Suzy had kept a diary, but it hadn't occurred to her it might still be around.

Betsy thought again of the note Suzy had left for her. What else had her youngest written before she died?

CHAPTER 24

After supper and Dat's evening Scripture reading, Nellie shut her bedroom door and pulled the diary from its hiding place in her side table drawer, under several Sunday hankies. Then, settling onto her bed, she tucked her legs beneath her and set the book in her lap, running her hand along its cover before opening the diary.

> *I figured I couldn't hold out till my birthday, so I bought this journal with some money I received for Christmas. Now that I'm nearly sixteen, I want to remember everything that happens to me. Especially the boys I meet once I'm old enough to go to Singings and whatnot all.*

Nellie smiled, torn between the satisfaction of hearing Suzy's perkiness in the words she'd written and missing her even more because of it. Suzy's writing was tiny and precise, like Suzy herself.

Sighing, Nellie began reading again.

> *Today is New Year's 1966. I will faithfully write each day no matter how busy I get doing chores with Mamma, or Dat, who needs me to help curry the colts and tend to the chickens. Of course, there is always baking to be done for Nellie, as well, which I like best, because I love*

Nellie Mae so. She's the dearest person I know, except for Mamma.

When I've got time, I like sewing, too—and embroidering. Right now I'm stitching some pillow slips secretly for gifts, and I have some tatting started. Doilies will make nice surprises for my sisters' hope chests. A hopeless chest, really, as far as Rhoda goes. I'm laughing a little as I write, which ain't so nice, is it? And now I'm talking to myself! I just don't understand why a boy hasn't invited her driving after Singing or frolics—she's always home long before either Nan or Nellie Mae. Rhoda's as pleasant as the day is long, and right pretty in her own way. She's a good cook, too, so she'd make a fine wife. It's the strangest thing that no one else seems to think so.

Nellie paused, dreading to read Suzy's private thoughts further. She rose and went to the dresser, picking up the blue plate. "This feels like a betrayal," Nellie whispered, her heart pounding ever so hard. "Should I continue?"

After a while, she returned to the diary and began to read the third page.

I remember hearing the snowplow before ever laying eyes on it. Awful noisy it was, grumbling up the road behind me, making a clean sweep ahead. In more ways than one I need a clear path, too.

But finding that path seems nearly impossible. . . .

The sky was a shining arc of cloudless blue and the roadway was piled with snow on both sides, forming a wide tunnel. Suzy didn't mind whether the snow was knee-deep or plowed here on the road; she was having herself an adventure, headed to see her new friends this brisk January day. *A wonderful-gut way to begin the year!* she decided.

Congratulating herself on being sly enough to slip away from the house following afternoon chores, Suzy picked up her pace. She wanted to be where she'd promised to meet her friends at the appointed time, so she clomped over the snow-packed road all the way to the intersection of Route 10 and Beaver Dam Road. She caught herself grinning because Jay Hess, so blond and good-looking, would be driving today, or so she had been told by several of his school friends. She'd seen him around school two years ago when she was still young enough to attend—the People didn't go past eighth grade—but had never given him a second glance. That had changed when seventeen-year-old Jay spotted her walking in the square at Honeybrook before Christmas, enjoying her freedom and the fancy decorations. He'd asked her if she wanted to go for a ride in his car, and Suzy had smiled and accepted, eager for some excitement.

Today they were all going to that same square to mill around and have some ice cream, since school had let out for the day for Jay and his friends. Dat would find her easy way with Englischers another argument for why Amish pupils would do well to attend their own schools, no doubt. *A life set apart.* She'd heard this said so much she was tired of it. Tired, too, of being expected to grow up "in the faith." In short, Suzy was ready for some modern living, like some other Amish youth her age, though mostly it was the boys who pushed the limits. Boys got away with things girls could never get by with, like driving cars and hiding them from their parents.

Suzy often wondered why her older brothers had never strayed from the People. Or had they just kept it hushed up once they decided in favor of the church?

But no, she was mighty sure Benjamin, James, and Ephram hadn't sown wild oats. It was harder to know about the twins, because Jeremiah and Thomas were so much older, going on thirty now. Even so, they'd married before twenty, as had all her brothers. *Following the example of our parents by wedding young.*

Suzy knew she was being lured away from the Plain life by her own longing for freedom. She was reaching for a little heaven on earth, sowing her wild oats and hoping for crop failure, as some Plain boys would say.

Truth was she liked Jay and his friends—both the girls and the boys. Not a single one looked at her askance because she wore humble garb and pulled her hair back in a tight bun. They accepted her completely.

Darlene Landis and Trudy Zimmerman were the most interesting of the girls. Jay had whispered to Suzy they were "only friends," but when one day she'd heard Trudy talking to another girl about wanting Jay to kiss her again, Suzy'd gasped outright before she could stop herself. Even knowing that, she was curious about Jay and his ultra-casual way—what she supposed some called a "devil may care" attitude. If getting to know him meant associating with Trudy or anyone else he might have kissed, then so be it. She was not about to give up this chance.

Gingerly now she made her way over the thick coating of snow, slipping occasionally as she went. Enjoying the brisk air and the sun on her face, she looked toward the woods south of the road. Trees flocked with light snow glistened in the late afternoon sun. She assumed the majority of school kids had hoped yesterday for a snow day today, but Suzy was thankful the weather hadn't spoiled their plans.

Presently she stood waiting at the junction of Route 10 and the road she lived on, glad for some wind shelter. Scooting up close to the wide trunk of an old oak, she wondered how long she might have to wait for Jay and his buddies.

Assuming he would be along any minute, she breathed the icy air into her lungs and slowly exhaled.

She began to shiver but not from being too cold. Waiting there, Suzy felt the edge of the precipice on which she'd been balancing. She could nearly see it before her as she leaned over as far as she could—and then some—knowing there was no safety net at the bottom should she fall. Neither Dat nor Mamma would approve of her plans today—Nellie, neither. Nor would they have wanted her going anywhere with Jay's friend Dennis Brackbill, as she had for the past two weekends. Two long dates—two too many. Dennis was a fun-loving clown, but he had been reckless in his driving, even though she was in the car. *No regard for a girl's safety,* she thought.

Like Jay, Dennis had been her schoolmate before she was forced to leave and work with her mamma on the farm, as dictated by the Old Ways. The local school wasn't the best place to make friends with boys, her parents would surely say if they knew. But they didn't know, and they never would if she handled things right. Now if only Jay had remembered. . . .

Nellie closed the diary. She stared at the page, not sure she could bear to read any further. For the past couple of days, she'd glanced through the diary, reading stray lines here and there—accounts of quilting bees and walks with girl cousins—but until tonight she hadn't found anything out of the ordinary. Nothing at all like what Nellie had just read—at the start of the diary, no less.

How long had Suzy's interest in Jay or Dennis—or Darlene and Trudy—lasted?

Nellie wished she'd left the diary buried in the woods, but she'd started this troubling journey and now she must see it through, returning to it another day.

How on earth did I miss seeing this brazen side of Suzy?

———

When Nellie awoke earlier than usual Thursday, she felt ready to read more of Suzy's diary, but when she sought to do so, Nan stopped by. As much as Nellie longed for more interaction with her sisters, she couldn't help but wonder why Nan had to poke her head in the door. It was as if she suspected something.

Has Nan been spying on me?

Nellie tried her best to think back. Hadn't she been discreet enough, closing the bedroom door and sitting with her back to it as she had?

"Is it me, or are you up too early?" Nan asked, coming by yet again in her long white cotton nightgown. She hadn't taken time yet to slip on her bathrobe, and her hair was still uncombed.

Nellie was not amused and quite glad she'd kept Suzy's diary hidden from view just now. "The question is, why are *you* up three hours before breakfast today?" she asked. "You plannin' to help me bake some pies?"

Nan grimaced. "Couldn't sleep anymore, is all."

Nellie didn't know what to say to that. Nan had always slept longer and deeper than anyone she knew. Nan had once announced at the breakfast table that she wished she might sleep in longer of a morning, to which Dat had nearly choked on his coffee.

When Nellie offered nothing more, Nan padded back to her room. Nellie waited till the door to Rhoda and Nan's room clicked shut. She heard their bed creak and assumed

Nan had slipped back in for an added forty winks. She had little time left to read before she must begin the day's baking, so Nellie quickly found her ending spot from yesterday.

Suzy's written account took Nellie back to February and March of last winter, the time of year when their lives revolved around visiting family, butchering, and farm sales. Even the public schools closed for the latter, since teachers realized that a number of Plain and English students were involved in the auctions' social aspects.

All the while, Nellie's beloved sister had yearned after darkness, becoming ever more caught up in the world. . . .

For Suzy, every spare moment these days was spent with Jay Hess and his "clique," as those outside his group referred to the six students who went nearly everywhere together. Suzy had gladly gone with them to the movies, to bowling alleys, and even several times to a dance hall. Wherever Jay chose to go, Suzy aimed to be right by his side, soaking up his modern life like a dry sponge.

She remembered how light-headed she'd felt the first time she'd puffed on Jay's half-smoked cigarette, his face close to hers, as if he longed to somehow be a part of her first smoke. They'd laughed at her momentary dizziness and he'd kissed her later, long and lingering. In a few days she'd adapted, eager to have a full smoke of her own when with Jay. He was on her mind all the time now as she cooked and cleaned with Mamma. In her free time, she artfully drew his name and wished she were still in school waiting for him after the bell.

Dat would more than have my hide if he knew.

Anxious to maintain her secret, Suzy promised herself not to become too keen on Jay's smokes; nor would she drink more than two beers at once. For his part Jay never suggested she bring a change of clothes when they went out, something she viewed as a sign of his affection—he liked her enough to be seen with a Plain girl, of all things. Besides, there were others like her. Suzy wasn't alone in her search for a way out of the dead-end street she'd been born on.

The two other Amish girls who ran around with Englisch-ers never dressed Plain when they did so—they let their hair down, too, and even cut and styled it. Both had downright shallow boyfriends who probably would have preferred to date a nice English girl if they could have gotten any of the fancy girls interested in them. At least, that was how Suzy looked at it.

Jay was better. He liked her as she was . . . though that was not how she planned to remain.

By late March, he wanted to spend more and more time alone with her. They drove the back roads, frequently pulling over to park. Together in the private darkness of his car, they talked and drank and laughed till Suzy cried, tarrying longer each time.

How alive Suzy felt with Jay, alarmingly so. The whole world halted in its tracks when she was with him. He admitted the same thing to her in so many words. *"You're my baby girl,"* he would say and reach for her, holding her so tight she believed he would never let her go.

When it came time for sowing alfalfa in her father's wheat field, Jay seemed put off by her absence. "You shouldn't have to do boys' work," he said at first. Soon, though, he was more relaxed about her chores, telling her all was well. "I'll wait for you, Suzy. You do what you have to, to please your family."

She warmed to his words as she had from the start. Fact was he could get her to see things his way just by the smooth way he suggested them, though she hadn't done all the things some schoolgirls succumbed to in the name of love. Still, she knew she was treading on dangerous ground, ever so close to getting the cart before the pony.

It wasn't that Suzy didn't trust herself to be able to keep resisting Jay. What worried her more than possibly giving in was the emptiness she felt, in spite of the thrill. Was this all she was willing to trade her wholesome, dreary life for? She'd longed for freedom from the heaviness she felt living Plain . . . bound to eventually dying that way, too, if nothing changed. Bored with life, she yearned for more than her roots could possibly offer.

But the more she reached for what she expected would fill her up, the more drained Suzy felt. All the same she simply could not go backward to the repression that had driven her away from her family and their beliefs, in search of light and love. The Old Ways were less appealing than ever.

Jay managed to get her talking about eloping one night after they'd fogged up his car windows but good. She told him she loved him, adding that she was interested in running away with him if he wanted. Just that quick, he changed the subject, muttering something about attending vocational school or a community college next year.

"You don't really want to get married yet, do you?" she challenged him.

"Why sure, baby. You'll see." But he had new excuses for her nearly every time they saw each other.

In early April when the tobacco farmers were sowing seeds in their sterilized tobacco beds, Suzy helped her parents and sisters plant potatoes. She had begun to chew gum nearly round the clock at home, pushing in a fresh stick every half hour or so in an effort to cover the smell of cigarettes. She chewed so many packs of gum, it was as though she were addicted to that, too.

Gum, cigarettes, and Jay Hess . . . but not in that order.

Nellie slammed the diary shut. She felt unclean, like she ought to bathe. *Poor Suzy . . . all mixed up, looking for acceptance far from the People.* She thought back to Suzy's wild days, stunned by her own naïveté—how little she as a sister had suspected. When Suzy's clothing had smelled a smidgen like cigarette smoke, Nellie never dreamed her own sister was the one smoking. To think drinking and necking—with an outsider, no less—were also to be counted among her dear sister's sins.

"Ach, why'd she feel the need to run fast with the world?" For the life of her, Nellie Mae couldn't begin to grasp that she'd shared this very room—and nearly everything of her own life and dreams—with Suzy, never once guessing her sister was so *ferhoodled.*

She stared at the diary. "This would not just break Mamma's heart . . . it might make her sick," she whispered.

Tears spilled down her cheeks. *You fooled me, Suzy! I thought you were merely childish, not this.*

"I trusted you. I thought I knew you."

The truth she had so desperately sought was too shameful to accept. Nellie slid from her bed and crumpled into a heap on the floor, burying her face in her hands and sobbing louder than she'd ever meant to.

CHAPTER 25

———

Early Friday morning, Betsy knocked on Nellie's door, asking to come in. Nellie mumbled a yes and rubbed her sleepy eyes, looking up from her snug spot in her big bed, as her mother entered. Betsy was struck by the fact the bed looked too large without Suzy in it.

She'd heard Nellie burst out crying early yesterday morning but felt she should wait a day, at least, before approaching her about it. She knew all too well that sometimes grieving people preferred to be alone. "Are you all right, dear?"

Nellie Mae nodded. "Are *you*, Mamma? You're up awful early."

Betsy couldn't help but smile. *Nellie, ever thoughtful . . .* "I heard you cryin' yesterday," she said.

"Oh jah . . . that."

"We all miss her terribly," she said.

Nellie sighed and rolled over, covering her head with the quilt and saying no more.

"I'll help with your baking today," offered Betsy, but Nellie only grunted slightly in response.

Closing the door gently, Betsy wondered if Nan was right about Nellie's reading Suzy's diary. If so, it didn't seem like such a good idea for Nellie Mae in her susceptible state. *Seems like a lesson in futility, really.*

Nevertheless, Betsy could not deny her own curiosity about Suzy's Rumschpringe.

———

As Betsy and Reuben dressed for the day, she knew it was time to tell her husband of her prayer in the attic—she'd waited too long as it was. She had been hesitant, wanting to keep it to herself, so foreign the experience was to her. She couldn't help but wonder how she and Reuben would find their way together as new believers.

She finished placing her Kapp on her head and went to him, reaching for his big callused hands. "Reuben, I must tell you that I understand what you feel when readin' the Good Book."

His eyes met hers. "You do?"

She could hardly go on. "I believe . . . just as you do," she whispered. "I couldn't put it off . . . didn't want to wait any longer to receive this blessed salvation."

His smile spread clear across his ruddy face, prematurely wrinkled from long hours in the sun. "Ach, this is the best news, Betsy." He wrapped his arms around her, enfolding her.

"I'm ever so glad you got me thinkin' . . . I best be catchin' up with you, love."

Reuben laughed heartily and leaned down to kiss her cheek. "Our eyes have been opened wide by the grace of our Lord." He beamed into her face. "I daresay there may be more than we know."

"What will happen to us all?" Betsy asked.

"We'll simply go about our business and family, trusting God to make the way clear and straight before us."

228

"Will we leave the church?"

He frowned momentarily. "All the present upheaval in our midst . . . I say we bide our time, wait till things calm down some before pulling up roots."

"It's not like we're ashamed. . . ."

"Not at all, Betsy. What makes you say that?"

"We could simply leave the church and face up to the Bann. Look at Cousin Jonathan and almost the whole of his family . . . all of them shunned."

"'Tis mighty disheartening to think of us—all the People— treatin' him so."

"Seems we're kinder to outsiders who burn down our barns and run over our buggies with their cars—never pressing charges—than we are to our own." Her words caught in her throat.

"Forgiveness is the expected way." He picked up the Bible on their dresser. " 'Tween you and me, Betsy, I've never fully embraced our shunning practices. I've got private opinions 'bout that."

"Oh?"

"Our boys know this. The twins are more inclined to see eye to eye with me, but Ephram's downright outspoken against my views." Reuben looked at the floor and then raised his eyes to meet hers. "We cut off our own folk . . . and for what? Too short a haircut on a man . . . too wide or narrow a hat brim, for goodness' sake? What difference does any of that make in the eyes of the Lord?"

"Ach, Reuben, I never knew this of you."

"Well, I take issue with some of our rules, puttin' it mildly. But I've held my peace for this long, love. Time I began declaring what I believe to someone, starting with you. Upholding the rules of the Ordnung is not vital to salvation."

Betsy turned toward the window, watching the horses grazing in the distant paddock, the early-morning sun making their hides shine. "We've been taught all our lives that it's not God's will for folk to get together to study the Bible . . . but I honestly feel the need for it."

Reuben agreed. "I've been talkin' with Preacher Manny about this very thing."

She gasped. "Your cousin Manny knows of this?"

He took her hand and sat with her on the loveseat near the window, sharing all he had discussed with both Manny and Cousin Jonathan. "No matter whether we get the bishop's approval—and we won't—we'll start up a Bible study right here ourselves."

Reuben was a man of surprises, for sure and for certain. She felt more love for him than ever before . . . knowing he'd gently yet consistently shown her the truth. To think she was God's child, just as her husband was—this man who had led her to drink of the living water, like the woman drawing well water in the biblical town of Samaria.

"I can hardly keep from tellin' our girls what's happened," she said softly.

Reuben grinned. "We can tell our family together."

"All of them?"

"What's to lose?"

She touched his hand. "Oh, my dearest love . . . just about everything. Look at Cousin Jonathan and his family." Pausing, her eyes rested on her dear husband. "Jonathan lives among the People, yet he and his family are alone in their beliefs."

Reuben shook his head. "Jonathan won't be alone for long."

A heavy silence ensued as Betsy pondered all that her husband had shared.

———

At breakfast Betsy offered to help her husband mow hay, since last evening Reuben had announced this would be a "good, clear day for it."

By late that morning, the hay was out drying in the sun. Her husband had indeed chosen a fine day—sunny yet cool enough to make hard labor comfortable.

All during the noon meal, whenever Reuben looked her way, he was smiling. His eyes simply danced with joy.

Nan got up to serve the dessert she'd made, urging them to stay put.

Betsy noticed again how empty their long table looked most of the time now, what with the boys grown . . . and Suzy gone. But she was determined to look at life differently. Instead of dwelling on what she didn't have, she wanted to embrace what she did have, and to the full. Since yielding her life to God, she felt a stirring within.

Is God helping me find hope amid my grief?

She glanced at Nellie Mae, who looked utterly miserable, her eyes tired and downcast as though she was trying hard not to let her distress show. Betsy's heart went out to her.

Nan was more talkative than usual, mentioning several of the morning's customers at the shop. Much as Betsy enjoyed hearing her describe the regulars, she hoped they weren't becoming too important in Nan's mind. She mustn't fall into the curiosity that had surely pulled Suzy down.

Rhoda began talking about the many tall martin birdhouses in the Kraybills' yard.

"Like we have," Betsy said, finding this tidbit interesting.

"Well, Mrs. Kraybill's about as Plain as you can get and still be English," Nan said.

"What do you mean, dear one?" Betsy asked.

"She cooks from scratch like we do," Nan said, glancing at Rhoda, who was nodding. "And she sews the children's clothing, too."

"Most by hand," Rhoda piped up.

"Now, that is surprisin'," Betsy admitted.

"She's even tried making her own paper—imagine that!" Nan laughed softly.

Betsy smiled at her daughters and at Reuben, who looked to be about ready to pop his suspenders. Twice during the meal he'd actually winked at her. Once he reached for her hand and covered it with his own, squeezing it quickly before letting go.

So great a secret we share, she thought, looking fondly at her daughters. *O Lord, please show your narrow path to our dear girls. . . .*

Nellie Mae didn't want to stare, but she couldn't help but notice the affectionate exchanges between Dat and Mamma during the meal. What was going on between them? With all she'd learned of Suzy's life, she felt still more troubled by Dat's incessant Scripture reading. No matter that his waywardness pulled him in a different direction than Suzy's—it failed to follow their tradition just the same.

She hadn't even considered opening Suzy's diary this morning before getting out of bed. No, she wanted to rest her mind, hoping to erase the troubling visions her keen imagination provided. Her once-innocent sister had willingly dabbled in sin, and because of what? Simple boredom with the Plain life?

The very notion angered Nellie, and she hoped what she felt was more on the side of righteous indignation than resentment. There was no point in allowing anger over the revelation of Suzy's iniquity to cause her to sin, as well. Thankfully she was not the ultimate judge.

Unable to sit still and hide her feelings a moment longer, Nellie rose abruptly from the table. "Who wants ice cream with Nan's cake?" she asked.

Nan frowned, obviously not pleased at Nellie's attempt to usurp her role of server. Rhoda's mouth gaped open, and she appeared ready to reprimand Nellie. Of course, she had every right to, being older.

"Girls, please sit down, the both of yous," Dat said, surprising Nellie and obviously Mamma, too, who wore a concerned look on her sweet face.

"I've got something on my mind," he continued when Nellie and Nan had taken their seats. "Something that will change the direction of our lives."

Suzy's shenanigans lingered in Nellie's mind in spite of her father's words. What possibly could alter her life more than what she'd already discovered? "Your mamma and I have accepted all the teachings of Jesus." Dat's face turned solemn as he spoke the words, and Nellie's stomach clenched. "We want to know more, to study the New Testament with others who are saved, as we are."

Rhoda raised her eyebrows, and Nan turned white.

"Saved?" Nan blurted out.

Nellie gulped, immediately thinking of Caleb. *Ach no, not that!*

CHAPTER 26

Nellie felt as though she were drifting, her mind pulling her backward to Dat's frightening announcement . . . and forward, into the future, which seemed less clear than ever. She tried her best to get her bearings in the midst of a steady stream of customers all Friday afternoon. But her attempt to remain rooted in the here and now was futile.

It seemed inevitable that the People would band together against this notion of Dat's and follow the bishop on the matter of salvation. Declaring it as a completed act was ever so prideful, or so they were taught. Yet the way her father talked, one of their own preachers wanted to have meetings to study the Bible with as many families as were interested.

Dat had quoted the verse "as for me and my house, we will serve the Lord" as his prayer for his family. Naturally he would desire his offspring to follow him in his beliefs, although it would be a real miracle if all five of her brothers abandoned their baptismal vows for this. Ephram, for one, was headstrong—and firmly tied to the Old Ways. So was Benjamin. Wasn't the Ordnung supposed to be obeyed, without exception?

Ach, how can Dat expect us to follow in this?

Between customers, Nellie stepped outdoors to soak in some of the sunshine and promptly developed a headache. A tightness wrapped around her head, like a wide rubber band pressing on her brain. Still, she lingered outside, inhaling the spicy fragrance of midautumn. The sky shone as if newly washed.

Suzy's first missed autumn . . .

Nellie spotted several sugar maples, their leaves turning to reddish orange at the edges. She took heart in the promise of blazing splendor soon to come.

Her thoughts turned to Mamma. No good thing could come of handing over the diary to her mother or anyone else. And Nellie knew she should not have given in to such impulsive crying yesterday.

Watching a car filled with more customers pull into the lane, she realized suddenly that their English neighbors, or even some of the People, surely must have bumped into Suzy last spring in town during her wild times. She would have been difficult to miss, spending time with such a crowd in her Plain attire.

Suzy did nothing at all to conceal her rebellion. How far did word spread?

Nellie feared that this, coupled with Dat's announcement at the dinner table, was merely the beginning of their sorrows. "So the rumors were true," she said to herself.

Do I dare admit this to Caleb?

Nellie couldn't help but think the life Suzy had lived—as well as the one Dat seemed determined to live—could doom her chances with her beau.

Betsy had never dreamed she would do such a thing as violate the privacy of a daughter's bedroom. Yet she felt convinced this search for Suzy's diary was justifiable. Even so, she hadn't decided how she would explain the deed to Nellie Mae. In some strange way, Suzy's writings struck her as Nellie's rightful possession.

She had sensed something change in Nellie nearly overnight. Her daughter appeared terribly depressed, and it worried Betsy no end. She felt the tension in her neck and shoulders as she relived the heartbreaking sound of her Nellie-girl crying her eyes out.

Betsy stood at the threshold and scanned Nellie's room— the bed, the dresser, the large rag rug. *Am I strong enough for this? Do I really want to read Suzy's account of things?*

Betsy knew what to look for because she'd seen Suzy writing in her little book . . . her head tilted down close to the page, hand fisted around a stubby pencil. Oh, but the very memory triggered pain—an intense one at that. *Do I need to know whose influence our Suzy was under?*

She wondered where Nellie Mae might keep such a book of secrets . . . and why Nellie herself had felt the urge to learn more about Suzy's rebellion.

Going to sit on the bed quilt, Betsy touched the small table where Suzy had set the lantern at night. Betsy recalled the many times she herself had sat in this very spot, soothing Suzy's feverish brow with her hand or bringing a homemade chicken corn soup to either daughter when she took ill. Her heart felt a pang at the memory of Nellie Mae and Suzy sitting on the bed, dangling their short legs as they hugged each other, giggling over their little-girl secrets.

This room holds so many memories. She rose and went to the dresser, seeing an unfinished circle letter lying there. She picked up the small hand mirror and frowned into it, aware of new lines in her face—all the not-so-subtle changes created by the sadness around her mouth and eyes.

Setting the mirror down, she wanted more than anything to know what would have caused Nellie Mae to weep here, in this room.

Both Nellie and I want answers, evidently, she thought. Even Reuben had so many unanswered questions; he just hadn't voiced them, at least not to her.

Betsy walked back to the bed and gently lifted both pillows, glancing beneath them. Moaning softly without meaning to, she worried she might be walking over Nellie Mae's still raw emotions if she pressed forward. It wasn't like her to trample on the trust of her daughters. Nellie might be horrified to know her mamma was snooping about while she was out closing up the bakery shop for the day.

Such a hardworking girl she is.

Fluffing the pillows and smoothing the coverlet quilt, Betsy eyed the bedside table yet again. *Would Nellie bother to hide the diary? Or simply keep it nearby?*

When she opened the drawer of the small table, the air went out of her for a moment. Slowly she reached for it, lifting Suzy's journal to her lips and pressing it there for ever so long, like clasping a gem to her heart.

It was enough to merely feel the book in her hands, against her cheek. "Oh, Suzy, I wish I might've helped keep you innocent. . . ."

She placed the diary back in the drawer. She was not as upset with herself for intruding on Nellie's special bond with her sister as she was sorrowful for a life lost for all eternity.

Lingering there, her eyes fixed on the diary, Betsy decided not to read a single page unless Nellie offered it. *Otherwise, I might lose her, as well.*

Caleb lifted the reins and clicked his tongue. *Four months ago this week, Suzy Fisher drowned,* he thought. *How's Nellie Mae taking the terrible anniversary?*

The hay wagon jolted forward, and he remembered precisely where he'd stood in the tobacco-drying barn when the astonishing news had reached his ears. *A group of carefree Englischers drove to the lake at Marsh Creek State Park for a day of fun. None was wearing a life jacket. One Amish girl drowned.* . . .

For days he'd walked in circles, concerned for the girl who'd stolen his heart in a single glance, realizing his pursuit of her would have to be pushed back. He'd thought at the time that it didn't matter what you'd done up till the point of your death—when your number was up, that was that.

Yet deep inside, where he squelched the more difficult questions, Suzy's death was to him like a night without a single star. Venus snuffed out, never to shine like the white jewel it was.

His gaze roamed over the alfalfa field. He had always enjoyed the way the breeze rippled through it in waves. All the many acres surrounding him called to his sense of beauty . . . and pride. To think this fine spread would someday be his. He was ready to claim his inheritance, even though it would be yet another year before he could do so, Nellie Mae by his side. Daed had said at breakfast that any day now they'd sit down and talk over the plan for the farm's transition to Caleb. He couldn't imagine being more grateful for the gift that was to be his. For this reason alone, he would always defer to his father, including him in the day-to-day management of the farm. Daed and Mamm would be well cared for. He'd see to that.

He chuckled outright. His hope of writing Nellie Mae a letter had not been acted on as the busy week wore on. No time had surfaced to sit privately in the kitchen, what with Mamm and his sisters hovering. Besides, he saw more wisdom in directly telling Nellie Mae the things in his heart.

Jah, all the things . . .

He looked forward to the day when he could make her his bride . . . but first things first; he had yet to pinpoint the location of her bedroom window, for when the big day arrived. Of course he could learn it by merely waiting around after letting Nellie out by the road tomorrow, following the hog-butchering frolic—watch to see which window lit up. *A good plan.*

Caleb thought how ridiculous he must look out here in the middle of the field with the mule team and a big grin on his face.

Daed will think I'm a man in love . . . or a fool.

————

Reuben rode fast after an early dinner Saturday, passing Ephram's place as he headed toward his firstborn sons. Jeremiah and Thomas would hear from him today about God's plan for man's salvation, as stated in the Good Book.

Although he had been praying for this encounter for a while, he asked now for divine wisdom and the right words to say.

Thomas and Jeremiah were the best starting place among his grown children, because if he could persuade them to get involved in Bible study, they would more than likely encourage their younger brothers to follow in their footsteps.

Reuben's heart sang with praises as he rode toward the sunset, making his way along Beaver Dam Road, then turning south on Plank Road. God had already worked a miracle by turning Betsy's heart toward Him so swiftly—Manny's, too. He noted a few dozen feathered stragglers perched high on a telephone wire. When all was said and done, how many of the People would heed Preacher Manny and pursue saving grace? He couldn't help but wonder how he'd feel if he and Cousin Jonathan were the only ones sticking their necks out; he was mighty thankful they had Manny to look to for direction.

He thought of Bishop Joseph, concerned about his older brother's health. Would he respond soon to his and Manny's request? Perhaps having a minister conducting the studies would somehow suffice. He could only hope for a yea.

All in God's hands . . .

Spotting his sons' big farmhouse on the left, he slowed the horse, seeing his eldest sons putting away the sickle-bar hay mower. So they'd been making hay today, too. *The apple doesn't fall far from the tree.*

Though eager to share those things Reuben wished he'd known years ago, he took his time turning into the drive. He marveled at the brilliant orange, gold, and white mums in the flower beds in front of the porch and running alongside the house; nearly the same color arrangement as Betsy's own flower garden. Esther and Fannie—Thomas's and Jeremiah's wives—were known to work well together, painstakingly planning the color scheme. A laughing good time they always had, especially with their daughters alongside.

O Lord, help us keep our closeness as a family in spite of the upheaval ahead.

"That wasn't so bad, now, was it, Nellie?" asked Caleb as they rode away from the hog butchering.

Nellie had to admit she'd enjoyed herself, thanks in no small part to Rhoda. Her eldest sister had chosen to work alongside her, mixing seasonings into the sausage, while Nan spent her time with Rebekah Yoder, helping grind the meat.

For a change, Rhoda didn't seem like a stranger, thought Nellie, happy for some time with her.

She leaned close to Caleb presently, her hand in his. "Thank goodness for that good, stiff breeze . . . it cleared out the awful smell."

"You and your smells."

"Must run in the family," she said, thinking of Suzy's famously sensitive nose—quick to savor a lovely fragrance, swift to wrinkle at a foul one.

"Aw, love, maybe that's partly why you enjoy bakin' so much—all the wonderful-gut scents."

Love? Her heart sped up. *Dat calls Mamma that!*

He let go of her hand and slipped his arm around her. "Come here closer."

"Closer?" A giggle burst out. "That's just about impossible, Caleb."

He kissed her cheek. "Well, now, it won't have to be like this forever."

He's thinking of marriage, surely he is!

He leaned his head on top of hers. "You're my girl, Nellie Mae. Don't forget."

She sighed, fully content to be riding into the twilight with him. She didn't want to ruin the special moment, but she felt she ought to be forthright about the things happening with her parents, and the sooner the better. *Better he doesn't hear more tittle-tattle 'bout our family from the grapevine.*

"Um, Caleb, mind if we talk frankly?"

"Why sure. What's on your mind?"

She took a breath for courage, hoping what she had to say wouldn't create a wedge between them.

"My father's taken a shinin' . . . well, to studying." That was all she could get out at first.

"You had me uneasy there for a minute. I thought you were goin' to bring up all the tractor talk." He turned to look at her.

"Jah, but Dat has no interest in goin' fancy. What he's mighty interested in is the Good Book." She continued, her heart in her throat. "He's waitin' on word from Uncle Bishop to see if he and Preacher Manny can hold meetings on the no-Preaching Sundays."

"What for?"

"Bible study."

Caleb fell silent.

He's displeased. She could almost hear the beating of her own anxious heart in the quiet.

"I've heard of Amish in other districts wanting this," he said at last. "But I can't imagine our bishop allowing it. It's not in keeping with the Old Ways."

"Seems so." She sighed sadly. "What do you think will come of this, Caleb?"

He squeezed her hand. "No matter what, you and I won't be affected by it. Will we?"

She loved Caleb and wanted to say it right then, but now wasn't the time. Such a profession of devotion must come from him first. "I hope not," she said softly.

Truth was, Dat's determination to have the entire family follow his beliefs could pose a problem. She dearly hoped Caleb's and her relationship would not suffer as a result.

CHAPTER 27

This was a day of wonders, the way Reuben saw it. Not only had his twins eagerly joined ranks with him, but James and Benjamin, as well—his youngest son a bit more hesitant—agreed to unite in learning Scripture at the meetings Preacher Manny planned. They'd also voiced keen interest in tractors and electricity, but Reuben hoped that was not the motivation for his four sons' ready agreement. Still, he was anything but ignorant.

It was Ephram who would have to see the light, in good time, he told himself as he made his way toward his father's place. Ephram had refused to hear him out, as Reuben had supposed he might; his son had not wanted to make any trouble with the bishop. Reuben could only pray that his father would not greet this unexpected news the selfsame way. For certain, he felt as nervous as a young boy just now.

Mamm ushered him into the front room, where Daed was reading *The Budget*. Reuben sat down across from him, praying silently for wisdom.

"How's Betsy?" asked Daed right off.

Reuben guessed his reason for asking. "Well, she's surely missin' Suzy yet." He paused. "We all are."

"'Tis God's doin', and we must accept it as His plan." Daed hung his head for a moment. "Mighty hard to understand why she'd go off with worldly folk, though."

"Daed . . ." Reuben didn't want to get his father worked up before he'd even begun. "I came to talk 'bout other things."

"Oh?"

Reuben leaned forward. "I want you to hear this from me . . . from your son who loves you and respects all you've done for me." He paused briefly. "You and Mamm, well, you brought me up in the fear of the Lord God. I appreciate that. But there's more to God's ways."

"What're ya sayin', son?"

He stopped, weighing the moment, then continued. "I'm a believer, Daed—saved by the blood of the Lord Jesus Christ."

Daed rose swiftly, his face nearly ashen. "*Nee*—no, Reuben! This is the last thing I want to be hearin' from you." He walked away, stopping to stare out the window, his back to Reuben.

"Hear me out, Daed. I want to explain what I've learned . . . all that God is teachin' me through Scripture." Reuben went to his father and placed a hand on his shoulder.

"Get out of my sight!" Daed spun around, frowning. A glint of a tear was in his eye. "Be gone!"

Reuben did not want to risk upsetting him further, though he would have welcomed a conversation without such turmoil on Daed's part.

How did I expect him to respond? Reuben wondered, stopping to kiss his trembling, bewildered mother on the cheek before heading out the back door.

Long after supper and spoken evening prayers, Reuben sat with Betsy in their bedroom. "Ephram flat-out rejected the idea of attendin' any Bible study, just as I supposed," he told her. "Said he didn't want to make trouble with the bishop, which is understandable."

"That one has always clung to the Old Ways . . . much like our Nellie Mae seems to be doin'. She's come right out and said she's opposed to anything involving change," Betsy remarked.

"I pray she'll come around in time," Reuben said, glad for this moment with Betsy. He needed her comforting presence after such a day. "At least Nan's showing some interest, but Rhoda's a harder one to read. Do ya think she'll embrace the gospel?"

Betsy shrugged. "Still findin' her bearings, I daresay," she said.

"Seems so." He reached for her hand. "Let's pray for the Lord to lead all our dear ones to Him."

She nodded, tears welling up. "Jah, pray I will."

Reuben held her hand, looking down at their intertwined fingers. "We've been through some awful hard things, love." He paused, attempting to stay composed. "I hate to say it, but the days and months ahead could be ever so trying."

Betsy's eyes filled with tears. "Don't know how I'll manage. Yet somehow . . ." She tightened her lips. "Jah, somehow we will."

"We've placed our trust in our Savior . . . and I'll do everything I can to spare you more pain." Reuben didn't go into what he foresaw in the near future, but just the same, he sensed it was coming. Like a bolt out of the sky, lightning would strike and divide the People smack down the middle.

The first sign of serious trouble came in the form of a reply letter from Bishop Joseph the Tuesday nearly two weeks after Reuben had sent his request. It seemed his brother's health had taken a swift turn for the better, and he and Anna were heading home right quick. *Just so you know—Preacher Manny, too—it cannot be God's will for any of you to come together to study that way, preacher or no preacher,* the bishop wrote. *Folk who do don't stay Amish. I've seen it time and again. . . .*

Reuben's courage wavered briefly as he read the short and pointed note. So that was that: His brother had denied them. Reuben had expected as much, but there had remained a small spark of hope.

Reuben knew precisely what would happen if he and Manny forged ahead, disregarding the bishop's wishes. Reuben had heard of families elsewhere who had held Bible studies and were found out, never having asked permission. Eventually, if they refused to "come under" the Ordnung, a six-week probationary shun was slapped on them. If that didn't teach them, then they were shunned for life. The only way to get back into the church and the brethren's good graces was to repent and say you were back on the straight and narrow.

The Gospel was divisive; no questioning that. In some cases in Scripture, following God severed offspring from parents, and spouses from each other. Abram of old, for one, had followed the Lord God out of his father's house and country, forever away from his kindred.

Am I willing to obey God at any cost?

Forcing air out of the side of his mouth, he decided that the minute his hay was raked for bailing, he would go and talk things over with Preacher Manny, who was also in danger of being ousted if he crossed this line.

Yet to stand still is to go backward, Reuben realized.

———

Nellie exercised patience at the cash register while their English neighbors, Mrs. Landis and her daughter, Joy, chattered on and on right at closing time. Tired from being on her feet, Nellie was anxious to sit at Mamma's supper table and enjoy the juicy ham she knew was roasting.

Mrs. Landis swept back a strand of raven-black hair—noticeably dyed—into her neatly flipped shoulder-length hairdo. "Joy tells me her cousin Darlene knew your sister Suzy from school," the woman said, startling Nellie Mae. "Quite well, in fact."

"Oh?" Nellie's throat pinched up. *What does she know?*

The woman's daughter blushed quickly and shook her head. "Mom, *please* don't bring that up."

That silenced Mrs. Landis, and after the two of them had left the shop, Nellie pondered what could have been on Joy's mind. But her curiosity was not enough to make her crack open Suzy's diary again. No, she would not open *that* wound tonight. She was much too tired to contemplate the further transgressions of her sister. Was her lifelessness, even melancholy, due to what she'd discovered through Suzy's words, or was she coming down with something? She had been known to absorb tension in a way that made her ill. *Come to think of it, is that what happened to Uncle Bishop?*

What on earth will he think when he finally returns? she wondered, what with Dat—a stalwart church member—making prideful talk of being "saved." What would their bishop do about that?

Going to the shop door, she stood on her tiptoes and turned the Open sign around to Closed.

Oh, how she wished she could take comfort in Rosanna's company. She wondered how things were for her friend as she readied her household for the coming babies. *Won't she have fun with two to care for!*

Nellie thought ahead to what it might be like to hold a baby of her own . . . hers and Caleb's. She smiled in spite of herself. She and her beau planned to ride over to the millstream this coming Sunday afternoon in broad daylight—Caleb's suggestion.

He's getting mighty bold. Nellie laughed softly, pulling the door shut before heading toward the house.

Supper was set out—pork chops, fried potatoes and onions, and buttered lima beans, with a small dish of chow-chow. Rosanna had taken great care to prepare a fine hot meal for her husband.

Before they could begin eating, though, she quickly showed Elias the matching reversible cradle quilts she had been making for the babies. One side featured a pattern in pastel pinks and green, the other one in blue and lavender. "That way if we have two boys, or two girls, or one of each, we'll be just fine," she said, putting them away before she sat down.

Elias frowned at the head of the table. "Two girls, you say?"

She nodded, hoping her husband wasn't opposed to the idea of daughters.

"These are to be our firstborn, Rosanna."

"Jah."

"For pity's sake, do we want girls, really . . . if we have a say-so?" His frown grew deeper.

"Well, I figure if we can't ever have any babies of our own, then why on earth not take what we're given? Besides, the more the better." There—she'd said at last what she had been wanting to say for days.

Elias rose abruptly. "Why not wait and decide when your cousins' babies are born? See what they turn out to be."

"Wait till they're born? But, Elias—"

"No, you ain't listenin'." He stood with both hands on the back of the chair. "I aim to have a son. At least one."

She didn't understand what was bothering him so. Surely the possibility of their raising two girls wasn't all there was to it.

He marched to the back of the house, where she heard him muttering out in the summer porch. She knew better than to go to him. He obviously was trying to hold his peace about something. Elias was not a man who would usually quibble, and initially he had appeared as grateful as she for Kate's offer—maybe even more so. But the past few weeks had been a trial for him.

Was it the slim harvest? Even with less of a hay crop to bring in than usual, he was beyond tired. They all were, working from sunup to sundown.

Lord, won't you bless my husband . . . give him peace?

She didn't know what had come over her, thinking a prayer like that. Maybe she'd secretly visited Jonathan Fisher's place one time too many. Dear shunned Linda was a fountain of information on canning pureed food for babies, though Rosanna'd never once let it be known that all the questions she was asking were for herself.

So much to learn . . . and Linda is ever so prayerful.

As far as she knew, Cousin Kate had not yet told anyone that she planned to give her babies away. *How will the womenfolk react, especially with twins? Everybody loves two little ones in a baby buggy, side by side.*

Sighing, Rosanna ate the delicious meal alone, not happy about the idea of sitting here while Elias fumed. *Will he settle down tonight long enough to eat supper?*

Surely his hearty appetite would bring him back to the table.

Jah, he'll return in a few minutes. Then, when he's filled up, he'll tell me what's really troubling him.

———

Caleb headed toward the barn to check on the bedding straw for the animals, particularly for the new calf. He whistled a tune he'd heard in town, a snappy melody he'd liked immediately. His Mennonite cousin Christian Yoder had told him it was a "jingle" often used on radio stations right before the news or a sports report. Of course, not having been around radios much, Caleb wasn't aware of such things. The tunes Cousin Christian liked to whistle were as foreign to Caleb as the worldly jingle he found himself whistling repeatedly tonight.

The young calf seemed to like the sound as Caleb moved into the pen with her and petted her soft coat. He gave her more straw, pushing it around to even it out, and was getting ready to return to the house when he heard his father talking to someone up in the upper level of the two-story barn.

Not one to eavesdrop, he almost headed out of the barn, but the topic of conversation swayed him. A man whose voice Caleb could not place was talking about someone who'd served out his conscientious objector status in Civilian Public Service years before. While doing so, the young man had been introduced to lively prayer meetings and Bible studies. "He even started watchin' television," the man said, sounding indignant. "Well, if this here fella didn't start second-guessin' the absence of a tractor in his father's fields and the lack of electricity flowing through the house, mind you."

"I've heard similar tales," Caleb's father replied. "Too much mixing with Englischers 'most always comes to a bad end."

"No doubt of that, David. And same thing can happen when the youth start attendin' gatherings where the Good Book's discussed every which way. A march starts toward this enticing new path—a new order, some call it—and you hear every excuse under the sun for changing the Old Ways. 'Tis harder to turn your back on 'thus saith the Lord' than on 'thus saith the church,' some say. You just watch, David, if it don't come to that here . . . that tabernacle nearby's invitin' trouble."

Caleb realized he was holding his breath. He slowly exhaled, waiting to hear what Daed might say. "We were all young once, so I can't be talkin' against the youth. But to go against the Ordnung as a baptized church member? There's just no excuse for crossin' *that* line."

"I say it's Uncle Sam's fault all this got started," the unfamiliar man replied. "Far as I can tell, trouble reared up when he forced our hand and made us serve our time, even though we were conscientious objectors."

"Jah, look where that got us." Daed huffed loudly, and Caleb darted out of the barn while he had his chance. He felt terribly guilty for listening in as he had, but with Nellie Mae's family stepping so close to this same dangerous edge, he was anxious to know all he could.

CHAPTER 28

———

Sweet breads and anything made with pumpkin were the most-requested items at Nellie's Simple Sweets now that they were into deep October. The demand for such goodies moist with pumpkin always rose near Halloween, though Nellie Mae never cared to acknowledge the day. While the practice of trick-or-treating mystified her, Nellie found the idea of dressing in costume to be most curious—she especially couldn't picture grown-ups dressing like storybook characters or favorite animals the way neighbor Diana Cooper described.

She expected the market for harvest-time desserts to last well into November and the start of the wedding season. Keeping up with the ever-increasing orders was so much of a chore for both Nellie and Nan that Mamma sometimes helped with the baking. Nellie could scarcely keep count of the quantity of pumpkin whoopee pies she was making between her dates with Caleb. They aimed to see each other every few days now that the silos were full.

Twice this week, Caleb had surprised her with thoughtful notes, none marked with a return address. Unable to wait until Sunday afternoon after all, Caleb had taken her driving last night to their spot near the picturesque stone mill.

There they had huddled against the cold on the wrought-iron bench, sitting so close they could have squeezed into Caleb's heavy woolen coat if they'd tried. They had wandered up and down the creek after a time, walking over to the mill-race and back, talking and trying to keep warm by moving alongside its gurgling waters.

Nellie had noticed how Caleb reached for her hand almost absentmindedly. *Like I'm a comfortable part of him somehow.*

There had been moments during last night's conversation, though, when Caleb had seemed tentative, as if holding back something important, although she wouldn't think of pressing him. He would tell her when he was ready, and until then she must simply swallow her fears that it concerned her parents, who were planning an upcoming meeting at Preacher Manny's . . . minus the blessing of Uncle Bishop. Might Caleb have heard of that?

She did not understand her parents' decision, but it was not her place to question. Dat and Mamma had made their promise to the church and to the Lord God long ago—who was *she* to remind them? According to Caleb himself, as well as her customers in the bakery shop, there were plenty of people who were still holding firm to tradition.

Here lately, she was glad she hadn't been born a boy and therefore more privy to the bishop's fury as his will clashed with those pushing for change. She'd heard Dat and Preacher Manny describe it in just that way as they talked openly yesterday morning while drinking coffee in Mamma's kitchen. They had not pretended to talk of other things when Nellie came to fetch a batch of pumpkin sticky buns for Mrs. Kraybill.

"*Listen, Manny, the lines have been drawn and erased and redrawn near endless times over the years,*" Dat had let fly from his lips. "*Don't you see the contradictions?*"

Preacher Manny had wholeheartedly agreed, which was evidently part of the reason the two of them remained so determined to begin their Bible-study meetings, starting on this next no-Preaching Sunday. To Nellie the whole thing sounded dangerously as though they were not only questioning the Ordnung but outright refusing to obey the bishop, too.

Setting themselves up as God . . .

Nellie shivered and glanced around the shop, taking inventory of her bakery items. Being out all hours last night had sapped her energy today for sure . . . though she wouldn't have minded the weariness if things were more settled at home. She couldn't begin to fathom why Dat and Preacher Manny would want to willfully go against the grain, so to speak.

———

Elias held Rosanna in his arms on this first no-Preaching Sunday in November, and as they relaxed, waiting for the morning sunrise, he spoke. "It's not so important that we get boys or girls or one of each, dear," he said. "Tell ya the truth, I'm still hopin' we'll have some of our own."

She cherished his nearness, relieved to know at last what had been troubling him. "Jah, doctors aren't always right . . . and we're still young, too."

"Lots of years ahead to keep tryin' for a little woodchopper." He stroked her long, thick hair. "Was it almost four years ago we got hitched?"

"I'm not a bit sorry for not waitin' longer, are you?"

He kissed her again, lingering this time. "Who'd be sorry to have such a pretty wife?"

She smiled. Elias had a way of saying the right things at the right time. "Well, maybe, Lord willin', we'll have us a baby someday. But won't it be fun having two wee ones here, right quick? Special delivery in a way."

"Not soon enough for you, that's for sure." Elias grinned in the dim light.

"Well, since twins tend to come early, it's a good thing we're all ready with the cradles and whatnot."

He leaned up on his elbow, looking down at her with adoring eyes. "We'll fill this old house with lots of little ones, jah?"

She hoped so, partly to please Elias. Truth be known, she would rather have a baby in her arms than most anything. But for now, Elias was cradling her in his, drawing her ever so near. His lips found hers again, and Rosanna was heedless to the dawn as it crept under the window shade and spilled light over their bed quilt. Not even the rooster's crowing succeeded in getting the two of them to rise and shine.

With a sense of joy mixed with trepidation, Reuben rode up with Betsy to Preacher Manny's farmhouse. Bishop Joseph had returned from Iowa mighty upset, far beyond the proverbial righteous indignation. Now Manny was under a watch for the Bann by his own ministerial brethren. They had warned him that he would be brought before the membership if he did not cease his activities.

But Manny had made his stand—he was immovable. To some extent it was Manny's doggedness to "push forward with God's calling" that had brought them here today.

Reuben paused at the back stoop with his Bible. "O Lord, go before us," he whispered, noticing seven buggies parked off to the side.

"The People are hungry, looks like to me," Betsy said softly as they made their way into the preacher's roomy kitchen.

By now a dozen or so folk were seated on folding chairs in the next room, rather than the long wooden benches common to Preaching services. Many had their Bibles open on their laps, ready for Preacher Manny to begin. Among them were Reuben's own four sons, Ephram being the only one missing.

Spotting his cousin in the corner of the kitchen, Reuben hurried to his side. "Manny, are you ready?"

The preacher's eyes were bloodshot. "I was up most of the night prayin'," Manny said, wearing his best white shirt and black broadfall trousers. "Will you offer a few words before I say what the Lord has put on my heart?"

Reuben flinched. "You want me to speak?" He shook his head. "I'm no preacher, mind you."

Manny gripped his arm. "I said nothing about preachin', Reuben. Just talk some about what God's been showing you in His Word."

"Well, I s'pose . . ."

Manny leaned closer. "Nothin' at all hard about it. The power that raised up God's Son from the dead lives right there in you." Manny pointed to Reuben's heart. "Remember that."

Straightaway Reuben breathed easier. Putting it that way, sure, he could tell the group how God was working in him. Standing in the threshold between the kitchen and the large sitting room, he recognized several more of his own kin, including Cousin Jonathan and his wife, Linda. These hearty souls were his brothers and sisters in the family of God.

I can do this, he decided. *With the Lord's help.*

Preacher Manny stood before them, cheerfully welcoming each person. Then he bowed his head for a prayer of blessing, encouraging all of them to open their hearts "to the tender witness of the Father's presence in our midst."

This was a far cry from what they were accustomed to hearing in prayer of a Sunday, and for this wonderful-good start to the meeting, Reuben was thankful. He and Betsy sat close to the front, in one accord, sharing the Good Book when Manny read from the verses that had transformed his life in the past weeks. The reading was powerful to Reuben, as well as to others, some of whom were sniffling. Tears spilled down his own Betsy's cheeks. *They're starving for this, just as I am,* Reuben observed, his heart filling at the very thought.

CHAPTER 29

On the day before they were to move Reuben's parents into the Dawdi Haus next door, Betsy had an unexpected visitor.

Heavy snow had fallen in the night, a good six inches by the looks of it. A gray November haze sagged over dormant fields like a dark blanket, making it difficult to see.

Betsy was both surprised and concerned when she heard a horse neighing in the lane. She hurried out to see Reuben's mother making her way toward the back door. "Well, hullo. What brings you on such a Wednesday?" asked Betsy.

Hannah leaned on the crook of her cane, all bundled up in her heaviest woolen coat. *"Wie geht's?"*

Betsy hurried down the shoveled walkway and took Hannah's arm to lead the dear woman up the steps and into the house. "You want something hot to drink?" she asked.

"That'd warm me up a bit, jah."

"You came all this way by yourself?"

"Me, myself, and the horse." Hannah smiled momentarily as she lowered herself into Reuben's rocker with a groan.

Betsy couldn't help wondering why she'd risk traveling alone. "How were the roads?"

"Just terrible." Suddenly Hannah's eyes were bright with tears. "Ach, Betsy, we best be talkin'."

The poor woman looked so completely distraught, Betsy assumed someone had died.

On edge now, she pulled one of the chairs away from the table and settled in beside Hannah. "What is it, Mamm?" She reached out to touch her arm.

"Oh, Betsy, word has it that you and Reuben . . ." Hannah stopped, hanging her head. Her shoulders trembled. "Oh, goodness me."

"What 'bout Reuben and me?"

Hannah slowly raised her head. "Ain't you with that bunch who's plannin' to jump the fence? Over there at Preacher Manny's?"

Betsy said, "Now, Mamma, we're all sincere . . . all of us growin' in the Lord together."

"You'll grow right out of the Amish, then . . ." Hannah lowered her gaze, shaking her head. She began to rock in the chair. "Movin' far away from the church of your baptism. It's just as Noah said."

"Oh, Mamm, don't be sad. I've never felt so happy . . . truly."

Hannah reached into her dress sleeve and pulled out a folded hankie, dabbing her eyes. "You'll be shunned if this keeps up."

Betsy knew as much. She and Reuben were waiting for the deacon to come knocking any day with a warning.

"I hate to say it, but I doubt we'll be movin' in here with you and Reuben after all."

All the plans they'd made—everything was set in motion to bring Noah and Hannah under the covering of this house. "No . . . no, yous mustn't change your mind on that."

"Ain't for me to say." Hannah wept openly. "And you neither."

Getting up, Betsy went to boil some water, having forgotten to put the kettle on. *Well, we ain't shunned yet!*

"Our attending Preacher Manny's meeting last Sunday doesn't have to affect you and Noah." Betsy realized she was pleading. Hannah was as stubborn as Reuben and his brothers had always been. Being a saved man hadn't changed Reuben's tenacity, and she knew what he'd say about his mother's visit.

When the teakettle whistled, she poured the boiling water into her pretty yellow teapot for brewing. Then she went to sit again with Hannah. "It would be wonderful-good if you came to hear what we're learnin'," Betsy suggested. "I never thought I'd be sayin' such a thing, but there's so much that's been . . . well, kept from us, it seems." There. She'd said right out what was on her mind.

"We'll be doin' no such a thing," Hannah said, her eyes flashing. "And looks to me like we're gettin' *naryets*— nowhere—on this."

"Reuben said believin' was likely to bring a separation"— and here she touched her heart—"but I was ever so hopeful . . ." She couldn't finish, lest she weep.

Hannah rocked harder in the chair, gripping both of its arms, her lips pursed. "Let's say no more on this for now. I'll have that tea, Betsy."

She rose and went to pour the water, putting a little extra sugar in Hannah's cup for good measure. Then she took the matching teacup and saucer to her, gently placing them in her wrinkled hands. "Here you are, Mamm."

Hannah accepted it, had herself a sip, and blinked her eyes at Betsy. "Speaking of partings, have you heard what Kate Beiler's plannin' to do?"

Betsy shook her head. She found it interesting that Hannah had so quickly abandoned her dispute. "What 'bout Kate?"

"The strangest thing, really." Hannah frowned deeply. "She's going to give her babies to Elias and Rosanna, but it's all hush-hush."

Betsy was stunned and almost asked Hannah if she was sure . . . if she wasn't mixed-up, as she sometimes could be.

"Seems your Nellie Mae has known of this for some time. Rosanna told her, as I understand it from Kate's midwife, Ruth Glick."

My girls and their secrets . . .

"Nellie hasn't said a word."

"Well, Ruth thinks the twins will be comin' sooner than was first thought."

Dear, dear Rosanna, keeping wee ones all bundled up in this cold. "Guess Rosanna will be ever so happy. Sure has had a time of it, jah?"

Hannah nodded, drinking some more tea before answering. "I daresay Elias will be sleepin' in the spare room some."

To this both women smiled.

"Poor man has no idea what he's in for," Hannah stated flatly.

"Do you know why on earth Kate would give her babies away like this?"

"Kate loves her cousin is all I know. Like I said, it's a secret . . . not even Rachel knows."

"Kate's own mamma doesn't?" Betsy shook her head. "That's mighty surprisin', ain't so? Best we be keepin' word to ourselves, then." Betsy didn't want to think of Rachel's possibly hearing such news from someone other than Kate.

Truly, the midwife should know better than to be speaking of it to others.

Hannah nodded. "When the news is out, some will take it in stride; others will be flabbergasted." Hannah wiped her eyes with her hankie again. "I say it's just the nicest thing, truth be told. Rosanna's getting her heart's desire, two wee, perty babes."

Betsy had to agree with pretty, because every one of Kate's brood was just that—as fine-looking as any children she'd ever seen, including her own. "Such a generous thing to do, jah?"

Hannah drank the rest of her tea, pausing to look over her cup at Betsy. "Wonder if the babies will know who their real parents are." Her hand trembled.

"That'd be a good thing, given they're all cousins."

But Hannah thought differently. "Those poor young'uns wouldn't know who to mind, though, would they?"

Betsy hadn't thought of that. She couldn't imagine what Rosanna might face if that were so. "I hope all goes well, but I could never do what Kate's doin'. And I'd be nearly beside myself if any of my children were to hand off my grandchildren to someone else!"

Hannah nodded slowly, finally agreeing with something Betsy had said. They talked about less contentious things for a while—the next quilting bee and how many weddings were coming up this week.

"Would you like a quick visit with Nan and Nellie Mae?" Betsy looked out the window. Unless someone had arrived on foot, there didn't appear to be a single customer at the bakery shop.

"Sure I would." Hannah brightened significantly.

"I'll go and call them."

Unexpectedly, Hannah remarked, "If her sisters don't mean to be on hand, your Nellie's goin' to look mighty lonesome during Preachin' next Sunday, I daresay."

At the comment Betsy stopped in her tracks as she was heading out to get her shawl. Turning to stare at Hannah, she wondered why she'd brought this up. "Why would ya say this, Mamm?"

Hannah ignored the question. "I daresay sensible Nellie Mae's goin' to marry herself an Old Order fella, and you and Reuben won't even be welcome at the wedding."

Betsy had heard all she cared to. "Well, for goodness' sakes."

"Now you be thinkin' good and long 'bout this, Betsy. You and Reuben need to consider what you're givin' up." Hannah had scooted herself to the edge of the rocking chair. "You think on it real hard, ya hear?"

Betsy bit her tongue and hurried to get her wrap. Stepping into the cold, she realized she had been thoroughly reprimanded and humiliated by her mother-in-law. In the past she would have given the woman what for, but today she decided to offer the utmost kindness to Hannah and prayed to that end, making her way to the bakery shop.

Nellie saw Mamma approaching the bakery shop around the time she'd told Nan they ought to slip away to see why Mammi Fisher had come on such bad roads. Now here was Mamma hurrying into the shop door, her face redder than it ought to be from the short jaunt.

"Girls, your grandmother's eager to see you." Mamma put on a smile. "Go down and see her once."

Nan nearly ran for her shawl and out the door, but Nellie paused. "Why on earth . . . today of all miserable days?"

"For a visit." Betsy turned away.

"You're upset, ain't so?" Nellie went to her.

Mamma breathed visibly. "Your Dat said things like this would happen. I never dreamed . . ."

Nellie leaned her head against her mother's. "What did Mammi say?"

"She and Dawdi won't be movin' back here. We're as good as shunned."

Nellie struggled with the lump that threatened to close her throat. She felt frightened to think of such a thing happening to her parents . . . to their family as a whole, as would likely be the case. "Is there no stoppin' this?" she whispered.

Mamma shook her head, clearly trying to keep her composure. "Go visit with Mammi now."

Nellie nodded, willing to obey her mother on this account. But unbaptized though she was, she wouldn't think of abandoning the Old Ways—not for the world, nor for Dat's faith.

CHAPTER 30

Snow fell in thick, fluffy flakes as Nellie Mae closed up the bakery shop that Wednesday. She had a hankering for a walk, and since she'd already enjoyed a short visit with Mammi Fisher earlier, she bypassed the house and headed toward the road for a breather, ready for some time alone. She could see through the window that Mamma and Mammi still looked to be hashing things out in the kitchen.

Mamma's all fired up, she thought, taking in the sight of waning maples outlined against the frosty curtain of snowflakes. *Dawdi and Mammi refuse to move here. If that don't beat all!*

Nellie pulled her shawl more tightly around her, against the chilling air. She wondered how many folk would be affected by the commotion in their midst. How far would the disagreement over the rules of the Ordnung spread?

Putting that out of her mind, she breathed in the refreshing frostiness of the late afternoon, watching the heavy snow and remembering the many times she and Suzy had caught snowflakes on their tongues. Such wonderful-gut growing-up years.

The account of Suzy's slide into sin still gnawed at Nellie, keeping her awake at night. She hadn't decided whether to bury the diary again or completely destroy it, but she was going to do something. She couldn't risk anyone else in their family reading about Suzy's disgraceful behavior.

Mrs. Landis's comment about Joy's cousin Darlene and Suzy came back to her just then, haunting her.

Suzy's past is nobody's worry now. Even so, it was dreadful to know others remained all too aware of her younger sister's wicked behavior.

She forced her thoughts back to Mammi Fisher and her grandparents' sudden decision not to live here. Had Dawdi sent her to confront Mamma?

Nellie pushed through the snow, moving faster as her head cleared. She had not heard yet this week from Caleb, even though he had written three letters to her last week. The weather being this cold, they hadn't seen each other for seven days, despite their original plan to go to the millstream together last no-Preaching Sunday. She missed him, wondering when their special night might come. When would they talk quietly in her room while sitting on the little loveseat? Cousin Jonathan's father and brother were well-known in the area for upholstering these beautiful pieces of courting furniture with their delicate oak arms and legs.

Smiling momentarily, she wondered what she would have done if Caleb's flashlight had shone on her window while Suzy was still alive and sleeping soundly in the room. She supposed she might have asked her sister to sleep in the spare room for that particular night. The way she'd heard it from Maryann and her other sisters-in-law, most girls could sense when their beau intended to propose.

Caleb loves me. What's keeping him from asking me to be his bride?

She'd had fears that Caleb was upset at what she'd told him about Dat's keen interest in the Good Book. More than likely, he knew of her parents' connections to Preacher Manny by now. It seemed nearly everyone was aware who had attended the meeting last Sunday.

And who hadn't.

Lately she felt nearly frayed, loving Caleb yet wanting to obey her father in his leanings, as she'd been taught to do. Rhoda and Nan were planning to join their parents and older brothers at Preacher Manny's house come this Sunday. A bold and foolhardy move, holding a meeting on the actual day of Preaching, of all things!

As for Nellie, she planned to walk alone to Preaching service, where she assumed Uncle Bishop would give the main sermon—his first since returning.

What will Caleb's family think if I show up by myself?

Even though courtship was usually to be kept confidential until the planned marriage was announced, Nellie was fairly sure that at least Rebekah had an inkling Caleb was seeing her. That girl didn't seem to be one to miss anything.

Up ahead the roof of a tobacco drying barn glistened thanks to an ample layer of snow, and she was struck by how picturesque it was, though she must have seen the same barn hundreds of times.

She continued walking briskly, the dense cold penetrating her bones. When she sighed, her breath nearly froze in midair, and she wished she'd worn a scarf to wrap around her face.

A good half mile later, she spotted Rhoda's distinct silhouette coming up the road's shoulder. She called "hullo," glad she'd stumbled upon her. Even though they lived in the same house, recently she'd scarcely spoken two words to her oldest sister. "Hullo!" she called again.

"Nellie Mae . . . where're ya goin'?" Rhoda crossed the road toward her.

"Just needed some fresh air."

"Well, you've picked icy air." Rhoda laughed.

Nellie smiled. "You must be workin' a lot these days."

Rhoda hugged herself, rubbing her mittened hands against her arms. "It seems best, well, to be away from the house as much as possible here lately."

"Are you really goin' to Preacher Manny's with Dat and Mamma?" asked Nellie.

"Only out of respect for Dat. Aren't you?" Rhoda asked.

"Can't."

"Must be you've got yourself a beau, then?"

Rhoda sounded like Nan had some weeks back. Nellie wouldn't be tricked, however; she would not say a word about Caleb.

"Well, do you?"

"Look, Rhoda, I don't ask you 'bout your friends or what you do away from home, do I?"

Rhoda shrugged. "I'd tell ya. Ask one question you're dyin' to know."

"All right." The air stung Nellie's lungs. "Why's it so important to work away from home . . . for Englischers, of all things?"

"That's two. I said only one," Rhoda snipped.

Looking at her, Nellie was shocked at Rhoda's sassy, even worldly response. She flinched, shying away. "Never mind, I guess."

"Aw, come now, Nellie Mae. What's wrong with you?"

With me? Nellie stared.

Rhoda sighed. "Dat's sure been ferhoodled lately."

"Ach, now you're bein' rude."

"Well, you and I know better than to say we're *saved*. I'm surprised Mamma's putting up with it, even sayin' she believes such things, too. What's happening to our family, anyway?"

"I s'pose I could ask you the same, Rhoda. Seems you're gone an awful lot."

Rhoda's eyes flashed her frustration. "I like workin' . . . making some money, is all."

"Savin' up for something?"

"Maybe so." Rhoda gazed at her. "But it ain't for what you might think."

Nellie Mae had no idea what she meant. "Well, I didn't mean to pry."

Rhoda huffed, walking past her. "I'll see you back at the house, sister," she called. "Don't stay out too long, or you'll catch a cold and miss goin' to your precious Preachin' come Sunday."

Nellie sputtered, her breath turning to ice crystals before her. *She's just dying for electric, no doubt.*

Walking faster, she felt terribly annoyed. "Who does she think she is, livin' a double standard?"

Just ahead a buggy was swiftly heading this way, through the shroud of snow and fog. "Hullo, Nellie Mae!" came a familiar voice.

She recognized the woman in the buggy as the midwife— Mary Glick's granddaughter Ruth. "You look to be in a hurry," Nellie called to her.

"Kate Beiler's wee ones are a-comin'!"

So soon? Turning, she watched the enclosed gray buggy as it sped by. "Ach, Rosanna. Today's your blessed day." She wished she might run and catch up with the carriage to ride straight to her dearest friend, but the horse had already galloped past.

Nellie stood there in amazement. "I hope Kate's—and Rosanna's—babies come healthy and ever so safe."

She rushed back to the house to divulge the startling news, glad she'd have something worth writing to Cousin Treva and the others in their circle letter. Out of breath, she spotted Mammi's buggy still parked near the back door.

Maybe I can borrow it to run over to Kate's, where Rosanna surely will be.

But when she arrived inside mere moments after Rhoda, Mamma was tending to Mammi Fisher, laying a wet cloth on her forehead and soothing her with her gentle hands and voice. Rhoda knelt at her feet.

"What's happened?" Nellie rushed to the rocking chair, shocked at how red and stricken Mammi's face was.

"Will one of yous ride for the doctor?" asked Mamma.

Nan brought another damp cloth. "What's wrong with Mammi?"

"She nearly collapsed," Mamma explained. "Limp as a dishrag now."

"I'll go for the doctor." Nellie turned and ran for the back door, throwing on her winter things. She was glad a horse and carriage were already hitched as she hopped inside and picked up the reins.

All the talk of shunning . . . no wonder Mammi's ill, she thought, feeling sick herself as she headed toward a completely different destination than Kate and Rosanna's tiny babies.

———

Having alerted the doctor, Nellie dashed back down the steps outside the doctor's cottagelike office, anxious to return to Mammi's side. She watched the doctor's car speed out from behind the building and turned to see Mrs. Landis coming up the walkway, her arm in a sling. "Hullo, neighbor," she said to the older woman. "What did you do to yourself?"

"Oh, it's so embarrassing, really. I fell on the sidewalk in front of my own house. I'm just heading in for a follow-up appointment," Mrs. Landis told her. Then she lowered her voice. "I'm so glad I ran into you, Nellie Mae. My daughter was terribly self-conscious at your shop, you must know."

"Oh?" Nellie fidgeted, eager to be off, but she was polite and listened.

"Fact is, your sister Suzy saved my niece Darlene's life. Suzy made all the difference to a girl who was sinking fast."

Saved her life? "Your niece . . . did she get into a bad crowd?" Nellie felt she was sticking her neck out by asking, but she had to know.

"Oh, mercy, yes! But Suzy kindly helped Darlene see the error of her ways."

Thunderstruck, Nellie had almost forgotten why she was standing there. "Ach . . . I'm awful sorry to have to run off, but my grandmother's ill. The doctor's already on his way over to our place."

"Well, I hope she's all right," Mrs. Landis offered. "I'll be sure to say a prayer for her."

Nellie thanked her and waved good-bye as she raced down the walkway. *My sister must've fooled Mrs. Landis but good. What's she mean by saying Suzy helped Darlene?*

Nellie was mighty sure—Mrs. Landis had the wrong Suzy.

CHAPTER 31

By the time Nellie arrived back at the house with the horse and buggy, the country doctor's car was already parked in the lane. Swiftly she tied the horse and hurried indoors, relieved to find Dawdi Fisher there, as well as Dat.

Dawdi Noah leaned over Mammi. "Poor, poor, dear," he said as he fanned her. All of them were hovering until the doctor shooed everyone into the front room so he could take her blood pressure and try to determine if she'd had a stroke.

Anxious, yet relieved to see Mammi more coherent now, Nellie headed to her room for some quiet. Observing her grandmother so incapacitated at first had been frightening. She would stay put until the doctor was finished with his examination.

Her worry for Mammi alternated with her curiosity about the twin babies Rosanna would soon hold in her arms. Of course, it was too dark to venture over there now. Besides, the midwife at John and Kate Beiler's place might be saying the selfsame thing as the doctor here, scooting everyone out till the babies came. She could only hope and pray the wee ones were strong enough, being born so early.

With troublesome thoughts swirling in her head, she decided to add to the circle letter. This time of year, once the harvest was in, the circle letters fairly flew back and forth, and her cousins would be expecting news.

Finding the lined stationery in her dresser drawer, Nellie Mae felt a strong need to narrate her day, to keep her mind occupied.

Picking up her best pen, she began to write.

Dear Cousins,

Hello from Honeybrook.

There is so much to tell you, starting with the most wonderful news: Kate Beiler's twins are soon to be born—I haven't heard if they have actually come today, but the midwife fairly flew past me when I was taking a walk a while ago. I'll give you the firm details in my next letter. All right?

We've other interesting news here, too. Our bishop is back from a long vacation in Iowa. His trip wound up being longer than planned due to an illness, but I hear he's healthier now.

My sister-in-law Maryann's baby will be the next one to arrive, at least for our family. Of course, there are oodles of little ones on the way. And, oh goodness, all the weddings! Mamma said we've been invited to three on a single day next week. Not sure which one they'll pick, but it'll surely be fun.

She paused in her writing, wondering which weddings Caleb and his family might attend. If Caleb happened to be at the same one as she and her sisters and parents, would she end up at the feast table across from him, maybe?

Sighing, Nellie contemplated the pleasure of seeing Caleb at an all-day wedding celebration now that they were truly a couple. But that wasn't the kind of thing she would share with Cousin Treva and the others who would receive this letter.

Thinking again of her very sick Mammi, Nellie struggled to remain upbeat—she didn't want to spoil the tone of the letter. After a moment, she resumed her writing, apologizing for bearing the sad news about Mammi Fisher. *We're still awaiting the doctor's word as to what she's suffering from.* She added a few more lines before signing off, asking Treva and the others to please keep the letters coming "nice and fast." Then she folded the letter.

With Mammi's health still weighing heavily in her mind, Nellie Mae slipped the folded letter into the drawer of the small bedside table. Pausing there at the sight of Suzy's diary, she reached in and picked up the book, terribly aware of the guilt that yet lay hidden inside her—the anger, too, which made her impulsively lift the bed mattress at one end and shove in Suzy's diary.

There. That's where it stays till I burn it up.

She straightened the quilt coverlet and headed out of the room to see how Mammi was doing.

The labor was intense for her cousin, and Rosanna cringed each time Kate stirred from rest to moan. Rosanna sat in the corner of Kate and John's large bedroom, not close enough to see the babies crown and be birthed, as she was hesitant about being present at all. Yet Kate had insisted she be in the room once word had reached Rosanna that the babies were most likely coming today. Ephram had received a call on the community telephone up the road from Rosanna and Elias's place, and Maryann had rushed over to deliver the news. Upon hearing it, Rosanna had offered nary a word of explanation, other than to say her cousin surely needed her help.

When will Kate reveal her plan for her babies? Rosanna wondered. Perhaps her cousin had decided it best to wait until the babies were actually born.

Several times Kate's cries jarred Rosanna so much that she held her breath, feeling more and more as if she, too, were a part of the birthing process. As if in some strange way, she were the babies' mother, too.

O Lord, please help them to arrive safely....

Kate moaned again, and Rosanna's heart went out to her suffering cousin. She would stay by Kate's side as long as it took, waiting patiently for the twins' birth.

Reuben hadn't seen so many folk in his house since before James and Benjamin had married and moved away. More were on hand than could possibly be of help, yet he was grateful for their presence, a sign of their care and concern for his mother. Presently, he attempted to occupy his father's attention even as his mother was seriously ailing, but it was nearly impossible to keep Noah Fisher away from his bride of over sixty years. How thankful Reuben was that he'd fetched his Daed right quick after arriving home and learning of Mammi's condition.

Reuben struggled with the lump in his throat as Daed checked in with the doctor for probably the tenth time this hour, getting reports every few minutes. At last the doctor determined his mother should not be moved—at least not tonight. With Mammi ordered to bed rest, his parents would stay in the downstairs bedroom whether they liked fellowshipping with "Preacher Manny's bunch" or not.

Reuben helped the doctor get his mother into the spare room and settled on the edge of the bed. She was more coherent now and the color had returned to her face. The doctor had administered a diuretic to lower her blood pressure, as well as a medication to open her blood vessels, assuring them that, in time and with rest, she would recover.

Betsy, ever thoughtful and kind, helped dress Reuben's mother, offering one of her own nightgowns. Once she had settled her under the covers, she left Mamm alone with Dat, who remained there all during supper.

After the trying events of the day, Reuben was eager to retire early for the night and told Betsy so. He would not tell her, however, of his encounter with outspoken Ephram this afternoon, because it would only serve to upset her more. Ephram had been awful hotheaded, saying some mighty hurtful things. *"Best be cuttin' the cord with Preacher Manny and come back where ya belong,"* his son had spouted off, a deep frown of condemnation on his ruddy face. *"You're embarrassing your family . . . bein' the focus of community criticism 'n' all."*

No doubt Ephram's anger and disappointment had compelled him to say the disrespectful, even harsh, words. Yet Reuben had heard nearly the same from a whole group of men in Bishop Joseph's barn, armed with spiteful threats. Preacher Lapp himself had put pressure on Reuben to sever his ties with Preacher Manny and return to the fellowship of the brethren. But that hadn't smarted as much as his intimidating remark—*"We'll starve you out if you're not careful, Reuben Fisher!"*

Never had Reuben thought someone's beliefs could cause so much loathing. He'd headed home to seek refuge, only to find his mother suffering the aftereffects of an apparent stroke.

What he needed most was Betsy's tender touch on his brow, the loving way she had of caressing his cares away. Reuben went around extinguishing the gas lamps and then took Betsy by the hand to lead her upstairs.

"Oh, he's so tiny," Rosanna said as Ruth Glick, the midwife, placed Kate's son into her arms. She fought back tears, wanting to clearly see his wee red face, so wrinkled and sweet.

"Say hullo to your first son," Kate said weakly between more labor pains—the second baby was coming fast.

Rosanna was surprised at how very light he felt in her arms. Nearly as tiny as a baby doll. Oh, the joy of cradling him so near! And to think a sister or brother was on the way.

Soon her attention turned back to dear Kate, who was clearly struggling harder with this second birth. By the time the blanketed baby boy was replaced with an even smaller infant girl, Kate was unable to control her mournful cries, which shortly became muffled shrieks of pain.

Something's terribly wrong, thought Rosanna, wanting to shield the infant in her arms and to ease her poor, dear cousin's pain.

———

Rosanna did her best to keep her emotions in check as she held Kate's hand. Her cousin reclined slightly in the backseat of the English neighbors' car, groaning and gripping her abdomen. John was at her side, while Rosanna and Ruth Glick each held one of the babies. Rosanna wasn't even sure which twin snuggled in the crook of her arm; they looked that much alike. But as rosy-faced as the babies were, they were too early and small, and their lungs might have difficulty with breathing. The hospital would keep them in an incubator for some days—possibly longer.

This was not as disappointing as it was worrisome, but Rosanna would not borrow more anxiety than she was already experiencing, what with Kate bearing such enormous pain next to her.

Kate's neighbors had kindly offered to drive all of them, including helpful Ruth Glick. Such a crowd for one vehicle! On a day like this, Rosanna was thankful for the speed and warmth of the car as it raced toward the hospital. Anything to spare Kate's life.

I wish there was a way to alert Elias, thought Rosanna. She would like for him to join her at the hospital somehow, to meet their perfect children. Probably he sensed something was up, what with her still being away at this late hour.

Are other couples as closely connected? she wondered.

Outside, the shadowy landscape and occasional lights seemed to literally fly by . . . she'd never gone so fast in her life. Goodness, but she could scarcely focus her eyes on the lit houses and other cars. Was this what it was like to be fancy?

She'd heard tell of a group of folk meeting over at Preacher Manny's house and wondered if all of them would be driving cars next thing. Tractors, surely, as that was all *es Gschwetz*—the talk. She wondered if Elias might not have been upset at supper a couple weeks ago about all that ruckus, more than worried about not getting a boy.

Well, he's got himself a son after all . . . and I've got me a daughter.

Now if the doctors could just help Kate . . . and get these little ones to a healthier weight, Rosanna and Elias could bring them home to the snug oak cradles Elias's father had made. Then, and only then, would all be well.

CHAPTER 32

An hour before dawn, Nellie Mae rose and dressed to do all the baking for the day. When the last five pumpkin pies were out of the oven and cooling, she began mixing the eggs and milk for scrambled eggs for everyone.

In spite of Dawdi's protests, Mammi Fisher walked slowly from the bedroom to the kitchen table with the help of her cane. Looking much better this morning, she seemed terribly reluctant to sit at the same table with all of them, even though they were kin and had bedded her down for the night. This struck Nellie as ridiculous, but she had no desire to laugh. Who was her grandmother to arbitrarily slap the Bann on *all* of them, for pity's sake?

Dawdi was less inclined to hover today, Nellie noticed, and he and Dat slipped out to the barn together following breakfast, probably for a man-to-man talk.

Rhoda and Mamma began to wash and dry the breakfast dishes as Mammi headed back to the bedroom for some more rest. Nan politely offered to tend to the bakery shop so Nellie could go and see if she could help out at Kate's. Nellie could hardly wait to set eyes on the babies, so she took the pony and cart over to Beilers', glad for her sister's easygoing manner today.

The pony cart shifted and skittled over the snow, and she wished she'd brought Dat's old sleigh instead. Even so, the cold tranquility was soothing, just as her walk had been yesterday—prior to having words with Rhoda. She shook her head, wondering when Rhoda had become so direct.

Like Mammi Fisher was with Mamma . . .

When Nellie arrived at the Beilers', she was stunned not to see a single buggy parked in the yard. She wouldn't jump to conclusions, but she couldn't help but think Kate might have needed some medical help birthing the twins.

Curiously, she peeked in the back door and saw Kate's niece Lizzy playing with two of the younger children.

"Come in," Lizzy called at her knock, meeting her at the door. "If you're lookin' for Kate, she and the babies went to the hospital last night."

"Are the twins all right?"

Lizzy grinned. "Ach, though ever so tiny . . . a boy and a girl."

Oh joy, one of each!

"Did Rosanna King happen to stop by, do you know?" asked Nellie.

A warm smile spread across Lizzy's face. "Oh my, did she ever. Rosanna said the midwife handed the first twin—the boy—right into her arms nearly the second he was born."

Nellie felt like crying. "That's so dear, ain't?" She assumed Lizzy knew why Rosanna had been on hand for the births.

Nodding, Lizzy agreed. "Kate's the one they're most worried about, I guess."

"Oh no. What's a-matter?"

"All I know is she needed to get to the hospital along with the babies, and right quick."

"Well, it's a good thing you're here," she told Lizzy.

One of Kate's toddlers howled in the kitchen behind them. "I'd better get back to bein' a mother's helper," said Lizzy. "Come again, if you want."

Nellie said good-bye and returned to the pony cart. The hospital was much too far for this colt, even though it was one of Dat's best trained. Had she brought the enclosed family buggy she might have considered making the trip to town. Besides, it was treacherous on the roads, especially with all the traffic and impatient Englischers.

Somewhat disappointed, Nellie headed home, wishing she could offer something besides the rote prayer that now sprang to mind.

———

The rooster's sharp crowing nudged Nellie Mae awake at the break of dawn, and she jumped out of bed, having overslept this Lord's Day.

Mamma was waiting in the kitchen, already laying out fruit and cold cereal, her expression as gray as dusk. "Dat and I would like you to come along with us to Preacher Manny's."

"I'd rather go to Preachin', really." Nellie disliked standing up to Mamma this way, torn between loyalty to her family and love for her beau.

"Well, remember you live under the covering of your father, dear."

Nellie wasn't surprised at Mamma's words. After all, a young woman her age was expected to follow the rules of her father's house without question.

Mamma stood behind Dat's chair at the head of the table, her eyes softening, as if she might be thinking that maybe, just maybe, Nellie had found a beau. "I hope we won't be divided on Sundays . . . you, Dat, and me on the opposite sides of the fence, ya know?" she said sadly.

But she and Dat have moved away from the right side, thought Nellie. *I haven't gone anywhere.*

Without saying more, Mamma turned quickly to make her way out to the summer porch to don her work coat—going to feed the chickens, no doubt.

Feeling glum, Nellie moved to the window. *Oh, the weight Mamma must carry, and now I'm adding to her sorrow.*

Later, after washing and dressing, Nellie was met with a cool response from Nan, who glared at her when they passed in the hall. None of her usually cheerful, "How'd ya sleep?" or *"Gut Mariye,* Nellie Mae!" Nan must've had an earful from Rhoda, for certain.

She felt terribly alone as she left the house to make the long trip on foot to Caleb's uncle's house for Preaching service, glad for her warm snow boots and knitted mittens. Just as her grandparents had refused to live with them because of her parents' beliefs, Nellie was turning down her parents by striking out on her own today, following her heart. *And the tradition of the People,* she thought as she slipped along the snow-packed road.

I'll look ever so odd, sitting alone without Mamma and my sisters, she realized. Odd . . . and a magnet for attention, which she despised.

She hadn't walked but half a mile when Ephram and Maryann, with their children huddled near, came along and stopped the horse and sleigh for her. "Hullo, Nellie Mae! Want a ride?" It was Maryann, looking ever so sympathetic.

Nellie got on board, and chubby Katie crawled over to snuggle on her lap.

"Such a perty Lord's Day, jah?" Maryann said, turning to look at Nellie, but her sad eyes and lifted brow seemed to say, *Sorry you're all alone today.* . . .

Filing into the house with Maryann and her little ones, Nellie felt nearly as conspicuous as if she'd been by herself. She noticed that John and Kate Beiler were absent, and she hoped Kate was improving quickly and that the babies were all right, too. All told, there were several dozen folk missing, and she assumed most were over at Preacher Manny's and not at the hospital with the Beilers. Even Nellie's own grandparents were absent, though on doctor's orders. *Dear, dear Mammi,* she thought, hoping her grandmother would remain on bed rest for a while as suggested. *She'll be fine if she does.*

Fine physically, but what about otherwise? How can Mammi and Dawdi reject their son and family?

The service began, and Nellie Mae sang every song, as she always did; however, she was conscious of the tightness in her throat during silent prayer, when they knelt at the wooden benches. And she was ever so conscious of Caleb . . . and his family. What must they be thinking?

After the first sermon, offered by Preacher Lapp, the bishop rose and began to speak in more conversational tones than she'd ever heard at a Preaching service. He even read the Scriptures in English rather than High German so everyone could understand. She realized at once why he had chosen to do so as he read from the third chapter of Colossians: " 'And let the peace of God rule in your hearts . . . ye are called in one body. . . . ' " He went on to build his sermon on that text, admonishing them to avoid disunity and to steer clear of those claiming "a strange belief."

Nellie found it interesting that the entire sermon was, in fact, pointing fingers at Preacher Manny and his group.

The bishop's stern words—"those who uphold such a way of thinking put on a treacherous kind of pride . . . as unto death"—echoed in her memory all through the common meal.

Settling in at the table with Ephram and Maryann, she felt as if all eyes were on her. Some of the older folk went so far as to extend their concern to her, coming up and inquiring of Mammi Fisher, which dispelled some of the tension.

But the awkwardness returned when Maryann took the children off to the washroom, leaving Nellie alone with her obviously brooding brother.

"Dat's mighty foolish, I have to say. I pity you, havin' to live at home."

She wouldn't agree with him, so vicious were his words. "Looks like our grandparents won't be stayin' with us, after all."

"Well, it's Dat's fault, don't you know?"

"Nothin' either of us can do." She looked at him. "Is there?"

He ignored her. "Dawdi Fisher's havin' to move all the way back to Bird-in-Hand, mind you." Shaking his head, he mumbled something she couldn't make out. Was he cussing under his breath?

"Look on the bright side," she said softly. "They're goin' where they'll fit in."

"Puh! They belong in Honeybrook—not clean over there, where we have to go so far out of our way to visit and whatnot."

"So it's an inconvenience, is that it?"

Now it was his turn to pale at her remark.

"You're not thinkin' of Dawdi and Mammi at all."

"Just like Dat ain't thinking 'bout all the trouble he's in," he shot back. "Or 'bout how all this affects us."

So he's peeved because what Dat does reflects poorly on him.

"By the way," Ephram added quickly, "I'm mighty glad to see you here, toein' the line, Nellie Mae."

You sure have an interesting way of showing it, she thought, ever so glad when Aunt Anna Fisher came over and sat next to her. Anna asked about the possibility of Nellie's helping with kitchen cleanup at one of the upcoming weddings, and Nellie was quick to agree. All the same, secretly she hoped this wedding wouldn't be one that Caleb and his family might attend. If so, she would not be able to see him much at all.

When Aunt Anna rose and moved to another part of the long table, Nellie noticed her brother had disappeared. She sighed with relief, well aware of her own floundering feelings this day . . . something akin to swimming up a stream, the current so strong it threatened to drag her under.

She considered Preacher Manny, her own relative, of all things—the man of God's choosing for the People. She felt terribly frustrated, suddenly wondering if she shouldn't hear him out. After all, he had been appointed by God, so what did it mean that he was moving away from his original calling? Here where so many were still honoring their life vow to God and the church.

Preacher Manny was partly the reason her parents had abandoned the church of their childhood and hers. Where was she expected to take her kneeling vow to the People now? Where was she to make her marriage promises someday, to become a good Amish wife to her dear Caleb?

Right here, she told herself. *I'm staying put.*

She was about to help clear tables when Caleb's father stormed toward her, wearing what looked to be an out-and-out scowl. She turned to glance behind her, certain he was heading for someone else.

She was just getting up when he surprised her by speaking to her. "Nellie Mae, mind if I sit with you a minute?"

It was highly unusual for a married man to talk with a single, unrelated young woman. At the request, her neck felt too warm and her heart thumped much too hard. And Caleb . . . where was he?

"Nellie Mae," he began, "I'm mighty curious—where might your parents be today? Your family, as a whole?"

She wanted to remind him of Ephram's family and their presence here, but she felt terribly awkward speaking up to this man.

"My father's . . ." If she finished by telling the truth, she might not see Caleb again, and she was fairly sure that's where this conversation was leading. Oh, she wanted to search out her darling with her eyes. Where was he?

"Nellie?" David Yoder leaned forward, expression sober. "Has your father joined up with Preacher Manny?"

She looked at him, afraid she might burst out crying.

"Would it trouble you to ask Dat instead?" It took all she had, but she'd said precisely what she wanted to—what she *had* to. She must put him off somehow. Would this suffice?

"Well, Nellie Mae Fisher, I believe I'm talkin' to you here and now."

She could not keep her tears in check any longer. Just when her lip began to quiver and she felt as though she might either rise and say something out of order—either that or bawl like a child—just then, Caleb appeared at the back of the room, coming her way.

Ach, thank the Good Lord!

Fearless, as if he'd encountered such confrontations himself, Caleb walked right up to the table and stood to his father's left. "Nellie? I'd like to have a word with you."

He's as forthright as his father. Yet she knew without a doubt he was rescuing her, and she loved him all the more for it.

"Daed," he said, turning to face him, "Nellie Mae's comin' with me for a while."

She wanted to laugh—oh, she wanted to clap. This beau of hers, wasn't he the best? She knew she'd follow him no matter where he led her today, which turned out to be clear to the end of the cornfield and beyond, to the high bluffs overlooking Honeybrook. It was a spot she'd always loved, and there she stood, hand in hand with Caleb . . . then swiftly she was in his arms.

"You are one brave girl," Caleb whispered in her ear before kissing her forehead.

"I was so . . . speechless," she admitted.

He nodded, his forehead pressed against hers, seemingly already aware of the line of questioning his father had taken with her. "Don't feel put upon, Nellie Mae. Please don't."

Well, she *had,* but no longer, not with Caleb's kind and comforting manner. Goodness, she believed she could go through most anything with him by her side . . . with his encouragement. She could tell by his admiring glances and the squeeze of his hand that he adored her all the more for choosing the Old Ways today. And him.

But eventually Nellie had to return home and endure the disapproving glances of her family, knowing Dat would give her a good talking to sooner or later. Suddenly, waiting a full year to wed Caleb seemed much too long.

CHAPTER 33

All Dat could talk about upon arriving home was Preacher Manny's meeting . . . how it had nearly doubled in size this Lord's Day. "What will it be like by next Sunday, with word spreading as it is?" he wondered aloud. Mamma was simply glowing. As for Rhoda and Nan, they seemed to have been won over by a single visit.

The four of them chattered excitedly at the supper table, but Nellie did not feel too left out—not with Caleb's support. She would not embrace the "strange belief" Uncle Bishop had hammered against for two full hours in his sermon.

With the family's topic of talk seemingly limited to one thing, nightfall couldn't come soon enough to suit her, and Nellie slipped away to her room. On the way, she spotted Rhoda and Nan in their own room, their heads bent low over Dat's King James Bible. For this further proof of their companionship, Nellie was envious. Wasn't it bad enough to lose Suzy? Now must she also lose the remainder of her family . . . and to a foreign faith, at that?

She lay down to rest, clinging to the hope of having some good fellowship with Maryann once again—and Rosanna, too, when the new babies were safely home. Perhaps she would spend time with Kate once she was completely well again. She didn't see much chance of enjoying that with Ephram, as it didn't seem to matter which side of the fence you were on with him. Either way, she could not seem to please *that* brother!

She turned on her side in an attempt to get more comfortable, willing herself not to think about Caleb's father's approaching her. She took solace from the fact she would soon put an end to Suzy's dark secrets . . . tomorrow, after she closed the shop for the day, she would destroy the diary.

Suzy's wicked life will never touch another soul. . . .

———

Washday dawned mighty quick, and since Mamma was in bed and under the weather, the time-consuming chore fell to Nan and Nellie, because Rhoda had to leave for work earlier than usual. Rhoda didn't say why, which annoyed Nellie, what with having to juggle the washing and the larger-than-normal amounts of baking.

Down in the cellar, Nan talked to Nellie of wishing for an electric washing machine—"maybe even a dryer, too, someday. Lots of folks at yesterday's meeting said such things matter little in the eyes of God." Nellie sighed inwardly and was mighty sure this sister had missed out by not being present for the bishop's warning yesterday at Preaching. *Goodness—seems she's already set on goin' fancy.*

As kindly as was possible, she put up with Nan's evident enthusiasm for modern conveniences, paying closer attention when Nan said she saw "two new groups rising among those at Manny's gathering."

"What do you mean?"

"Just what I said." Nan pushed more clothes into the gas-powered wringer washer. "There's one group that's mostly concerned about knowledge of salvation, like Dat. And there's another group wanting to own tractors and cars and other useful things."

"What's Preacher Manny think of all this?" Nellie had assumed Preacher Manny's splinter group would be consumed with Bible study, like her parents were—not the yearning for fancy things like Nan indicated.

"I don't know exactly," Nan admitted. "He talked only about Scripture, really."

"Can you imagine Dat ever drivin' a car?" Nellie had to ask.

Nan shook her head. "Never."

"But he could fall prey to the other group eventually—like the Beachy Amish—and desire those things, ain't so?"

Nan laughed a little. "Mamma will keep that from happening, don't ya know?"

Nellie agreed that was probably true.

"I've heard some talk of Dat's cousin Jonathan bein' interested in cars," Nan added.

"Does he own one yet?"

"He will soon, I 'spect . . . according to the grapevine. Doubtless he'll have himself electric next and a tractor with rubber tires, too. Why not, when he's already shunned."

Nan went on. "You should go to Preacher Manny's with us and see for yourself, Nellie Mae. I think you'd be surprised, just maybe."

She stiffened. "I'm not interested in turnin' my back on the Old Ways."

"Ach . . . the Old Ways." Nan chuckled. "Just imagine not havin' to hang all these clothes on the line, and on such a frosty day, too." With that she flounced upstairs with another wet load, leaving Nellie to ponder every speck of their conversation. If nothing else, she was glad Nan was at least speaking to her again.

———

Rosanna sat in the hospital waiting room, exerting some degree of patience as she awaited further word on Cousin Kate's condition. Being the only Amishperson in the room made her feel like a pea out of its pod, yet she was determined to see Kate. Unfortunately, she didn't know precisely how to go about requesting a visit, what with so much hustle and bustle in the hallways as doctors and nurses came and went.

After a time, she rose and searched for what looked like an information desk to ask about her cousin.

"Are you related to Mrs. Beiler?" the woman asked, recognition in her eyes.

It's the head covering, no doubt.

"I'm her first cousin," Rosanna replied.

The woman paused, nodding and glancing down at a list of names. "Mrs. Beiler's one popular woman, or so it seems. She's had a total of nine cousins visit her already."

Rosanna didn't see how she was going to convince her that she, too, was a cousin. She might have turned to leave without seeing Kate at all, if Aunt Rachel hadn't walked toward her at that moment. Rachel came up and slipped her arm around Rosanna's waist, leading her down the hall. "Are they keepin' you from Kate?" she asked.

"Not sure, really." Rosanna paused. "Is she goin' to be all right?"

"Well, she's terribly weak . . . they're watchin' her closely. She lost an awful lot of blood. You haven't heard?"

Rosanna shook her head. "I'm so sorry to learn of it. Will she be able to go home soon?" She didn't dare ask about the twins, because she wasn't sure if Aunt Rachel even knew yet that her grandbabies were going to be raised by Rosanna.

"Jah . . . soon." Rachel gazed seriously at her, then whispered, "Ach, Rosanna, I think what Kate's doin' is downright peculiar, 'tween you and me. I just yesterday heard from John what he and Kate decided to do for you and Elias." Her aunt seemed a bit put out; then her eyes brightened some. "Even so, it seems the twins will know who their first Dat and Mamma are, jah?"

Rosanna recalled that awkward conversation and nodded her head. "That's what Kate wants."

Aunt Rachel touched her hand. "I'll be wantin' to see my grandyoung'uns quite a lot, I'm sure you know."

Rosanna agreed, feeling sorry for Rachel, who was only now getting used to the idea of her flesh-and-blood grandbabies going home with someone else. "You can come see them anytime. In fact, I'll be happy for the extra help."

Rachel smiled suddenly. "Oh, you'll have all kinds of help, trust me."

"Denki," whispered Rosanna, grateful Rachel seemed accepting of the plan. "Thank you ever so much."

———

Nellie was grateful when Nan stopped by the shop mid-morning with the last of the baked goods, even going so far as to help unload them into the display. Once her sister left to start cooking the noontime meal for Mamma, however, Nellie took great care to rearrange the gingerbread and oatmeal cakes. "I'm a fussbudget," she muttered, knowing it was ever so true.

Going around the front of the display case, she stepped back, pretending to be a potential customer, surveying the place. Just then, dark-haired Joy Landis entered. Nellie was surprised to see her on a school day. "Hullo," she said. "Can I help you?"

The girl smiled shyly, and Nellie caught sight of the tiny American flags on her earlobes. Nellie must have stared too long at her earrings, because Joy reached up to touch one ear and asked, "Do you like these, Nellie Mae?"

Nellie felt her cheeks flush red and forced a smile. "Jah, they're perty."

"I'm wearing them because it's Veterans Day. We're off school today."

Nellie vaguely remembered having a day's break on a November Monday back when she was a student. The teacher had told her the holiday was to honor soldiers who'd fought in America's wars, so it wasn't one a peace-loving Amish girl was likely to recall.

Joy suddenly seemed awkward, looking away as if perhaps she had something on her mind but didn't know how to express it.

"Care for a sample?" Nellie offered, thinking that might be what she wanted.

"No . . . but thanks anyway." Joy strolled nearer the display case, eyeing several kinds of cookies.

Nellie went around the counter to stand and wait, wishing she could think of something to say to fill the silence. She thought of bringing up Joy's cousin Darlene, wondering how she was doing *this* school year, but then felt she had no business inquiring.

Just when she thought Joy was going to stare a hole in the peanut blossoms, she looked up, meeting Nellie's gaze.

"I'm not here to buy anything today but because I promised my mother I'd set the record straight."

Listening, Nellie did not move an inch.

"I know some people around town thought your sister was a wild one, but Suzy helped a whole bunch of kids from school. I'm not kidding."

Nellie studied her. "Why are you sayin' this?"

Joy looked over her shoulder at the car parked outside. "My mother didn't think you believed her."

"Why should I?" Nellie's words slid out too quickly. Joy would surely know by this that Nellie assumed her own dead sister was as wayward as gossip had her.

"You thought she was a rebel?" asked Joy.

Nellie couldn't admit this to an Englischer. "Ach, I didn't say that."

"Well, just so you know, Suzy was the best thing that ever happened to Darlene." Then, without saying good-bye, Joy turned and left the shop.

Nellie watched the slender girl slip into her mother's car. It was obvious Joy had been coerced into coming here, and Nellie felt sorry for her. Yet she was glad, too, that Joy had found the courage.

"Goodness' sakes," Nellie Mae murmured aloud, rather stunned. "I guess it's time to read the rest of your diary, Suzy . . . ain't so?"

CHAPTER 34

Nellie Mae raised the bed mattress and tugged on Suzy's diary. She would give it one more look, hoping to find something good in her sister's story. Even so, she dreaded wading through more of the muck and mire of Suzy's Rumschpringe.

Flipping through the pages, well past the spot where she'd given up before, Nellie began to read again, hoping to find something good this time.

> *Today I spotted a weasel's footprints in the mud along the stream on the other side of the road. Of course I had to follow them. Such natural things are so appealing. Honestly, it's like there are two of me. . . .*

Suzy's work boots squished in the moist soil along the creek as she followed the footprints, wondering where they might lead. She had wandered away from the house, wishing Nellie might come exploring with her, but there were customers, so Suzy didn't bother to ask. She followed the weasel's footprints all the way through the expanse of field adjacent to the neighbors' land.

As she did so, she pondered the weasel-like way Jay Hess had behaved in recent weeks. She had not seen this side of him before—a spoiled child throwing a tantrum . . . and all because he couldn't have his way with her.

To top things off, she'd happened upon some clean-cut boys passing out invitations to a "lively meeting," as they called it. Truly a temptation it was, especially since the invitation came from the tall blond boy, Christian Yoder. His face reminded her of someone, though she couldn't place who. She supposed if he hadn't been so nice and talkative, she might not have accepted.

Naturally she knew better than to tell Jay of her Friday evening plans, lest he fly into a rage as he did if she so much as looked at another fellow. She'd wished he'd play by some of his own rules, since *he* flirted with other girls till the cows came home. She surprised herself by looking forward to an evening without him.

When that Friday evening arrived, Suzy slipped away after supper to the meeting, taking the pony cart. There were lots of young people—English and Plain—in attendance. Not many were in Amish dress like she was.

She'd noticed before merely in passing how pretty the Tel Hai campgrounds were. The cedarwood tabernacle building, with its open sides, drew her as she walked in behind a group of distinctly Mennonite girls, their hair combed straight back and topped by their cup-shaped, pleated white head coverings.

The music was as lively as Christian had said it would be—and inspiring. A young evangelist wearing a black suit shared God's words, fervently urging repentance. Hundreds were present, including many couples and families sitting in lawn chairs—even buggies parked along the road so their occupants could listen in. Folk were transfixed by the sober words coming from the young minister, and many wiped their eyes, brushing back tears.

Suzy sat upright, captivated by the passion emanating from the preacher behind the wooden pulpit positioned in the center of the long platform. She was amazed to see dozens of weeping people rushing to the timber altar at the end of the sermon . . . and so many teenagers gripping hands, leading friends to the front.

Suzy couldn't miss Christian in his yellow shirt. He sat nearby with three other young men, all apparently without girlfriends. None of them responded to the call at the altar, so Suzy assumed they were already among the "saved." Christian held his Bible open to share with the boy seated next to him, occasionally bowing his head in prayer as the evangelist addressed the group kneeling at the front.

With a name like Christian, he must be from a Plain background, she guessed, but his loud shirt indicated otherwise. *Unless he's as unruly as I am.* But she doubted a wayward boy would be promoting an event like this—a church service in a lovely, peaceful setting like none she'd ever been to.

The evangelist left the pulpit to walk back and forth. "Listen to the Bible: 'These things have I written unto you that believe on the name of the Son of God; that ye may know that ye have eternal life, and that ye may believe on the name of the Son of God.' Notice the words 'that ye may know.' "

I want to know.

Suzy thought of her boyfriend—his reckless behavior, the wild friends she and Jay ran with. Then she thought of her family, steeped in tradition. Were they *all* lost, as this preacher declared? What did the Good Book really say?

She clenched her hands, repressing her desire to get up and walk to the front, rejecting what the evangelist called "the convicting power of God." With tears threatening to spill down her cheeks, she rose and slipped out the back.

The next day, she wandered off to the wooded area beyond the paddock after chores, watching for springtime birds.

Everywhere she looked, she saw God's handiwork. The truth of His creation surrounded her; even the cross-shaped limbs on the oldest oak tree reminded her of the young minister's sermon. *"Nailed to a tree, the Savior died for you. Because of His life sacrifice, you can have salvation in His name."*

She thought again of the tearstained faces of the young people rushing to the altar, their obvious relief and joy after they prayed with the evangelist. Maybe the boyish preacher really did know what he was talking about.

Although she'd always sensed it, Suzy saw a fundamental order in the woods this day, from the tallest, most stately tree to the smallest woodland mouse.

Order is everywhere, she thought, spotting a grouping of tulip poplars, or whitewood trees, as Dat called them. Their highest branches swept together in one direction, and they made the maples and oaks seem small.

Why, God even directs the smallest sprout in and out of dormancy, she thought as she walked, embracing the beauty and grateful to have heard such wonderful-good news of God's love. The words of the young preacher persisted in her memory. *"Read for yourself—don't take my word for it,"* he'd said.

Wavering back and forth, Suzy struggled, knowing she was at a crossroads. Either she could continue down her present path with Jay and his friends, or she could grab hold of the Savior's hand and come out of the darkness.

She longed to know this Jesus the preacher had talked about. Her whole life, she'd never heard such things.

Jay caught up with Suzy on Tuesday when she was running errands in town. He asked where she'd kept herself on Friday night and why she hadn't shown up at the appointed spot. She invited him to come along with her to hear "something truly good" but stopped short of saying it was a church gathering, hoping to win him over by telling about the exciting music.

When he asked where this cool place was, she said east of Route 10 on Beaver Dam Road. He must have put it together, because he sneered and said, "You must think I'm stupid, Suzy. I wouldn't be caught dead with a bunch of fanatics."

"Then you won't be seein' *me* anymore!" She turned on her heel and started to leave.

At that Jay began to ridicule her fiercely, gouging her with every conceivable slur. She had never expected this kind of treatment from someone who had once claimed to love her. Now she doubted he had ever cared for her at all.

When later Darlene asked if she'd broken it off with Jay, Suzy admitted she had. As much as she wanted to have a boyfriend, the tug toward the rustic tabernacle was stronger.

As the week wore on, Suzy sneaked peeks at Dat's English Bible, folding slips of paper into it to mark her place— especially in the New Testament, where her father wouldn't see them. She found several of the verses the evangelist had referred to and copied them carefully in her diary. She was eager to learn more, but her loss of Jay was in the back of her mind. She thought of all the pieces of her heart she'd given him, wishing she could do most anything to have them back.

While Suzy wanted to share her loss with her closest sister, she didn't tell Nellie what was happening, fearful Nellie wouldn't understand—not when the boy involved was English. And not when her heart was being pulled in a new, equally forbidden direction . . . away from what she'd always been taught.

How she wished her family had more religious understanding. As far as she could tell, they merely lived in accordance with the teachings of their ancestors. Sure, Dat and Mamma took the family to Preaching every other Sunday, but it felt to Suzy that they were simply putting in their three hours. There was no talk of a relationship with God's Son, no urgency toward Christ. No, the way they were going, bound by the rules of the church and the bishop, nothing apart from a divine miracle could save her family.

They're lost to tradition.

That second Friday evening at the tabernacle, Suzy was one of the first to walk "the sinner's aisle." Even though the minister was older this time, and possibly wiser, the message was the same. "God's promise of salvation can be trusted," he stated. "It is clear—'Verily, I say unto you, He that heareth my word, and believeth on him that sent me, hath everlasting life, and shall not come into condemnation; but is passed from death unto life.' "

No condemnation . . . She wept, thinking of this. *Lord Jesus, I trust in you as my Savior today,* Suzy prayed from her heart. She rose from the altar with tears on her face.

The very next day she set out to share her new faith with her English friends, inviting Darlene to go to the Honeybrook Restaurant to have ice cream. Darlene immediately agreed—

a surprise, since she typically had been reluctant to spend any time at all with those she called "goody-goodies."

"You're not happy with the way your life's goin', are ya?" she asked Darlene.

Tears sprang to her friend's eyes.

"Won't you come with me to the meetings?" Suzy asked.

"I can't."

"You won't be sorry," she urged. "Just this once?"

Darlene shook her head. "I'm into things you can't begin to know about."

"Well, I don't have to . . . and God already does."

They talked together till their ice cream was nearly soup. Even though Darlene had refused her invitation, Suzy prayed she might change her mind.

At the next revival meeting, Christian Yoder noticed Suzy and went to sit with her. They got to talking, and it turned out he was Rebekah Yoder's second cousin, Christian's family having left the Amish decades ago. Soon Suzy had met his siblings—all boys—and their friends, finding fulfillment in the wholesome company of this brand-new group.

As her life began its compelling new chapter, Suzy spent quite a lot of time praying, asking God to bring her family to salvation. "Whatever it takes for them to come to you, Lord, I am willin'." She longed for her family to experience this rebirth, and she made a point of praying nightly for them over in James's former bedroom, the most secluded spot in the house.

A few weeks later, Darlene stopped her on the street. "Do you have time for a soda?" she asked. Suzy nodded, and when they'd settled into a booth at the restaurant, Darlene broke down and revealed how hopeless her life was. "I've been watching you lately, Suzy, and . . . whatever you've got, I want it," she admitted.

Suzy could hardly walk for flying. God was already answering her prayers!

She even had a new boyfriend—Christian's brother Zachary. Zach's goal in life was to make it to the mission field, an idea that appealed greatly to Suzy.

It was Zach's idea for their entire group to go out row boating on Saturday afternoon, June ninth. Suzy decided it would be the perfect opportunity for Nellie Mae to meet the Yoder brothers. Truly, she had no reason to be ashamed of this circle of friends.

When Suzy invited Nellie to go along, asking on behalf of Christian, she was surprised at her sister's strong disinterest. Nellie was obviously put out, even defensive toward the suggestion, and Suzy wondered if perhaps her sister had a beau she didn't know about. They argued about Suzy's plans, Nellie huffing about the room, saying, "It doesn't look right for you to be runnin' with a group of mostly boys—and Englischers, too—for pity's sake! What are you thinkin', Suzy?"

"But the boys are all brothers, and there'll be girls along, too. I thought it was kind of Zach's brother to offer to pair up with you. It would be just as friends. He's ever so nice . . . his name's Christian, and he certainly is that."

"I don't accept blind dates," Nellie replied, frowning. "'Specially not with worldly boys."

Suzy had known it was rather optimistic to hope Nellie might join them, but she'd honestly hoped—and prayed— her sister might say yes. She was completely taken with the idea of getting her sister out on the water, surrounded by her believer-friends. After all, Jesus had taught His disciples in a boat out on the Sea of Galilee, hadn't He? Honestly, she felt called to this day.

If only Nellie Mae hadn't gone and spoiled things by being ever so stubborn!

Nellie rose, the diary clasped tightly to her chest. She didn't know what to think, yet the tears flowed all the same. *Suzy ran wild for a time but found something far better in the very strange beliefs our own bishop preaches against,* she thought.

It was impossible to disregard Suzy's zeal. And to think that God had seemed to answer Suzy's constant prayers for Dat and Mamma . . . why, nearly the whole family looked to be headed down that selfsame path.

Whatever it takes, Lord, Suzy had prayed.

Nellie stopped for a moment and looked at the diary in her hands. Had Suzy unknowingly offered up her own life for her family? Was such a thing even possible?

Lo and behold . . . she knew. Dat's and Mamma's grief over Suzy's death had opened their hearts wide. They had feared the worst possible loss—everlasting punishment for their youngest. If what Dat and Mamma believed was right, then Suzy was with the Lord. *Oh, to think . . .*

Nellie moved to the window, opening to the last page of the diary. She brushed her tears away so she could see the words, the final writings of a girl who had fallen in love with God's Son.

I wish Nellie and I hadn't fought this morning. I wish she would change her mind and go along with Zach and me and the others. She wouldn't have liked Jay and his friends, I know that. But my new brothers and sisters, so to speak? There's no question she would be ever so fond of them.

Maybe someday she'll meet the Yoders . . . in God's good time.

Ach, but I love Nellie Mae. She's simply acting like a big sister, trying to keep me safe—always worried about appearances, and all.

So it's all right. I forgive Nellie, dear sister of mine.

Nellie cried, unable to stop the tears. "Oh, Suzy, how I wish now I'd gone. I didn't know it was so important to you, that these weren't the reckless Englischers the grapevine whispered about." Her shoulders shook as regret once again engulfed her. "I'll never understand why you went boating in such deep waters without a life jacket. . . . I would've made sure you had one."

Nellie threw herself on the bed and wept, with every sob slowly releasing the guilt that had bound her. Suzy's precious, life-giving words echoed in her mind: *It's all right. I forgive Nellie. . . .*

CHAPTER 35

At first light Tuesday, Bishop Joseph held a meeting in the barn between those who were "causing a nuisance" and a group of men who supported the Old Ways. He'd spread the word the day before, and no matter their opinion, Reuben noted the men of the community had complied by showing up.

The scene unfolding before him was more cantankerous than any he'd experienced, including the meeting some years earlier, when the church district had divided after growing too large to accommodate house meetings. There had been a heated squabble that day, too, what with people wanting to go with this or that relative or friend.

Yet that was almost comical compared to this, he thought, looking at the now thirty or so men lined up along one side. If Reuben hadn't known which of them belonged to Manny's group, he might've spotted the believers by their meek demeanor and the tractor-lovers by their set expressions and arms over their chests, as if ready for combat. The bishop's stern bunch were generally the eldest among them, and some looked downright befuddled as they tugged on their long beards.

The bishop began by making a declaration. "Some of yous are here because your wives want electric and you want a car to drive. Others want to do missions work overseas or win your neighbors to a new gospel." He paused to inhale audibly, as if he were making a point with his very breath. "All of you dissenters are less than satisfied with the way things have always been. Don't say this ain't so!"

Reuben saw the fire in his older brother's eyes and wondered how he could ever salvage his relationship with Joseph after these weeks of infighting.

When the bishop was finished, he allowed discussion. First one spoke, then another, in an orderly fashion, until Old Joe Glick aligned himself with Preacher Manny. All of a sudden Reuben's father spoke out sharply against them, his face growing so red that several men on his side had to restrain him. Even at this early-morning hour, the uproar had been ignited.

Reuben couldn't have gotten a word in edgeways if he'd wanted to. He would've liked to defend his cousin Manny, and he would also have liked to see his eldest brother have a tender heart toward the Lord Jesus.

A sudden flutter of wings startled him and the others, and their gaze followed to the wooden rafters, where two barn swallows flew round and round, as though frantically searching for a way out.

"Well, lookee there." Preacher Manny pointed upward. "Those birds are like me . . . like some of the rest of you, too. They feel as trapped as if they were in a silo—can't find the door."

"*Himmel,* there 'tis!" hollered one, pointing to the barn doors as guffaws erupted.

"Jah, be gone . . . get thee behind me, Satan!" said another, thrashing his black hat.

Manny attempted to still the crowd. "Come now, brethren—"

At this, the bishop waved his arms. He bowed his head, working his jaw while the crowd silenced. When he raised his eyes and spoke at last, his words were barely audible. "Does it not matter, beloved, that you are in danger of losin' your very souls?"

Unexpectedly Reuben thought of Suzy. He leaned his head back to look at the long rafters supporting the barn above, wondering when the swallows had flown away. And to where?

The bishop continued. "You leave me no choice but to—"

"You're goin' to shun us all?" asked a man smack-dab next to Preacher Manny. "Then we'll take the whole of our families with us!"

A roar of support filled the room.

Reuben locked his knees. There was no way out . . . not the way this was going. They were devouring each other.

The bishop stepped forward. "But you're not taking *all* your family. Many of them are already alienated from you. Will you trade the fellowship of your extended family for tractors and cars?"

The roar faded.

The bishop turned to Preacher Manny. "Will you abandon your grandsons for an arrogant gospel?"

Reuben shuddered. *Arrogant?*

David Yoder placed his hand on the bishop's shoulder, eyes blazing. "Look how you're divided amongst yourselves. For this you'll abandon the tradition of our ancestors? For this you'll risk losin' your families?" He fairly growled. "As for me and my house, we will choose the Lord."

Reuben's face burned with resentment. Choosing tradition was not choosing God. To Reuben's dismay, the crowd of men began to argue loudly again.

At last the bishop stepped forward, his hands raised high.

A hush spread over the barn as he went around, pointing to each man to inquire of his decision. After the first man, the bishop literally began to take roll, asking for a "yea" or "nay" on upholding the Ordnung. Some clearly felt put on the spot, and Reuben, for one, disliked his brother's approach.

When Joseph came at last to Reuben, his jaw quivered. "Where do you stand, brother?"

Reuben fixed his eyes on the bishop. "The Ordnung is not the way to salvation. I say 'no.' "

His older brother nodded, jerking his head. "Well, then. We have a split down the middle . . . nearly fifty-fifty."

Once more bedlam erupted in the barn.

After several attempts to regain control, the bishop merely shook his head. In dismay he turned and headed for the barn door, yet the arguing continued.

That's it, Reuben thought. *We're as good as excommunicated!*

He'd prayed before arriving today, asking God to give him insight and the wisdom to make a suggestion to the bishop at the right moment, if indeed the time came. He stepped forward now, calling for peace. "My brother—our bishop—needs a reprieve." He waited for them to turn to look at him before adding, "Don't you see we're gettin' nowhere?"

"We'll have the way of our forefathers," David Yoder shouted.

Cheers backed him up.

"Let's be respectful 'bout this, brethren—for the sake of our families and our heritage, if not for the Lord God almighty." With that Reuben left to find Joseph.

When he found him in the woodshed, the bishop was pacing. "Bishop Joseph," he said. "My brother by blood and under God, may I have a word?"

The bishop looked his way, eyes moist. "What is it, Reuben?"

"I appeal to all that is good and right. Not only are families rending asunder, but the conflict is eatin' all of us in this community alive." He stopped, praying silently, then went on. "If I might be so bold, a wide-scale shunning may not be the answer. It was never meant to be used in this way, was it?"

Joseph frowned.

"The best chance for those who are in error to see the light—if indeed we're in error—isn't to shun us, but to keep lines of communication open, jah?"

"What do you suggest?"

The man of God is inquiring of me? "Why not encourage harmony . . . so desired amongst us?" Reuben said.

The bishop's eyes were kind; the fire was tamed.

"While in prayer the past weeks," Reuben continued, "the Lord revealed a plan to me. I've told no one . . . 'cept now I'm tellin' you. Why not offer a peaceable parting? Let each man choose his path, under God, for his own family."

"Sounds like the children of Israel—every man doin' what is right in his own eyes."

Reuben should've seen that coming.

The bishop stood tall, his jaw set. He squinted at an uncut log, then he picked up his ax and flung it deep into the piece of wood, where it stayed. "I've got loose rocks to haul out of my fields today—work to be done. Come. I need to finish what's been started."

The men immediately ceased their talking when the bishop walked into the barn with Reuben at his side. Reuben joined his cousins Jonathan and Preacher Manny, not knowing what the outcome would be.

His elder brother straightened, his mouth a thin line. "Those of you who insist on following your own way unto perdition, so be it. If you're askin' for my say-so to abandon the beliefs of your fathers and the Lord God and heavenly Father who brought our ancestors out of martyrdom, then you have three months to choose your side without penalty of the Bann. Either go or stay—leave the Old or embrace the faith of your fathers. If you wait longer than the ninety days, you'll be shunned. Now, I wash my hands of this."

Bewildered, yet thankful, Reuben hurried home to Betsy and breakfast. *'Tis nearly a miracle. . . .*

———

Over a breakfast of fried eggs, German link sausage, waffles, and black coffee, Reuben shared the bishop's surprising announcement with Betsy and the girls. His wife said little, but he could tell by her raised eyebrows that she was as shocked as he was.

Nellie spoke up, though. "It's about time for all this to settle down, ain't so?"

That's the truth, he thought, truly relieved. Now he could continue to have good fellowship with Ephram and others, including his parents, who were scheduled to move to Bird-in-Hand tomorrow. He'd offered to help with his parents' relocation, but the way things had gone with Mamm's last visit here, Reuben's younger brother thought it best to "leave things be."

His thoughts turned to the upcoming Sunday meeting, and he felt energized whenever he pondered hearing the teachings of the Good Book with like-minded souls.

Now that their path was clearer, Reuben anticipated a call at some point for the ordination of a second minister in addition to Preacher Manny. And years down the road there might be need for a bishop, as well. For now, odd as it might be, his brother would no doubt continue to oversee them.

Silently, he offered a prayer of thanksgiving for God's prompting him to propose a peaceable schism. Who'd ever heard of such a thing? But the bishop had heeded, and for that there was much cause for praise.

CHAPTER 36

Nellie was both intrigued and nervous about going to Preacher Manny's house the Lord's Day following the bishop's declaration. Suzy's diary had awakened in her an intense curiosity, and she intended to find out more about the reason for her sister's devotion to her faith.

Dat said not a word, but Mamma smiled and nodded when Nellie followed Rhoda and Nan into the horse-drawn sleigh. The day was brisk and dark clouds threatened flurries, yet Nellie had an air of anticipation as they rode over the snow-packed roads already heavily rutted by steel buggy wheels.

Arriving at Manny's, she noticed right away the fifteen or so gray family buggies lining the side yard. It felt odd not to file in after the men and boys, as the womenfolk usually did. In other ways, though, the house-church gathering was less like the informal Bible study she'd imagined it to be, and more like an Old Order service, with the men and boys sitting on the right, and the women, young children, and babies on the left.

Preacher Manny's words and the verses he read and explained in the packed-out house moved Nellie to tears as she sat between Mamma and Nan.

Do I feel like Suzy did . . . her first visit to the tabernacle?

The singing was hearty—two songs from memory from the *Ausbund*, their old songbook, and another she'd heard only at one of the more lively Sunday Singings—"What a Friend We Have in Jesus."

Preacher Manny mentioned briefly the coming church split, advising those present to search their hearts for their future. Most likely the group would eventually become a new order—a designation Nellie had never heard before. "Each man and each woman must make this a matter of prayer."

Each woman? Now, Nellie found that interesting.

Certainly Suzy had embraced salvation for herself, not waiting for a man—the brethren or her future husband—to impart it to her. The road of Suzy's life had curved, then turned again.

Nellie Mae tried to look about her discreetly, aware of Ephram's and Maryann's absence. Dat must be feeling it even more so, with his family incomplete here in this meeting place. As for herself, Nellie yearned more for Caleb's presence. What would he think of hearing Scripture passages "read in context," as Preacher Manny made a point to say. She wished, too, that Caleb could witness the enthusiasm springing from their minister as he instructed them, his face shining like a lighthouse beacon.

The longer the meeting lasted, the more Nellie understood why these people sought to experience God's grace, something she'd failed to comprehend before reading Suzy's diary. She confessed to herself that she wished to know something like it with Caleb; such a blending of hearts would be the icing on the cake for their relationship. *And for our future,* she thought.

And yet Nellie wanted to know whether giving herself over to this still-foreign belief was the only way to know the grace her dear sister—and parents—seemed to have found. *Is this for me?*

When it came time to pray, they turned and knelt at their chairs as was their usual custom, but Preacher Manny led them aloud. Dare she learn how to pray like this, just as Dat prayed—not to receive answers so much as to reveal her heart?

Hesitant as she was about appearing to turn away from what she had been taught, Nellie Mae wanted to know more. It was impossible not to sense the joy of this gathering. Caleb should see it for himself.

She would write to Caleb this afternoon and invite him to attend with her next Lord's Day.

————

Caleb was not surprised to see a letter from Nellie Mae in the mailbox Tuesday afternoon, but he was astonished at her bold request.

Dear Caleb,
 Will you consider going to Preacher Manny's for church next Sunday? I want to know your honest opinion. . . .

Caleb could not believe his eyes. What had happened to the girl who'd assured him of her faithfulness to the Old Order? How could she be interested in Preacher Manny's rebellious talk?

His temples throbbed. Reading the letter again, he noticed she'd signed it, *With love, Nellie Mae.* Seeing that, he took hope.

Our love is still alive, he assured himself, determined to talk her out of this impulsive idea.

He stuffed the letter into his pants pocket and returned to the barn, recalling their walk to the bluffs behind his uncle's farmhouse, after Daed had confronted Nellie Mae at the common meal. How was it possible for her to open her mind to change when she had been so strong in her stance that day? Hadn't she vowed her loyalty?

If Daed gets wind of this . . .

Caleb scarcely knew how to persuade his father of the depth of his love for Nellie . . . the rightness of his choice. It was a rare departure from the norm for a son to confide such matters, but his father had obviously figured out whom he was seeing—thanks to Rebekah, probably. "I shouldn't need to defend my preference for a mate," he muttered, heading out to the far pasture to tend to the cattle's water.

He must see Nellie, and before next Sunday. No doubt she had anticipated some resistance from him. Perhaps she'd hoped he would mull over the letter and acquiesce, if only for a single Sunday.

Caleb couldn't begin to read her mind. Even so, he knew one thing: He would follow the mandates of the Ordnung at any cost . . . and once he had talked sense into Nellie, he was sure she would, too.

———

Nellie Mae still smelled the sweetness of the bakery as she hurried up the steps to her room. Tuesdays were exceptionally good days for selling pastries. Most people did their washing on Mondays around here—English folk included—making Tuesday the more popular day to get out and purchase goodies from Nellie's Simple Sweets.

Lighting the lantern, she happily settled into her room for the night. She began to take her hair down and brush it, thinking of Caleb. Her letter had surely arrived at her darling's by now, and she could only guess what he'd thought. The sad truth of the matter was that the planned split of the People was tremendously complicated, especially with her father and Caleb's going separate ways. Yet Uncle Bishop seemed to think it for the best, even though he was relinquishing his power by handing over the ultimate decision to the heads of households.

Dear Uncle, he must be relieved in a way. She would not want to be in his shoes, nor her aunt Anna's. The sanctioned split could not possibly go well. Already she'd heard from the grapevine that some were beginning to behave like sheep needing a shepherd. *Cars are an awful big enticement,* she thought.

She was glad Uncle Bishop was allowing people ninety days to make up their minds. *Will Caleb and his family cross over, too?*

The barbed manner in which Caleb's father had recently approached her seemed to make the likelihood of his ever leaving the Old Order extremely slim. All Nellie Mae could do was hope for a truly peaceful resolution in spite of Caleb's and her misery.

––––––

Nellie Mae had curled up in bed, snug in her warm cotton nightgown, yet unable to sleep. Having retired earlier than the rest of the house, she stared at the ceiling, not counting sheep but days.

What would Suzy have thought of all this?

She opened the drawer next to her. Suzy's Kapp strings lay in her diary as a bookmark of sorts. Nellie had wanted to mark the spot where Suzy's life had made a turn for the better. *Is she with the Lord because someone invited her to hear another side to things? Could it be?*

She wondered about that and pictured Caleb sitting alongside Dat and her brothers, all in a row at Manny's meeting. What would happen if he came?

Still imagining the scene, she fell into a deep sleep.

Some time later, she happened to hear a *tick-tick* on her windowpane.

Sitting up, she thought she saw a flicker of light, too.

Am I dreaming?

Heart in her throat, Nellie Mae scurried to the window and looked out. There, standing in the snow below, was Caleb, shining his flashlight into her eyes.

Ach, is this the night? Has he come to propose?

She unlocked the window, raised it, and poked her head out. "I'll be down in a minute," she whispered. "Will you meet me at the back door?"

Caleb turned off his flashlight just that quick, and she hurried to shut out the frigid air, pushing down hard on the window frame. "Oh, goodness . . . what'll I do?"

Nearly in a panic, she stumbled about, lighting the lantern and snatching up her white bathrobe and slippers—but no, she couldn't go down in her nightclothes. What was she thinking?

Lickety-split, she changed into her Sunday best and brushed her long hair, pushing it back over her shoulders. Only family members were supposed to see it hanging free of her bun and Kapp, but she'd already kept Caleb waiting long enough. Suddenly she laughed softly, realizing that Caleb would see her like this for many years to come. *I'm going to be his bride, for goodness' sake!*

After taking a moment to make her bed, Nellie snatched up the lantern, carrying it down the long staircase, glad for the solitude of the hour. She considered Maryann's emphatic remark—that the girl always knew, supposedly, when this night had arrived. *She* hadn't had the slightest inkling, or had she somehow missed it at the last cider-making frolic?

More fully awake now, she began to worry that Caleb might have been disturbed by her letter. Put out, even.

But he's here! What does it mean?

Tiptoeing across the kitchen floor, Nellie Mae hurried to the summer porch, eager to lead her beau to her room, where they would sit on the pretty loveseat, holding hands as he spoke tender words of love.

Nellie held the lantern high as she went to the back door, smiling her welcome. "Oh, Caleb . . . it's so good to see you!"

"You, too, Nellie Mae." He seemed surprised at her hair . . . first looking, then not looking. He rubbed his hands together, his cheeks rosy red, his eyes meeting hers.

"Come in and get warm," she offered. "We can talk in my room, if you want."

His face darkened, his eyes serious. "Nellie, I'm not here for that. . . ."

She felt her mouth drop. "All right," she said.

He's not going to ask me to marry him.

"We need to talk, Nellie Mae."

She paused. "Where?" She glanced over her shoulder. The kitchen was vacant and dark.

"Best not be wakin' up your Dat." Caleb glanced at her again, and his gaze admiringly followed the length of her hair. "Can you bundle up and go ridin'? I brought some heavy lap robes . . . and some hot bricks."

She forced a sad little smile. He waited for her to roll her hair into a makeshift bun so she could push it into her black winter bonnet. Then she donned her heaviest coat and other winter clothing, all the while her heart sinking.

What will he say?

They pulled out of the lane slowly, without speaking. Then, once they were out on the main road, Caleb began to talk. "I read your letter, Nellie." He reached for her hand, but his glove felt stiff against her mittens. "Don't you understand what this means . . . what you're asking?"

She swallowed hard. "Jah, but the meeting was ever so interesting. Nothing like what I s'posed."

"It's foolishness, that's what! Heresy—the things Preacher Manny's teaching." His voice was earnest, pleading.

She felt as if she might literally sink into the seat. She'd believed the same thing before reading Suzy's diary, but now she did not wish to swiftly dismiss the teachings that had transformed her sister's life. "But, Caleb, if you could just hear what I heard . . . if you could just help me understand."

"I don't need to go. I know what's bein' said."

She sighed. "You're judgin' by what others say? Ach, the rumor mill will be the death of us."

"Now, Nellie . . . love."

She was torn between the submissive way she'd been taught to speak to a man, and what she felt she must say. "Won't you hear Preacher Manny out, Caleb? Just this once?"

Once was all it took for Suzy.

He turned to face her, still holding her hand. "I woke you up tonight for a reason. I'm here to ask you to cling fast to the Old Ways." His voice grew stronger, ringing through the darkness. "I trusted you when you said Suzy was a good girl, no matter the rumors, and I've pursued you knowin' my Daed's concerns. I stood up for you with my father, Nellie—told him you're the kind of woman he should welcome as a daughter-in-law."

She was silent. She *had* insisted to Caleb the rumors about Suzy were false, but that was before she'd discovered everything about her sister. "I told you the truth about Suzy," she protested. "She wasn't a wayward girl when she died . . . she was—"

"I want you to turn from this nonsense, Nellie. The sooner the better."

"Have you closed up your mind . . . your heart, then?"

"My heart is for *you*, Nellie Mae. I want you to be my bride. Marry me next year, after baptism."

Marry me?

The words she'd longed to hear, yet he'd spoken them in the midst of an argument. Even so, how could she refuse him? She couldn't hold back the tears. "I love you, too, Caleb. Honest, I do. And I *want* to marry you . . . but . . ." She couldn't go on.

"Jah, we love each other," he replied. "That's why I'm here, to protect you . . . to keep you from makin' the biggest mistake of your life."

"I'm not sure I see it that way." She brushed away her tears. "Can't you just go and hear for yourself?"

He shook his head. "I know what I believe."

"Jah, tradition. Plain and simple."

"I'm not goin' to a silly meeting."

"You're diggin' in your heels like an obstinate mule, Caleb Yoder."

"Call me whatever you like, but it won't change my mind."

"Your ears are closed tight, ain't so? You don't want to know more than what we've always believed." She sighed. "Well, I'd like to know if there's more than that—if God's own truth's behind what Manny's preaching."

He let go of her hand and leaned forward, the reins draped over the lap robe. "Nellie, it all boils down to this: My father would disown me if I left the church for this newfangled whatever it is. I'd have no way to make a living . . . for us. I'd lose everything. The land, my immediate family. Daed's respect."

"Well . . . you'd have *us*. We'd find a way somehow. Love can win out, jah?" she offered tentatively, yet the words sounded hollow even to her. She touched his arm. "Your land's mighty important, sure it is. But how can land mean more to you than our life together?" Her voice shook with both sadness and frustration.

"I could ask the same of you. How can my goin' to a meeting mean more to you than my reputation with my father . . . or the life we planned?" He leaned back, regarding her, his eyes softer now. He turned then to stare straight ahead and was quiet for a good, long time. "I've heard you out, Nellie. Now I'll say what I must. I've never cared for a girl like I do for you." He looked at her again, the muscles of his face quivering. "I wish we hadn't fought . . . honest to goodness."

"I'm sorry, too."

He drew her into his embrace. "I'm fearful, love. I'm afraid of what could become of us."

"It's not enough that we love each other?"

He closed his eyes, blowing out a breath. "I think I'd best take you home now."

"Jah, 'tis best," Nellie Mae agreed. Quarreling had gotten them nowhere.

CHAPTER 37

The wind rose up in the night, bringing with it freezing rain and snow. The wedding season was off to a bitter start.

Nellie gladly fulfilled her promise to Aunt Anna to help in the kitchen at the wedding she'd mentioned, filling up the week before it with as much work as daylight would allow. Neither her path nor her family's crossed with Caleb's at any of the all-day wedding celebrations Dat and Mamma chose to attend on the first Tuesday and Thursday, days set aside for weddings. For that she was truly sad.

She did see Caleb at the weekend cider-making frolic, his furtive gaze meeting hers. He seemed as willing to invite her to ride into the night as previously, but he did not care to hear her talk about the upcoming New Order youth gatherings. Already, a small group of youth had formed, thanks to the decision of many families to immediately accept the bishop's offer. Nan had decided to attend tonight's initial gathering, and for the first time, Nellie had found herself on her own, without any sisters at a frolic.

Nellie was aware of a small sorrow growing within as she wondered how she and Caleb could ever truly unite as man and wife when everyone around them seemed bent on division. She had been wholly honest with him and now must attempt to trust the Lord God for the outcome as Suzy might have. Yet she found herself increasingly given to silence, lest their relationship continue to be strained. Truly, there was simply too much at stake.

———

Rosanna took care not to slip on the crusty ice along the sidewalk as she carried baby Rosie toward the waiting vehicle. Elias offered his free arm to her, cradling tiny Eli in the other.

"We've got ourselves a Mennonite taxi service." He smiled at her.

"Jah, I see that."

"I wanted their first ride home to be nice and warm for our son and daughter," he added as they walked. "They seem a mite too fragile for this cold, if ya ask me."

"The doctors said they're both perfectly healthy—strong, too. Bet it won't be long before you're chasing after that son of ours." Rosanna gave him a loving glance. "You must be mighty happy about your boy."

"Well, I daresay I would've settled for two girls, seein' that perty smile on your face just now, love."

"Aw, Elias." She didn't let on that she'd nearly held her breath for Kate to birth a boy. "Thank the Good Lord."

"Jah, you can say that again."

The driver stepped out to assist them into the cozy van, and Rosanna carefully slid inside, next to her beaming husband. Leaning down to kiss Rosie's rosebud face, Rosanna felt her heart fill with a love that went beyond any she had known . . . and was content.

———

On the first day of December, Nellie awakened to a landscape of white, the sky as colorless as the ground. The horse fence and every tree in sight—even the side of the barn—were completely covered with snow due to a blistering Nor'easter.

Nellie hurried to dress and ran downstairs to help Mamma and her sisters with breakfast.

"Just think, you get a day off from bakin'," Mamma greeted her, smiling.

"I sure won't be goin' to work in this weather," Rhoda said woefully.

"Oh, but the Kraybills will understand once they look out their windows," Mamma said, trying to cheer her up.

"Jah, I'll say. We're downright snowbound," Dat declared, and they all laughed at that, gathering around the table when it was time to eat.

During the meal of scrambled eggs, ham, and fruit, Nellie excused herself and scurried upstairs to retrieve Suzy's diary. *This is the perfect time,* she thought, opening her drawer.

She turned the book to the page that had changed her thinking about Suzy. For sure and for certain, there were oodles of pages chronicling Suzy's sins, but the joy lay in where her search had brought her.

Nellie returned to the kitchen and approached the head of the table. Taking a deep breath, she said, "Suzy believed like you do, Dat."

Dat leaned forward, spilling his coffee.

"What?" Mamm gasped.

"It's all here . . . in her diary. She wanted each of us to know the Lord she loved."

Not trusting her voice, she handed the book to Dat where he sat. "Will ya read this page?" she whispered.

Dat's eyes held hers in question. Appearing reassured that she was earnest, he nodded and began to read silently.

Nellie Mae returned to her spot at the table and sipped some orange juice. Watching his lips move, she could not keep her eyes off her father's astonished face. Soon tears flowed down his cheeks.

Mamma frowned, looking at Nellie.

When Dat finished reading, he handed the diary to Mamma. His face radiated pure joy.

Mamma started to read, as well, and soon reached for Dat's hand. "Suzy's prayers were answered," she said reverently. "Her faith . . . and God's great mercy brought us to our knees, ain't so, Reuben?"

Dat, who evidently still hadn't quite found his voice, managed to whisper, "'Twas Suzy, all right . . . and our dear Lord."

Then Nan asked to see the diary, followed by Rhoda. Nan's eyes filled with tears, and Rhoda shook her head in wonder.

Mamma could hold back her happiness no longer. "Oh, glory be! Our Suzy's safe . . . not lost forever as we'd supposed."

"She's with the Lord," Dat said, blinking back tears.

They joined hands around the table as Dat thanked the living God "for this best news of all."

———

Reuben left the kitchen the minute the meal was done and went to the barn to be alone with his thoughts. He moved in and around the horses, paying special attention to the young ones, all the while pondering the surprising revelation in Suzy's diary.

He leaned down to stroke the mane of his favorite foal. "God was watchin' over my little girl all those months," he muttered as though talking directly to the colt. "Now, what do you think of that?"

Embracing the hush of the barn, Reuben walked to the back, facing north toward the vast whiteness of the pastureland concealed by heavy snow. In awe of the stark beauty, he thanked God for His care of Suzy. "I will not doubt you, O Lord . . . I know I can trust you to watch over all of my family," he prayed. "Each and every one."

———

Rosanna was as tired as she'd ever been after the first week home with the twins. She sat on the bed, brushing her long hair, talking with Elias about their babies—the holding, changing, bonding, and feeding—all of it precious to her. "Did ya ever think we'd be so busy?" she asked. "Some call it a double blessing 'cause we waited so long and got ourselves two." She smiled at that.

When Elias didn't respond, she looked over her shoulder. He was sound asleep, still wearing his choring clothes, his mouth hanging wide open. And he was lying on top of the quilt, of all things . . . holding Eli in his arms. The infant's tiny face was peeking out of the handmade blanket, the pink side of the quilt out by mistake.

She tiptoed around the bed and stood there admiring this wonderful man who'd agreed to become a father to someone else's children. Gently she covered him with a spare blanket before wandering out to the next room, a small sitting room where they'd placed the homemade cradles. *Nice and close by . . .*

Leaning over, she looked into the tiny peach-face of dear Rosie, who was in all truth both her cousin and her daughter, just as Eli was. The faint smiles during sleep, the smallest hands she'd ever seen, all curled up in tiny fists . . . the sweet, milky smell on their breath. . . . oh, how she loved them!

"You did this most wonderful thing for Elias and me, O Father in heaven. I couldn't be more thankful," she whispered.

She'd heard from Linda Fisher that Preacher Manny prayed as though he were talking to a friend face-to-face. Elias had no idea she'd spent any time with Nellie Mae's cousin this past week since the babies' release from the hospital. Linda was the sole reason Rosanna had kept up with the washing and the cooking—there were never enough hours in the day. Linda had encouraged her to read the Good Book, too, when she had a chance. *"Start with the gospel of John,"* she'd suggested.

Rosanna returned to the bedroom, thinking how odd it was that none of the nurses, nor the doctor in charge, had been aware that Kate's babies were to become hers and Elias's. She wondered if it had been kept mum for legal reasons.

After all, what were the laws of the world to them—two cousins in complete agreement, and with the bishop's blessing, too? In the midst of folk leaving helter-skelter for a so-called new order, the bishop surely had wisdom from above . . . or so Rosanna hoped.

Immediately she felt distressed for having second-guessed the man of God. Bishop Joseph was the divine appointment for the People. *Ach, for certain.*

Presently she blew out the lantern and slipped quietly into bed so as not to waken either Elias or Eli. There were precious few hours before the babies would be crying for nourishment.

They'll never be this small again, she thought, glad they were thriving in her care.

O dear Lord, help us bring these wee ones up in your grace and loving ways. And may we be ever mindful of your salvation, full and free. . . .

CHAPTER 38

The snow stayed on the ground for nearly a week, and then a Chinook wind blew in—a snow-eater, Dat liked to call it—to the surprise of everyone.

Nellie was in dire need of a brisk walk, and since it was the afternoon of the Lord's Day, there was nothing to keep her tethered home or to the shop. Feeling out of sorts and missing Caleb, she turned in the direction of White Horse Mill on Cambridge Road.

Our special place, she thought of the secluded area behind the old stone mill.

She didn't know why she was struggling so, but since their disagreement, whenever she considered Caleb's and her love, she felt a peculiar inner tug. She wished she could talk to someone, but no one knew how serious Caleb was about her. Or how much Nellie cared for him.

Truth was, she felt alone, and she found herself talking aloud, as if the air, or God, might have something to say on the subject. "Honestly, I know what I want . . . it's Caleb for my husband. He says I'm the girl for him—the one he wants to marry, but how can that ever be?"

Since Caleb was the youngest son in his family, the land would normally fall to him; but if provoked, his father could easily decide to give Caleb's bequest to his next-older son. She contemplated Caleb's life without the land he longed for. He would be miserable . . . might even blame her for his loss of it.

The fluttering of a crow caught her attention, and she thought of Suzy, whose favorite bird had always been the reddish brown veery—a shy, even elusive bird often seen in the woodlands near their house. It flew far away in late September, but no one knew where it journeyed for the winter.

Just as none of us knew where Suzy was all those months she was running with Jay and his friends.

Nellie sometimes thought of going to search out Suzy's Mennonite friends, as she assumed they were. She even wondered if talking with Zachary and Christian Yoder and the others who'd gone with Suzy to the lake might provide her with some final answers.

Looking about her, she realized she'd lost track of where she was. She spotted the wrought-iron bench where she and Caleb had sat and talked so many times and headed toward it.

Can our love survive the church split? she wondered, knowing there already had been a vast parting of the ways for so many. Thankfully her own family had suffered little in comparison to others—there would be no shunning to keep them from spending time with Ephram and Mary-ann and their children, and they could still visit with Uncle Bishop and the many people who would surely remain in the original church.

If Caleb and his family came over to the New Order side *after* the ninety days the bishop had allowed for decision making, how sad for them. But no, Nellie Mae wouldn't allow herself to think that way. She must live a joyful life, all the while knowing if she converted, she'd be saying good-bye to Caleb . . . and if she remained, she would say good-bye to Suzy's gospel.

Pausing to sit on the bench, she closed her eyes. There was something sweet in the air, or was it the fresh smell of December after a bitter cold snap? Beneath the dampness of the creek bank, the promise of spring was buried deep within the soil. But the sweetness she sensed wasn't that found in the earth. Perhaps it came from knowing spring would come again, no matter how far off it now seemed.

Maybe our corn will reach its full height next summer. . . .

It was getting cold and Nellie hadn't planned to come this far at the outset of her walk. She thought she might end up crying if she lingered here in this place.

She rose, wanting to go have one last look at the mill creek. Walking to the bank, she leaned against the cold trunk of a tree.

A rustling sound . . . then a familiar voice.

"Nellie Mae, is that you?"

She turned and saw Caleb coming down from the frozen pond. "Hullo," she said, her heart in her throat.

Had she spoken his name aloud? She wasn't sure.

"Nellie, what're you doin' here?" His eyes were bright at the sight of her.

She laughed. "I should ask you that."

"So we're both here spontaneously," Caleb remarked.

They looked at each other awkwardly, almost as if they'd just met, so surprised were they.

"Would ya like to walk with me?" he asked at last.

Without waiting for her to respond, Caleb reached for her hand and they strolled together, like old times . . . re-experiencing the delight of first love.

Yet she knew as well as he that things were different. Preacher Manny had said in a sermon that the Word of God was as powerful as a two-edged sword. Were they about to witness this divisiveness firsthand?

"I couldn't stop thinking 'bout this place . . . wanted to walk along the millstream again," Caleb confessed.

She listened, enjoying the sound of his voice, the way his eyes twinkled when he smiled. "It's perty here, that's for sure. Even on a cold day."

"We sure picked a fine place, jah?"

She smiled at him. "You picked it, Caleb . . . remember?"

"I certainly do." He paused as though considering what he wanted to say next. "I must tell you something, Nellie. Something I despise saying."

She braced herself.

"My father forbids me to take you as my bride. He said so earlier today." Caleb shook his head, his eyes fixed on the ground. "He'll withhold his land and all he's promised me if I marry you, Nellie."

A fury rose in her, and she wanted to declare his father unfair. But that was false—David Yoder had every right. It was his land to give, and he *did* have other sons already married and walking in the way of the Old Order church.

"What will you do?" she asked, not sure she could bear to hear the answer.

He was silent for a time, clearly frustrated. "We must do as my father demands and part ways."

Ach, no . . .

She stopped walking to face him and study his dear face, his hairline, the way his eyebrows framed his beautiful eyes. "Are you goin' to—"

"Make it appear so," he added. "Till I can think this through."

"You've spoken up to your father on this?" It was forward, but she had to know.

"More than once. Believe me, it's not the wisest thing to do."

She understood. There were a good many stern fathers and grandfathers amongst the People, some harsher than others, but most unyielding all the same.

Unexpectedly Caleb reached for her, pulling her toward him. "I can't think of losin' you. I won't."

She pressed her lips together to make them stop trembling and willed herself not to cry. "I would never do this to my son or daughter, would you?"

He reached to lift her chin, his face ever so near. "We cannot be seen together . . . ever. Even though we might attend the same Singings and whatnot, I won't take you out ridin' afterward—not because I don't want to. Do you understand, love? Rebekah, who's always been fond of you, will now surely become a spy for Daed."

Nellie nodded, the lump in her throat nearly choking her so that she could not speak.

"Nothing will stand between us. I'll see to that . . . somehow." He pressed his forehead to hers, lingering ever so near. "We'll find a way, I promise."

"I pray so" was all she could bring herself to say.

Caleb kissed her cheek tenderly, holding her hand till her fingers slipped away.

Honor thy father and thy mother, she thought as she walked toward Beaver Dam Road alone, wondering how following that arduous commandment could yield a blessing of long life. The way Nellie Mae felt now, she couldn't imagine wanting to live to a ripe old age without her beloved by her side.

EPILOGUE

———

I dreamt of Suzy last night, at long last. She came walking toward me in a meadow of red columbines and bluebells, wearing a purple cape dress and white church apron. She was as radiant as a bride, and in the dream I thought she must be wearing her spotless heavenly robe, her tears over her misdeeds all wiped away.

Dat says Suzy's gone to Jesus, and I think of it every morning as I rise to greet a new day, wondering if it is true.

As for Mamma, she's ever so busy passing on her new faith. She and little Emma were doing a bit of stitching this morning when I left the house to go to the bakery shop. Emma was curled up on Mamma's lap, leaning on the kitchen table while my mother showed her how to do a simple cross-stitch on a pillow slip. I had to stop and listen when Mamma said, "You know Aunt Suzy's in heaven."

Emma looked up from her embroidery square and blinked her big eyes. "What's she doin' there?"

"Oh, all kinds of wonderful-good things, I 'spect."

"Like what?"

"Spendin' time with the Lord Jesus, for one," said Mamma.

"God's Son?"

"That's right . . . let me tell you more 'bout Him." Mamma's voice went on, but I had to leave.

Seems in this house, there is much talk of "the Savior." In all truth, my parents speak of Jesus quite a lot, which is very different from what I heard all of my growing-up years. I guess they think some of us have a lot of catching up to do, myself included, though I'm ever so guarded in my curiosity. How can I be otherwise?

Nan, surprisingly, is warming up to me; we've been distant for so long. Her heart must still be broken, though she won't come right out and say so. I sometimes see the pain in her eyes, just as I see my own in the small hand mirror on my dresser.

I've decided not to part with Suzy's Kapp strings. I've been slipping them into my dress pocket again. At times I think it's peculiar to keep them at my fingertips, an ever-present reminder, but they bring more comfort than sadness nowadays. Mamma would probably not care at all if she knew.

Besides, Mamma showed me something of Suzy's that she, too, sometimes carries with her. A small pillow, stitched as finely as any I've seen—one made to alleviate headaches, of all things.

Dat says he knows now why so many of our crops failed last summer. He believes we were supposed to learn something important about trusting God. It was a message of hope to look to in the time of struggle. He says it's as if our heavenly Father were saying, *Look to me, even amid your uncertainty and loss—whether crops or loved ones—I am here, calling you to my joy and peace.*

In spite of my bewilderment over Caleb's father's demand, I am hopeful as I go about the duties of my life, knowing love can win out in even the worst of circumstances. Of all the stories Dat reads from the Good Book, the best example of great love is God's Son, seems to me. To think He would give up all of heaven to meet us here—to court us, wooing our hearts. Such a surprising thing, really.

Mamma says the best part is we will never be separated from that love, neither here nor over yonder. She figures Suzy must know that already—she says she can't imagine what Suzy's experiencing. So now when I think of my departed sister, I try to think like Mamma does, with jubilation and maybe a bit of envy.

Soon it will be Christmas Day, and this year will mark a special celebration of the Lord's birthday round here. Sometime before then, I'm going to settle in my mind what happened on Suzy's final day on earth. I want to thank her good friends, too, for looking after my wayward sister, helping to rescue her from the evils of the world.

Sometimes I wonder if I ought to visit the tabernacle come summer, if for no other reason than to honor my close sisterly connection to Suzy. Ach, but I hope my reticence won't keep me from meeting Zachary and his brother. I've already avoided them once, not accepting the chance to go boating with them that dreadful day. I was selfish, not wanting to spoil my chances with Caleb by being linked to his English cousin. In the end, though, I paid a terrible price for not going—yet if I can follow through and find them, what will *this* meeting cost me?

No matter what the days ahead may hold, I will keep baking the goodies my customers crave, extending kindness and good deeds to all I meet. And somehow, I hope the Lord God will watch over Caleb and me, even though our future looks mighty bleak. After all, the peaceable parting offered to the People by the bishop was a true miracle.

Why can't Caleb and I be a miracle, too?

ACKNOWLEDGMENTS

While doing research for this series, I learned of two schisms that occurred among the Old Order Amish in 1966, a time of great upheaval . . . and saving grace. And the mercy of one Amish bishop.

Much gratitude to my cousins Jake and Ruth Bare for their careful research, as well as to those from whom they received valuable information and memories.

Many thanks to my wonderful editorial team—David Horton, Julie Klassen, and Rochelle Glöege—and everyone at Bethany House who helps make my writing journey a joyful one.

Loving appreciation to my husband, Dave, for his terrific plotting advice, to Carolene Robinson for her medical expertise, to Barbara Birch for her excellent proofreading, to each of my Lancaster County research assistants, and to my partners in prayer in various places.

Above all, my deep thankfulness to our heavenly Father, who guides me in all my ways.

CROSSINGS®
THE BOOK CLUB FOR TODAY'S CHRISTIAN FAMILY

A Letter to Our Readers

Dear Reader:
In order that we might better contribute to your reading enjoyment, we would appreciate your taking a few minutes to respond to the following questions. When completed, please return to the following:

Andrea Doering, Editor-in-Chief
Crossings Book Club
401 Franklin Avenue, Garden City, NY 11530

You can post your review online! Go to www.crossings.com and rate this book.

Title _____ Author _____

1 Did you enjoy reading this book?

☐ Very much. I would like to see more books by this author!

☐ I really liked_____

☐ Moderately. I would have enjoyed it more if_____

2 What influenced your decision to purchase this book? Check all that apply.

☐ Cover
☐ Title
☐ Publicity
☐ Catalog description
☐ Friends
☐ Enjoyed other books by this author
☐ Other _____

3 Please check your age range:

☐ Under 18   ☐ 18-24
☐ 25-34   ☐ 35-45
☐ 46-55   ☐ Over 55

4 How many hours per week do you read? _____

5 How would you rate this book, on a scale from 1 (poor) to 5 (superior)?
_____

Name_____

Occupation_____

Address_____

City_____ State_____ Zip_____